THE PLANTERS
A Ripple In Time Book 2

A Historical Novel of Survival

By

VICTOR ZUGG

The Planters
A Ripple In Time Book 2

VictorZuggAuthor@gmail.com

ACKNOWLEDGEMENTS

Many thanks to Brandi Doane McCann (www.ebook-coverdesigns.com) for another cover design masterpiece. And equal thanks to Tamra Crow (tcrowedits@yahoo.com) for the professional editing. I'd also like to thank Sarah Gralnick. She's always the first to read my work. I very much appreciate her suggestions. They all made this book infinitely better.

CHAPTER 1

Nathan Sims eyed the sword's sharp point, hovering inches from his throat. Sunlight gleamed from the few spots on the blade not covered in blood. A large drop of the viscous, red liquid paused at the tip before continuing with an audible *splat* on Nathan's cheek. The blood mixed with beads of sweat and formed a pink rivulet down his jaw. His hands trembled, and his lips quivered.

It seemed like yesterday that he was on the beach in Miami, having a grand old time with a few friends. He'd boarded the plane for home, was hurled through some kind of time warp, and deposited off the coast of the Carolina Colony, three hundred years in the past. He'd survived the plane crash, near starvation, disease-infested swamps, and Indian attacks, only to find himself at the end of a pirate's sword. It had to be fate that brought him to this point in time, and it had to be fate that had spared his life thus far. Perhaps there was more in store for him.

"I know where you can find the silver," Nathan said to the man staring down at him.

The man steadied his sword hand and intensified his focus. His black eyes bore into Nathan's soul.

Nathan, with his breeches, shirt, and coat splattered with blood not his own, lay flat on the deck of the eighteenth-century sailing sloop. He turned his head away and peered at the numerous men gathered around. They each held a musket rifle, pistol, or sword pointed at Nathan's head. Some were barefoot and clothed in rags. Others wore high black boots, breeches, and linen shirts, not that much different from what Nathan wore. Their sun-darkened skin glistened with sweat, and the air stank of body odor.

"He's talking shit," one of the men said. "Nick 'em, Ned. Watch 'em bleed." The man's lips spread into a wide grin of rotted teeth.

Several of the others grunted in agreement.

Nathan peered through the men's legs at the detritus of battle. Splintered wood littered the sloop's open deck. The single mast, shattered from its base, lay tangled in a mass of lines, with most of its length, along with the sail and boom, over the side. Several lifeless bodies bloodied the deck. Others, Nathan knew, were out of sight below, or in the demolished sterncastle. Nathan was the only one left with a heartbeat. And it was thumping a mile a minute.

"You're Edward Low, right?" Nathan said, as he turned his head back to the man standing over him.

Ned's eyebrows twitched.

"Your silver was in a chest. We found it in a jolly boat with two dead men."

Ned's eyes widened.

"We have the chest, Ned," another man said. He had a full beard, cut short, and wore a loose linen shirt and baggy pants with the legs tucked into his boots. The butt of a pistol protruded from his waistband and his hand held a short, curved cutlass. He was better dressed than most. "Kill 'em and let's be off."

"Not so fast, Mister Spriggs," Ned said to the man. His gaze turned back to Nathan.

"That's a small part of the silver," Nathan said. "The rest is near Charles Town, on a plantation. I can take you to the people who have it."

Ned sheathed his sword. "Bring 'em," he said, as he turned toward the larger ship, a schooner, grappled alongside.

"What about the sloop?" a man asked.

Ned paused as he glanced around the deck. "Let her drift. It will serve as a warning to any who would defy my flag." He spit on the deck and then climbed aboard his ship.

Two men lifted Nathan to his feet and tied his hands behind his back. One of the men gave him a hard shove toward the two-masted schooner.

Captain Edward Low, Ned, to those who knew him, stood on the schooner's deck above. The specks of blood on his blue long-coat were no longer visible from the distance. He adjusted his three-pointed hat as the last of his men removed the grappling hooks and vacated the sloop. "Put 'em below," he said, as he peered long and hard at Nathan being brought aboard.

Nathan glanced a final time at the sloop, as the two vessels drifted apart. He focused on Dorothy Weiss' body, sprawled lifeless and facedown on the deck. Too bad her expertise in history hadn't seen this coming. He winced at the sight of Manny Hernandez's severed torso. The two sections of his body lay several feet apart, in a mass of blood and tissue. Nathan's eyes darted to several other downed men and women. Maybe no one was supposed to survive for long, outside their normal place in time and space.

As the two men ushered Nathan across the deck, he locked eyes with Captain Low, standing at the helm. Dorothy had mentioned he was ruthless and prone to torture. Nathan didn't doubt it. The man wore a perpetual scowl. Somehow, Nathan needed to make himself a valuable commodity to Captain Low. He needed to prove his worth, to save his life. He just wasn't sure how to go about doing that, especially given that the balance of the silver he touted was no longer at the plantation. He didn't know where it was.

◆◆◆

Ditching a single-engine, fixed-gear plane at sea is no easy task. The various iterations of catastrophe cycled through Stephen Mason's mind as he stared down at the water far below. Flipping nose-first was the most likely scenario, in which case Mason could wind up unconscious. The plane would sink and Mason would drown. The trick was, as he saw it, to get the airspeed as low as possible, cut power, glide, and flare at the last possible moment. It sounded very plausible, in theory; execution might be a different story.

Mason had already verified that Charleston was no longer the bustling metropolis it would become. Mount Pleasant, from where he'd departed earlier that day, was a series of planted fields. There were no bridges or infrastructure, no highways, just trees. The small settlement where Charleston would one day be located was the only exception.

There had been no response to his radio calls, and no feeds to his navigational instruments after he passed through the storm over the Atlantic. Based on the evidence, he came to the only possible conclusion: he had succeeded with his quest to return to the past. He didn't know how it worked but, just as before, the storm with the blue haze had hurled him back in time. He only hoped it was the right time.

At his current altitude of twenty-five thousand feet, the top ceiling for the Cessna 400 TT Corvalis, he would have been a speck and a buzz to anyone in Charles Town who happened to have been looking up when he passed over. Hopefully, his arrival had gone unnoticed.

Well away from Charles Town, out over the water, he turned northeast and followed the coast. There would be merchant ships up and down the coast. He needed to find a spot devoid of such ships, to lessen the possibility of being seen as he descended. Off the coast of what would become Myrtle Beach came to mind. That's exactly where they had ditched the airliner on his first trip back in time.

He checked the gauges and determined he had less than an hour of fuel, which was plenty to cover the seventy-five miles. Along the way, he searched the ocean's surface for wakes left behind large ships. He saw several. But directly off the coast of Myrtle Beach, the water appeared deserted. There were no wakes, and no tiny dots indicating a ship, for as far as he could see. He scanned the coast and estimated he was fifteen miles out. He would be out of sight from shore for his final approach.

Mason put the plane into a tight spiral and circled down while he kept his eyes open for smaller vessels. The vista remained empty in all directions as the plane plummeted.

The fuel indicator was near zero when he finally leveled out a few hundred feet above the surface. He reduced power and pitch on the prop, feathered the flaps, and let the plane's speed drop until he was mostly gliding at fifty feet. He cut power and watched the rotation of the propeller come to a stop, finessing the stick to keep the nose up. When the gears were only a few feet from the surface, he raised the flaps a hair and let the airspeed drop even more. The moment he felt the plane was about to stall, he leveled the flaps for a second, and then jerked the controls for full flaps. The plane flared to a complete stall, pitched, and dropped.

The plane plopped into the water, nose first. The tail sprang up to almost vertical and gently settled back, without flipping. The plane immediately began undulating in rhythm with the waves. Thanks to the intact wings, every part of the plane was above the surface except the gears. It had been a perfect ditching.

Without hesitation, Mason released his seatbelt as he scanned the water in all directions. He flipped the pilot's side door up and stepped out onto the wing. He began hauling gear from the back seat, starting with the personal life raft. It was sized for two people and came complete with two paddles and a battery-operated inflation pump.

Mason removed the gray and blue raft from its plastic cover and unrolled it along the wing. He attached the pump and flipped the switch. The pump went into a loud, rackety hum. As the raft began filling with air, Mason lifted the two water-proof bags from the back seat, along with his canvas rucksack and several smaller canvas bags. The two waterproof bags contained all the gear and clothes he had assembled in preparation of a successful return to the eighteenth century. The canvas bags contained the four thousand one-ounce silver ingots he had accumulated during the planning phase, back in the future.

He couldn't help but think that fate had played a large part in his return. What else could explain his passing through a warp in time, three times?

He stood up and took a second to think. Anything linking him to the future would need to be discarded, with three exceptions. The bags contained several pairs of wool hiking socks and several pairs of cotton boxer shorts. Both were a luxury from the future that warranted the risk. They would be hidden beneath his period attire, so it was a small risk. He would also be keeping his Glock and its associated ammo and magazines.

He next examined what he was currently wearing. The jeans, t-shirt, puffy jacket, sunglasses, and lace-up service boots would have to go. He stared at the new dive watch clasped to his left wrist. As much as he hated to part with it, the watch would have to go as well. He released the stainless hasp, slipped the watch off, and dropped it in the ocean. He removed the sunglasses and dropped them in the water. He stripped out of his jeans, jacket, boots, and polyester socks, rolled them into a ball and tossed them into the airplane's backseat. Barefoot and wearing only his boxer shorts and t-shirt, he turned back to the raft, now fully inflated. He released the pump nozzle and tossed the pump into the backseat. He loaded the gear and bags of silver, attached the paddles, and stood up as he stared at the plane.

Its loss was a shame, but a necessary sacrifice. And that sacrifice was taking its sweet time. It had been twenty minutes since the ditching and the plane remained buoyant, with no sign of giving in to its watery surroundings.

Mason opened one of the water-proof bags and extracted the long, machete-like knife included among the essentials he thought he would need. He crawled back into the cockpit, opened the starboard door, and stepped out onto the starboard wing. Using the long knife, he punched several gaping holes into, and through, the thin composite material of the wing. After doing the same with the port wing, he returned the knife to the bag, sealed it closed, slid the raft into the water, and climbed aboard. The entire ditching had gone so well he was barely wet.

He rowed a few yards from the plane and stopped. He stared back at the instrument that had brought him to what he hoped was three hundred years into the past, and the woman he loved. He judged that the nose sat a little deeper in the water than before and the tail was a little higher. The waves lapped over the wing more than they had before. The plane was going down and its loss put a damper on what should have been a joyous occasion. He began rowing north, based on the position of the sun. He had considered bringing a compass back with him, but it would have been one more item he wouldn't be able to explain if it were seen. As he rowed, he thought about the plantation and its new owners. But were they the *new* owners? He had no idea exactly when the blue-hazed storm had dropped him in the past. He contemplated the timeline as he knew it.

The airliner passed through the portal on June 19th, 2019. He and the others arrived in the Charles Town area in the same month in what they later determined was 1720. The battle with the pirate, Edward Low, and Mason's departure from that time period, occurred three months later, in the month of September. But when he arrived in the future, he was back in June 2019. That part didn't make a lot of sense. But who was he to try to explain the details of time travel? He boarded the Cessna for his final flight on March 3rd, 2020. Would he now be in March 1720? His mind went in circles trying to grasp the concept. The air temperature would be cool for March, even for South Carolina. He lifted his face toward the breeze. The temperature was moderate, not particularly cold or hot. He recalled what he had seen of the ground when he flew over the Charles Town area in the Cessna. The ground cover was mostly green, but interspersed with fall colors. Definitely not March, more like September. Was it possible he had returned to the exact point in time when he'd left, sometime in September 1720? If so, the battle with Edward Low had just occurred. But how did that make sense? He had no explanation, and he was giving himself a headache thinking about it. He tried to clear his mind as he put more effort into rowing. He would know soon enough.

It was well into dark when he heard the surf breaking over the sound of his own rowing. He peered into the darkness. In the distance, a dull line of white stood in stark contrast to the pitch black beyond. He continued rowing until he felt the boat being lifted by the breakers near the shore. He stowed the oars and let the foam-fronted waves carry him the rest of the way. Finally, the water deposited the tiny boat upon the sand.

Tired from rowing but excited to be back, Mason leapt from the raft and pulled it up onto the shore. He turned slowly, in a complete circle, as he peered into the night, trying to get some idea of what part of Myrtle Beach he had arrived. He saw water, beach, and the dark hulks of trees. He didn't have a clue where he was in relation to the camp he'd shared with the other survivors of the airliner ditching. Hopefully, the light of morning would help.

He slapped his neck, but the mosquito had already taken its quota of blood. Mason scratched the spot and then slapped his leg, just above the knee. Deciding there was nothing he could do in the dark, he pulled the raft across the sand and into the trees. He positioned his rucksack on the sand as a pillow, assumed a prone position next to his gear, and pulled the raft over on top of him, muffling the sound of the surf. He slapped at a mosquito's barely audible whine near his ear. He missed him the first time, but apparently struck home on the second try. Mason closed his eyes and was soon fast asleep.

CHAPTER 2

A *thump* against the rubber raft woke Mason with a start. He heard tiny feet run across the bottom, hit the ground, and scamper through the leaves. *A squirrel*. He lifted the raft and gazed at the ocean beyond the trees while he scratched a bug bite on his jaw.

Breakers crashed to the sandy shore and immediately withdrew to deeper water. The sky was a bright blue; the air smelled of salt.

He turned in a circle as he got to his feet. His surroundings consisted of trees, thick brush, the beach, and the ocean. Nothing looked familiar. He strode to the water's edge and peered up and down the sand. All was deserted. He had no idea whether he was north or south of his former camp. It really didn't matter, since there was no particular reason for him to return to that camp. And there was really no reason for him to visit the village of the Catawba Indians he had befriended. He thought of his friend Mato. If Mason were desperate, Mato would help. But Mason wasn't desperate. He had food, and the necessary equipment to survive during his journey to the Jackson plantation. How to get there was the question. It was seventy-five miles back down the coast, and seven miles inland from Charles Town, along the Ashley River. He had two options: walk, or row the rubber raft. He turned and stared at the tiny boat. It would be impossible to row the blue and gray inflated craft eighty miles without being seen. It would also be impossible to walk the beach all the way to Charles Town. The shore was chopped up, with a multitude of inlets and marshes. And it would be impossible to walk inland, at least it was from where he stood. The entire area was an endless series of streams, rivers, marshes, swamps, and their inhabitants. Mason pictured a large, black cottonmouth moccasin striking at his leg.

He knew of a trail, the Kings Trail, used mainly by the Indians to transport trade to and from Charles Town. But Mason had no idea how to reach it from his current position. Mato would know. It appeared he would need his help after all.

Mason gazed up and down the beach again. Just finding Mato's village would be a chore. It was four miles inland from the survivors' camp. And that camp was toward the north end of the Myrtle Beach area, just south of a small inlet. Mason pictured his location along the shore when he'd put the Cessna into a spiral. It was more toward the middle of the fifty-mile long curve of shoreline. The camp had to be north.

Mason stripped out of his shorts and t-shirt and waded into the crystal-clear saltwater. At waist deep, he submerged to wash the sand from his body. He sprang up in a cascade of water droplets as he ran his fingers through his close-cropped hair. He ran his hands over his skin to remove any lingering sand particles and submerged again.

He returned to the beach, shook the sand from his shorts and t-shirt, and carried them to the raft. Using the bottom of the raft as a table, he rummaged through one of the water-proof bags and extracted a pair of buckskin pants, a matching long-sleeve, pullover shirt, and a pair of slip-on, hightop black boots. These were just a few of the items he had assembled for this very occasion. He also extracted a black leather shoulder holster and his new Glock 19 pistol, along with two extra magazines loaded with 9mm ammunition.

He slipped into the shorts, t-shirt, and holster. The buckskin pants and long-sleeve shirt came next. He rummaged through the bag again, came up with a pair of wool hiking socks, and slipped those on. He pulled the boots on and stood. Finally, he extracted a felt, three-pointed black hat, and positioned it on his head with a slight cock to one side. He grinned, thinking he must look like Daniel Boone. He lifted the edge of his shirt and holstered the pistol and the two extra magazines. He strapped a leather belt around his waist, under the shirt. Two sheathed knives hung from the belt: a four-inch, fixed-blade and the much longer, machete-like, premium-steel, heavy-bladed affair suitable for chopping. It would be equally capable of hacking down a tree, or separating a snake's head from its body.

He next contemplated the rubber raft. There was no place in this world for a synthetic rubber raft. He unscrewed the valve stem cover and let the air escape while he pulled a foldable camp shovel from the bag. He dug a hole on the spot, filled it with the rolled-up raft, and covered the shallow grave with sand. He dug a separate hole, about two feet deep, midway between two particularly tall pine trees. He filled the hole with most of the bags containing the silver ingots. Four thousand one-ounce ingots weighed two hundred and fifty pounds, which was too much to carry. He placed one of the bags containing a thousand ingots into his rucksack. He could deal with the extra sixty-two pounds. From the ten boxes of 9mm ammunition, he placed two in his rucksack and placed the rest in the waterproof bag containing his second pair of boots and the nicer of the two outfits he'd had custom made back in the future. He placed the other set of clothes into his rucksack. He lifted the rucksack with one hand to judge the weight. It was heavy, mostly from the silver ingots, but he would need everything in the ruck as soon as he arrived back at the plantation. The rest of the silver, and the remaining gear, could wait until he returned, hopefully in a matter of days. He tossed the two waterproof bags into the hole with the silver and covered it with sand and leaves. He made a mental note of the hole's location, between the two tall pines and directly inland from the beach. He noted a tall dead or dying oak, without leaves and nearly without limbs, that would be visible from the ocean. He was confident he could find the spot again.

He put his arms through the canvas rucksack straps and started off up the beach as he munched an energy bar and sipped from a stainless water bottle. The weight on his shoulders was considerable, but doable.

◆◆◆

Nathan sat on the deck with his back against a bulkhead and his hands tied. His torso leaned one way and then the other, in concert with the ship's motions. Vomit saturated his long coat, waistcoat, breeches, and the deck around him. Ashen-faced and eyes closed, it was hard to tell if he was dead or alive as his head rolled from shoulder to shoulder, seemingly of its own accord.

Suddenly he felt a pair of vises take hold of both biceps and lift him. Dizzy, with legs like rubber, he opened his eyes to the blurry surroundings of the dank lower deck.

Two men manhandled his dead weight up a ladder, to the breeze of a ship under full sail.

For the first time in at least two days, he felt the sun's warmth on his face.

The two men carried him aft, to the helm, where Captain Low waited patiently.

When the two men let go of his arms, Nathan wobbled a second and collapsed in a heap. He tried to focus on the captain's scratched, dull-black boots, inches from his face. When his eyes cleared, he raised his chin to the man in control of his destiny as he released the pressure in his bladder. Warm urine soaked through and darkened the crotch of his breeches and spread to the wood planking.

Captain Low wrinkled his nose as he shook his head side-to-side. "The man is soiling my deck. Mister Spriggs, if you please?"

Spriggs, standing next to the captain, motioned with his chin to the two seamen still beside Nathan.

One of the seamen grinned as he retrieved a nearby wooden spar and slid it between Nathan's elbows and his back. With his hands tied in front, the length of wood contorted his chest forward and his shoulders back.

The muscles attached to Nathan's shoulder blades spasmed. He grimaced. Despite the pain, he did not cry out. Even in his jumbled mind, he knew there would be greater cause for that shortly.

The seaman attached a line to each end of the spar. The lines were joined at a metal ring. A single line ran up from the ring, threaded through a block and tackle attached to a gaff pole, and down to the deck. He and the other seaman heaved on the line, which lifted Nathan by his elbows.

Nathan screamed in agony at the sudden stress on his shoulders. The pain intensified as his back muscles and ligaments tightened and knotted.

The two seamen swung his body out, away from the ship, until his feet dangled over the ocean.

Nathan stared back at the men peering up from the deck and lowered his eyes to the hull of the ship. His bowels released as he felt his body being lowered. His descent paused; his sandal-clad feet skimmed the surface. And then his body dropped.

Fully submerged, he held his breath and kicked in an uncontrolled frenzy. The seconds ticked by in slow motion as his head remained inches from the surface. He kicked harder and wiggled his body like a mermaid, but to no avail. The urge to open his mouth and breathe intensified. Water began to seep in through his nose. His throat spasmed as he fought to keep his mouth closed. Just as his vision began to dull, he felt the spar jerk against his arms. His head broke the surface. He coughed water from his lungs and gasped for air. His lungs filled. His vision returned. He breathed deeply.

"Again, Mister Spriggs," the captain yelled.

It was loud enough for Nathan to hear and it gave him just enough warning to take in a last deep breath before his head submerged once more. Just as before, he kicked, he writhed, and he fought to hold his breath as the seconds ticked by. He felt the water's pressure tug at his breeches, in an attempt to remove them. He wrapped his fingers around the thin material at his waist as the current forced its way inside, thankfully ridding the breeches of any lingering human waste. And just as his senses began to dull, his head broke the surface. He coughed, gasped, and took in several deep breaths.

When his head plunged below the surface for a third time, he was sure it would be the last. His ability to hold his breath had been reduced to seconds. Fate had, indeed, brought him to this final point in time. Images from his past flipped through his mind. He saw himself as a child, chasing the chickens on his grandfather's Iowa farm. His mother's face popped into his mind, followed by the face of the girl he'd assaulted as a teenager one night in a park. He saw himself as a young man behind a desk at his father's construction company. He pictured the secretary, the woman he'd wanted to take out but was always afraid to ask. His mind returned to the water. He tasted the salt. He lifted his eyes and saw the bright blue sky, almost in reach. The color faded to gray. His vision narrowed to a pinpoint and all went dark.

Muffled sounds were his first sensation as he clawed his way back to consciousness. They grew in clarity as he sensed the hardness of the deck upon which he lay. His realization that he was no longer in the water brought profound relief. He also no longer felt the spar pressing against his shoulder blades. His hands were free. Nathan opened his eyes as he pushed himself to a sitting position. He gazed at various men scampering about the deck. He heard the captain's deep voice.

"Hard to port, Mister Spriggs."

"Hard to port," Spriggs yelled.

Men scurried about; lines were heaved.

Nathan peered over the port gunwale and saw the ship swing around in relation to billowy, white clouds in the distance. He also glimpsed a mass of square sails in the distance. *Another ship.* Nathan watched the actions of the men onboard the schooner and deduced that Captain Low intended to attack.

"She's a fat merchantman," Spriggs offered, as he stood next to the captain. "Run out the guns?"

"You do that, Mister Spriggs," Captain Low said. "And put a ball across her bow."

Spriggs hurried amidships and crouched next to two men manning the forward-most starboard gun. He yelled something Nathan couldn't hear.

The gun crews rolled out all five starboard guns.

Spriggs tapped a seaman on the shoulder and stepped back.

The seaman touched the cannon with a short, smoking length of rope.

Almost immediately, the cannon roared and a thick cloud of smoke billowed forth.

Without hesitation, the gun crew set about reloading the gun.

Spriggs returned to Captain Low's side and they both watched the larger ship.

"She's not heaving to," Spriggs said.

Captain Low stepped forward. "All guns fire at will," he yelled. "Maximum effect."

All five starboard guns boomed in rapid succession. Thick smoke rolled across the water toward the merchant ship.

Nathan heard the impact of several balls as they smashed into the larger ship's wooden hull and infrastructure.

"She's turning to," Spriggs yelled. "Guns coming to bear."

Nathan got to his knees for a better view and saw the merchant ship's broadside squarely lined up with the schooner. He saw flames and smoke blast from several cannons, a millisecond before he heard the multiple blasts. An instant later he felt the deck shudder violently as a ball tore into the side, taking out one of the five cannon emplacements. The force lifted the schooner's cannon nearly vertical before it slammed back to the deck. Two seamen were knocked backwards and ended up against the port gunwale, unconscious.

Spriggs ran to port and ordered one of the gun crews to replace the fallen men. Four seamen rushed forth and began levering the large gun back into position.

"Fire!" Captain Low screamed above the turmoil.

The four remaining starboard guns spit forth their flames, smoke, and steel.

Nathan watched as three of the balls tore into the merchant ship. The foremast suddenly collapsed in a tangle of sheets and sail.

"Let's get that gun back in action," Captain Low said from behind the new gun crew. His tone was nonchalant, almost like he was ordering a sandwich. There was no sign of fear or anxiety as he stood gallantly at the starboard gunwale, peering at the enemy.

Nathan, on the other hand, shook uncontrollably. At the cracks of musket fire from the merchant ship, and the impact of lead balls pinging off the rigging, Nathan tried to make himself as small as possible, curled up and heaped low on the deck, just in front of the helm.

"Fire at will, gentlemen," Captain Low said.

Each of the five big guns roared in rapid succession.

Even from his position low on the deck, Nathan heard several of the balls slam into the merchant ship, with a chorus of breaking timbers and splintering wood. The musket fire ceased.

"We have her colors, Ned," Spriggs said.

"Right, Mister Spriggs, bring us alongside and prepare to board."

Nathan rose up and watched as Spriggs maneuvered the schooner toward the larger ship, while every member of the crew gathered starboard. Nathan estimated at least forty men, all armed with pistols and swords.

When the two ships were a few yards apart, several of the men tossed grappling hooks to the larger ship and anchored the two ships together when their hulls touched. Captain Low, with his crew behind him, scampered over the gunwales.

Nathan cautiously rose to his feet, but remained near the schooner's helm. He watched as Captain Low stepped up to the merchant captain. The merchant crew, all unarmed, stood behind their captain. Suddenly, without provocation, Low ran his sword through the merchantman's torso. As the larger ship's captain crumpled to the deck, Low's crew began hacking and slashing. Shots rang out. In a matter of a few seconds most of the merchant crew was dead, or bleeding and about to be dead. Captain Low matter-of-factly sheathed his sword, climbed back over to the schooner, and walked to the helm where Spriggs waited.

"Put all hands to their cargo," Captain Low said. "Let's see what she has." He turned his gaze to Nathan. "Take him with you."

CHAPTER 3

It was late afternoon when Mason came upon a familiar stretch of shoreline. Another mile brought him to the survivors' camp. Standing just inside the perimeter, Mason turned in a slow arc as he perused the bark-covered huts, the tripods used for smoking venison, and the barrier of brush, limbs, and palm tree trunks they had built for protection. Even the central cooking pit remained as it was the day they'd left. But which day was that? Had months passed, the period of time he'd spent in the future, or had the survivors boarded the sloop for their trip to Charles Town only a few days ago? Based on the condition of the camp, Mason judged it to be the latter. The camp's appearance was another piece of evidence that led him to believe he had been returned to September, 1720. Mason thought of the people who had perished during the battle with the pirate, Edward Low. He pictured Dorothy, covered in blood, and Manny's body ripped apart. He had no idea why or how he alone had survived.

Mason stepped over to his old hut and took a seat on the palm frond mat. He pulled a water bottle from the rucksack and drank the last of its contents. He retrieved a second bottle and took a long swig. He stared at the stainless water bottle in his hand. He didn't have a clue how he would explain his current situation to Mato. The sloop was gone, the survivors were gone, but Mason remained. And now he was well-stocked, equipped, and clothed. There was no explanation Mato could understand. Mason didn't even understand it. It would have to be another situation without explanation. What was it Mato always said? *Some day you tell me*. Not likely.

Mason took another long gulp of water, got to his feet, and with the rucksack in hand, set off down the well-worn path to the stream behind the camp. With the mini water filter from his rucksack, he was soon pumping clean, clear water into the empty water bottle. After topping off the second water bottle, he stripped, waded into the stream, and washed off the dried salt from his earlier ocean bath. He rinsed his shorts and socks in the clean water and hung them to dry. Dressed in fresh shorts, socks, and the buckskins, he returned to camp.

To reduce the number of mosquitoes, he lit a small fire inside his hut, piled it with green pine needles, and closed the makeshift door. Soon, thick smoke billowed from every crack. He let the smoke continue as he sat on the log next to the central fire pit and ate another protein bar. He would spend the night in camp and visit Mato's village in the morning.

❖❖❖

Nathan sat below deck, back against the main mast, with his hands tied behind him and around the mast. He wore his breeches, linen shirt, and sandals. His blue long-coat was now the property of another member of the crew. That member sat with a group around a common table near Nathan. They drank from mugs as they laughed and jeered at Nathan and hinted at his fate. His head being separated from his body dominated. Apparently, they were taking bets.

Nathan heard steps on the nearby ladder.

Spriggs stepped to the deck. He walked straight to where Nathan sat and withdrew a long-bladed knife from his waistband. He stared for several long seconds at Nathan, as if considering where best to insert the blade. Finally, he bent down and sliced through the rope binding Nathan's hands. "Captain wants to see you. On your feet."

Nathan rose as he rubbed his wrists.

"Care to wager on his fate?" the man wearing Nathan's coat asked Spriggs with a grin.

The other men laughed and grunted.

"That wouldn't be fair," another man said. "He probably knows what the captain has in mind."

"What's his fate, Mister Spriggs?" asked the man wearing Nathan's coat.

"You'll know soon enough," Spriggs said. "For now, Thomas, you have watch."

"Aye," Thomas said, as he rose from the table.

Spriggs turned to Nathan and gave him a light shove toward the ladder. "That way."

Nathan climbed the ladder, followed by Spriggs and Thomas, and stepped up on the deck. He immediately spotted Captain Low at the helm. Nathan hurried in that direction, without Spriggs' encouragement.

When Nathan stood before him, Captain Low slowly turned his attention from the horizon and locked on Nathan's eyes. "I haven't forgotten about my silver," Low said. "We will be returning to Charles Town eventually, but for now, we have prizes to find. You'll help Strop in the mess."

"He could use some help," Spriggs said with a grin.

Low continued. "You'll be free to roam the ship. One step out of line and you'll be tied and gagged." Low turned to Spriggs. "Get him out of here before I change my mind."

"You heard the man," Spriggs said, as he gave Nathan a hard shove. "The mess awaits."

Nathan scampered back down the ladder and made his way along the rolling lower deck until he stood before an overweight man in the galley.

The galley consisted of a corner of the lower deck, near the bow. Various casks and barrels lined one bulkhead. All were secured by rope. A work bench lined the other bulkhead. Nets containing an assortment of fruits and vegetables hung from various pegs. A few feet out from the workbench stood a cast-iron, wood-burning, four-legged stove-looking contraption positioned in the middle of a layer of beach sand. The sand was contained within wood timbers secured to the deck. A metal pipe ran from the stove, through the deck above, to vent the smoke. A large, cast-iron, round-bottomed pot hung above the stove from a metal hook. Steam from the pot exited through an open hatch in the deck above. Wooden bowls and metal mugs lined a shelf above the work bench.

"The captain sent me to help," Nathan said, as he stood there looking dumbfounded. "I'm Nathan."

"You're Jimmy Green," the man said with a thick West Indies accent. "You'll remain Jimmy Green until I say otherwise." The man was gruff, with a deep, raspy voice. His shirt had been white at one time but now the multitude of stains had turned it a dark brown.

Nathan peeked into the pot and saw a white porridge-looking mass. "What is it?"

Strop paused with his head cocked. "You've never seen burgoo?"

"Maybe," Nathan said, "what's burgoo?"

"So, the captain sent me an idiot then," Strop said. He took a wooden bowl from the shelf and tossed it at Nathan. "You'll need something to eat if you expect to work."

Nathan lifted the wooden ladle, swirled the pot's thick contents, and poured it into a bowl.

"You'll want some molasses with that," Strop said, as he pointed to an earthenware container on the work bench.

Nathan removed the top and used a wooden spoon to dip the black, viscous substance. He let it dribble over the burgoo. Nathan used the same wooden spoon to stir the mixture until blended. He lifted the spoon to his lips, blew on it, and shoved it in his mouth. He chewed the hot mixture quickly. "Oatmeal."

"Yeah," Strop said. "Finish it." He put his foot on a small cask. "This salt pork needs to be rinsed and soaked." He pointed to carrots and onions in a net basket. "Those need to be cut up. There's work to be done, Jimmy Green."

❖❖❖

"Where you people?" Mato asked standing before Mason in the center of the village.

"There was a battle at sea. They were killed by the pirate, Edward Low."

Mato cocked his head as if to ask how Mason survived.

"I was blown into the water by a cannon ball blast. Everything is rather fuzzy after that."

"Fuzzy?"

"I can't remember exactly what happened."

Mato put his hand on Mason's shoulder. "All you friends die?"

"Everyone except Karen, Lisa, and Jeremy. As you know, they remained behind at the plantation. That's where I need to go now."

"You walk?"

"Yes, if you can point me in the direction of the trail."

Mato shook his head. "Trail very hard. Many swamps and rivers to cross."

"I know," Mason said, "but I have no other choice."

Mato ran his eyes back and forth between the rucksack and Mason's new buckskin set of duds, including the three-pointed hat.

Mason thought hard for an explanation, but he came up with nothing. There was no way to explain the equipment and clothes. And Mato hadn't even seen the items that were even more unexplainable, such as the water filter and the protein bars in their colorful wrappers.

"First eat, then go," Mato finally said.

Mason was relieved Mato had not asked any direct questions.

After a bowl of thin fish stew, Mato led Mason through the brush several miles until they came to a trail. He pointed to the west.

Mason extended his hand.

Mato grasped Mason's hand. "Four days. Move fast. Sleep off trail."

"Thank you, my friend," Mason said, as he released Mato's hand. "I will see you again." Mason turned and started walking.

◆◆◆

Nathan spent nearly all his time in the galley. The only exceptions were the few hours he slept, and the occasional visit to the head to relieve himself.

He slept like everyone else on the ship; *rough*, they called it, on a thin mat laid out on the deck. Most slept on the main deck to take advantage of the ocean breeze. Nathan wasn't that secure yet with the crew, so he slept on the lower deck, next to the galley and near where Strop snored away the hours. At first, Nathan got very little sleep and a whole lot of soreness, mostly in his hips and shoulders since he tended to be a side sleeper.

A visit to the head was a bit misleading. There was no actual latrine on the schooner. Relieving oneself involved simply peeing over the lee side of the main deck. That had not been a problem, but emptying one's bowels was a bit more complicated. At first, Nathan found it impossible to even contemplate defecating while sitting on the designated slab of wood extending from the gunwale, near the bow. From what he had observed, it took some serious balance, and a firm grip on a rope, to keep from being flipped into the sea, with even mild wave action. But worse, the seat was in full view of everyone on the main deck, which in the best of circumstances meant at least a few men. And even worse, the men used a common rag to refresh themselves afterward. A *tow rag* they called it. It was tied to the end of a rope and dragged in the water alongside the ship. The agitated sea was supposed to cleanse the rag of debris.

The first time Nathan saw it being used he shook his head in disgust and nearly vomited. Hygiene aboard was atrocious. He constantly wondered why everyone in this time period had not died from typhoid or e-coli. The only thing he could figure was that their immune systems had to be off the chart.

Several days passed before Nathan even attempted a bowel movement. On the first try, despite stomach cramps from several portions of porridge, he gave up without success. With a growing urge, he tried again that night, but again with no success. His fifth night at sea met with partial success. Two nights later, he returned to his mat much relieved and with a sense of accomplishment. Rather than use the tow rag, he cleaned himself with a bucket of sea water. He ended up drenched, but it was better than the alternative.

During this time, Captain Low and his ship of pirates had accosted two additional merchant ships. Both gave up without a fight. Like the first one Nathan witnessed, neither of the ships carried what he would view as treasure, but they did provide plenty of provisions. The schooner bulged with casks of salted beef and pork, barrels of rice and oats, some fresh vegetables and fruit, and enough biscuits to fill a pickup truck.

A ship's biscuit wasn't the soft, fluffy biscuits like his grandmother made back on the farm. The one's Nathan enjoyed with butter and honey. Ship's biscuits were hard as a rock and composed of two ingredients: flour and water. They may have been baked and cooled more than once to remove as much moisture as possible. These biscuits were practically impossible to bite and chew. To try would likely result in a broken tooth. It literally took a mallet to break them into pieces. In order to consume a ship's biscuit, it either had to be soaked in a liquid, such as wine or brandy, or pounded into crumbs and added to stew or soup, either while being cooked or after the fact. Only when softened by liquid could the biscuit, as a whole or in crumbs, be chewed and swallowed.

Most of the biscuits Nathan had seen came with a morsel of protein, in the form of weevils. Even the freshest of biscuits usually showed evidence of the little bugs. The men didn't seem to mind. They chewed without hesitation, as did Nathan, after a while.

It took about ten days for the crew's ridicule, jeers, and sneers to stop. Nathan hadn't been accepted as a member of the crew by then, he was much too soft and foreign for that. The crew simply lost interest. But his situation improved the very next day when they encountered their fourth prize ship.

CHAPTER 4

"Sails broad to port," yelled the ship's watch, a seaman standing at the bow.

Nathan, who happened to be on deck at the time, turned his attention to the expanse of sea off the port bow. There, in the distance, was a two-masted ship with square sails. Other details of the ship were not discernible.

Captain Low, standing at the helm, turned his gaze toward the potential quarry. He studied the ship for a full minute before turning to Spriggs. "To port, if you will, Mister Spriggs."

"Ned, we're already busting at the seams," Spriggs said.

"You never know what she might be carrying," Captain Low responded. He turned to the seaman behind the wheel. "Bring her to port."

The man turned the wheel.

Slowly, the ship came around to an interception course.

Spriggs hurried to the gunwale and peered at the ship in the distance. "Any guns?" he yelled to the watchman.

"Too far to tell, Mister Spriggs," the man replied. "But she's a brig."

From his time aboard, Nathan had learned that the brigantine, a two-masted, square-rigged ship, was a favorite among merchantmen. They were slightly bigger than most schooners, and could carry more cargo, but they were a tad slower. And their ability for close-haul sailing was limited because of the square rigging.

"Gun ports," the watchman sang out, "five of them."

Nathan raised his eyes to the British flag waving from the schooner's stern. It was a common practice, he knew. Pirates would fly a friendly flag, usually British, while closing on a prize and then run up their pirate flag when it was too late for the merchant to escape. He glanced at the ship in the distance and shook his head. *They had no idea what was coming.*

When the merchant ship was nearly in range of the guns, Low motioned to the seaman next to him.

The man quickly lowered the British flag and replaced it with Low's flag—a red skeleton on a black background.

A few seconds later, Captain Low ordered the guns run out.

Nathan watched for the merchant ship's response. He expected the ship's captain to lower the sails and prepare to be boarded, but that didn't happen. Nathan saw the gun ports open on the merchant ship's port side. The menacing black barrels of five guns appeared. As before, Nathan saw flame and smoke blast from all five barrels, a millisecond before he heard their reports. He dropped to the deck just as a ball slammed into the side of the schooner.

"Those are eight pounders," Spriggs yelled.

"Return fire, Mister Spriggs," Low said.

"Fire!" Spriggs screamed.

In rapid succession, the schooner's five guns returned fire. Each cannon recoiled against its lines as fire and smoke blew from the barrel. The crews immediately began the process of reloading as the two ships crept closer.

The merchant ship's second volley was at nearly pointblank range. All five balls tore through the schooner's rigging and sails. One busted the foresail boom neatly in half, leaving the back half of the sail cloth to flap in the wind.

Nathan raised his head just as the schooner's gun crews sent their response. The balls hit the brig with equal effectiveness.

Nathan's face turned white at the sight of several of his fellow crewmen sprawled about the schooner's deck. One bled profusely from the stump left by his missing leg, severed just above the knee. In the melee, the gun crews continued to reload and fire. Other crewmen perched behind cover and fired muskets as quickly as they could reload. There was much yelling and screaming. Men scrambled about the deck; many were wounded from wood shrapnel. It was obvious, even to Nathan, that the merchant captain had no intention of giving up peacefully.

As the two ships continued to draw closer, both crews exchanged cannon and musket fire. Smoke enveloped both ships in a thick haze. Men dropped, mortally wounded, and moaned in agony before succumbing.

With only a few yards between the ships, the cannons ceased firing. Grappling hooks took hold and men crossed from both ships with swords and pistols. Each side began slashing and shooting. More men fell.

Nathan watched as one man bit the ear off another as they rolled on the deck in hand-to-hand combat. Blood poured over both men as they continued to wrestle.

Debris and human body parts littered the deck.

Captain Low, wielding a sword in each hand, quickly dispatched members of the merchant crew. He stood back-to-back with Spriggs, who was fighting his own battle with two worthy opponents.

Nathan scrunched in a ball next to the starboard gunwale, with his hands wrapped around his head. He opened his eyes at the sound of metal sliding across the deck. A bloody-handled sword, minus its owner, came to rest inches from Nathan's nose. His first instinct was to close his eyes and curl into an even tighter ball. Instead, he picked up the sword. For several long seconds he stared at the blood-stained blade. The weapon was heavier than he'd expected.

As the battle raged, with men from both crews dropping, Nathan rose to a crouch on wobbly legs. His hands shook and his stomach did somersaults. He watched as every man stood toe-to-toe with an opponent. Even Strop, one arm badly sliced, fought with blood-thirst.

Captain Low and Spriggs had worked themselves apart and were each fighting a member of the merchantman's crew. In Nathan's estimation, the battle could go either way.

Despite Nathan's trembling, and the intense desire to run, he recognized an opportunity. As Captain Low fought, shifting back and forth, the two men's backs were often exposed to Nathan. He alone stood on the starboard side of the ship. A blade to Low's ribs would go a long way in favor of the merchant captain. But a blade to Low's opponent would go a long way toward improving Nathan's standing with the crew, and more importantly, Captain Low. Nathan weighed the pros and cons of both decisions as the seconds ticked by. Finally, he made a decision. He hesitantly stepped forth and plunged the blade.

Captain Low's eyes widened as he watched the man suddenly drop to the deck. He glanced at Nathan before engaging another merchant seaman.

Slowly, the tide turned in favor of the schooner's crewmen. Twenty-minutes later, every merchantman lay dead or dying, except one. The merchant captain stood with his left arm hanging limp.

As most of the crew tended to their compatriots, those with a chance of survival, Captain Low pulled a dagger from his waistband. Without hesitation, he flicked his arm at the captain and then replaced the knife.

A thin, red line appeared on the man's throat. A second later, blood gushed from the wound.

The merchant captain dropped to his knees as he grasped his throat and fell face forward onto the deck.

Without even a glance at the man lying before him, Low turned in a slow circle as he scanned the deck. His eyes stopped on Nathan.

Nathan dropped his chin to his chest as Low approached.

"I'll be needing you on deck," Low said.

Nathan raised his eyes and peered at Low's expressionless face. Before he could say anything, Low walked away. Nathan wasn't sure what Low could have meant, other than a reassignment from the galley to the deck. That was a promotion, Nathan presumed. Nathan started his new career by helping other crew members rid the schooner of the carcasses, including their own crew members. The bodies were simply dumped into the ocean.

With that done, Low signaled for Nathan to follow him over the gunwales to the other ship.

Spriggs followed, as well.

Low led them down a ladder to the cargo hold.

The hold was crammed with large, wooden barrels.

Spriggs ran his hand over the top of one. "Rice, lots of rice. We can't carry all this."

"Pick as many men as you think necessary. Take her to New York and sell the rice." He looked around at the brig's interior. "Sell the ship, as well."

"And then what?"

"Take the jolly boat to North Beach. I'll pick you up there."

"That will leave you with a short crew," Spriggs said.

Low peered at Nathan. "We'll make do."

◆◆◆

Mason paddled from the aft end of the canoe. He glanced from side to side as he made his way up the Ashley River from the Charles Town landing. He was curious to see if anything had changed along the banks since his return to this time period. So far, he had found everything the same. The river was just as he had last seen it; Charles Town was the same. Even the tavern where he, Nathan, John, Dorothy, and Jeremy had stayed was the same.

Soon, the top floor of the plantation house came into view above the saw grass along the bank. As he approached, more of the plantation came into sight. He could see men toiling in the fields, just as before, but with one notable difference. A white man stood out among the blacks. Jeremy.

Mato was right. It had taken four days to reach Charles Town. The trip had been uneventful. He didn't even pause when he reached the town. He continued walking, exited the west gate, and rented a canoe at the Ashley River landing.

He saw Jeremy look up and start walking just as the canoe bumped against the dock. The two of them met at the foot of the dock.

"Where's the sloop?" Jeremy asked, as he glanced at the canoe.

"It's a very long story, my friend. I'll fill everyone in later. For now, I'm just glad to be back."

Jeremy clapped Mason on the shoulder and walked him toward the house.

Before they had gone ten feet, Mason saw the door swing open. Karen and Lisa emerged and ran toward them.

Mason and Karen came together in a tight embrace. Finally, Karen released him and stepped back. "I'll have to admit, I was a little worried," she said, as she studied Mason's face. After a few seconds, her expression turned serious. "What's wrong?" She glanced at the dock. "Where's the boat?"

Mason stroked his beard. "I'll explain everything later. Right now, you have a hungry and very dirty man on your hands."

"Eat or wash, first?"

Mason slapped at his sleeve and watched a cloud of dust catch the breeze. "Wash."

◆◆◆

The four of them sat on the porch, facing the river. Jeremy, Lisa, and Karen watched as Mason, freshly washed and dressed in his coat and breeches, finished the last of a venison stew, thickened with carrots, potatoes, and onions.

He pushed the empty bowl forward on the table and looked up.

Everyone stared, waiting for Mason to explain what had happened.

"We picked up the rest of the survivors, just as planned," he said, as he sat back in the chair. "That morning, as we all left the camp and stepped onto the beach, we saw a schooner waiting off shore. The captain turned out to be Edward Low, the pirate. It was his silver Nathan found with the two dead men in the dory washed up on the beach. He wanted his silver back."

"So, what happened?" Karen asked, impatient for Mason to move the story along.

"With everyone aboard, we made it out of the cove. John accomplished some magical maneuvers to dodge the ship, and we made it to the open ocean with only a single cannonball hole through the main sail. Heading out to sea directly into the wind, we were able to extend our lead for most of that day. Eventually the sail ripped, and we lost our speed advantage over the schooner." Mason dropped his chin to his chest. He rubbed his face with both hands as he looked up. He stared directly into Karen's eyes. "As soon as the schooner was in range, they began firing. Several of our people went down immediately, including Manny and Dorothy."

"Did any of them survive?" Jeremy asked.

Mason turned to Jeremy. "I took cover behind the mast and tried to shoot as many of the pirates as I could. A cannonball blasted the mast and me into the water. Given the amount of damage to the sloop before I blacked out, I doubt any of the others made it. Mister Low lived up to his ruthless, bloodthirsty reputation."

"You don't seem to have any injuries," Lisa said. "And your clothes."

"The next part will be difficult to understand," Mason said. He paused and looked at each of the others in turn. "For me, that battle with Edward Low occurred months ago."

"I don't understand," Karen said. "You've been gone only a few days."

"I don't really know what happened after I went into the water. I blacked out. I remember fleeting images and sounds. I finally woke up in a hospital in Jacksonville, Florida, back in our normal time."

CHAPTER 5

"You're serious?" Jeremy asked.

"Dead serious," Mason replied. "I don't know how, but somehow I was hurled back through that same warp in time that we all went through. I was back in our time for months."

"Wait, back up," Jeremy said. "Everyone is killed and you're blasted into the water and back through time?"

Mason gave a subtle nod.

"You're right," Karen said. "It would be impossible to believe, except that the four of us know quite well that it is possible."

"So how did you get back here, to this time?" Lisa asked.

"The doctors tried to convince me that my memories of the plane crash, the Indians, Charles Town, the sloop, plantation, and the pirates were all hallucinations. I knew different, at least I thought I did. Homeland Security declined to reinstatement me when I wouldn't let go of the time travel story. I ended up resigning, sold my condo, packed a few belongings, and headed north, with no idea where I was going. I was just beginning to believe all the doctors were right when I ended up in Charleston and came across something that proved I had gone back in time."

Three sets of eyes were riveted on Mason, waiting for him to continue.

"You remember that bracelet I gave Mato when we first met?"

Everyone nodded.

"Archaeologists in our time found that bracelet during a dig near Myrtle Beach. I saw a photo of it in a magazine."

"I'm not sure a bracelet would have convinced me," Lisa said.

Mason was about to describe his visit to the plantation three hundred years in the future and what he learned there, when he decided against it. To do so would mean revealing Karen's pregnancy and Jeremy's death. He preferred to let the news of her pregnancy come naturally. And he planned to do everything possible to prevent Jeremy from getting sick and dying, so there was no sense in mentioning it now.

Karen glanced at Lisa and back to Mason. "So how did you get back here?"

"I had passed through that time warp twice, so I thought a third time was at least possible. I knew it was a long shot, but I also figured it wouldn't hurt to try. So, I went about provisioning myself just in case, rented a plane, and began searching for that weird storm. I found it on day ninety-three." He looked around at the three faces still staring at him. "And that's it."

"Any chance you landed the plane on some remote strip of land?" Jeremy asked. "Maybe we could find that storm again."

"Sorry. I ditched off the coast of Myrtle Beach. Mato pointed me toward the trail to Charles Town, and voilà."

"Three trips through time," Lisa said. "Is it possible the four of us could do it again?"

"Who knows?" Mason said. "I have at least some idea as to my first and third trip, passing through the storm. My second trip while floating in the open ocean is a complete mystery. I wasn't even awake when it happened."

"So here we are," Karen said.

Everyone turned their eyes to Karen.

"Exactly," Mason whispered, barely audible.

Everyone was quiet for several moments, deep in their own thoughts.

"I have some ideas for the plantation," Jeremy finally said.

Mason, Karen, and Lisa perked up.

"Like what?" Mason asked.

"I'd like to expand the kitchen. Increase the size of the building, and get a stove. Maybe install a hearth."

Mason raised his chin.

"I think the workers should be eating as well as us. We prepare meals large enough to feed everyone. We should all be eating the same food."

"I like it, except I'm not sure home stoves have been invented yet."

"A hearth, then. And I think we should let them know that if anyone wants to leave, we will do everything possible to make it happen."

"With their freedom," Lisa said.

"Of course," Jeremy agreed.

"And if they all leave?" Karen asked.

"Maybe we should talk to Sylvester first," Mason said. "Get an idea of how everyone feels about being here."

"I understand why the former owner picked Sylvester as the lead slave," Lisa said. "He's smart and quite capable."

"His English is better than mine," Karen said.

"Let's expand the kitchen first," Mason said. "It will go a long way toward expressing our intent. Actions speak louder than words."

"We're going to need some wood," Jeremy said.

Mason stared at the existing kitchen structure. Only a portion was visible off to the left side of the house. "Maybe an addition, a covered eating area with tables, attached to the kitchen?"

"We'll need a lot of wood for that," Jeremy said. "And nails. There are some tools in the storage shed, but we could do with more."

"We need another boat," Mason said. "Something like the sloop, but maybe a bit smaller."

"It needs to be large enough to transport our crops to town," Karen said.

"How are we going to pay for all this?" Lisa asked. She turned to Mason. "What happened to the silver coins that were on the sloop?"

"I suspect Ned Low was able to retrieve those coins," Mason said. "But I brought four thousand one-ounce silver ingots back with me. Most are buried back at Myrtle Beach. Too heavy to carry." He stared at Karen and Lisa. "I hate to leave you two here alone, but I'll need Jeremy to help find a boat and gather supplies. It might take a couple of days."

Karen looked at Lisa and back to Mason. "We'll be fine."

"We leave in the morning, then," Mason said.

◆◆◆

Karen, Lisa, and Sylvester stood at the dock and watched Mason and Jeremy step into the canoe and push off, both silhouetted against the rising sun. They both wore the proverbial long coat, waist coat, neckerchief, breeches, and stockings. Mason wore his custom-made, high-top, black boots.

With a glance over his shoulder, Mason waved and began paddling. He focused on the river ahead as he contemplated all he needed to accomplish in town. A boat was the first priority. Operating the plantation without one was possible, but it would mean hiring a boat every time transport was necessary. Plus, Mason preferred the freedom of a personal boat. A sloop the size of the one they'd lost might be too big for a couple of men to handle. Mason hoped to find something similar in design, but smaller.

Jeremy barely spoke during the seven-mile trip to the Ashley River landing. Aided by the river's current, it only took a couple of hours. When they stepped out and pulled the canoe up on the sand, Mason noticed lines of worry etched across Jeremy's face.

"They'll be fine," Mason said. "If we can find and arrange for a boat, we might be able to go home and return tomorrow for the necessary supplies."

"Okay," Jeremy said, as he stood up straight. "Let's get this show on the road."

Mason smiled and turned to the attendant. "Are we square?"

The attendant, an elderly man, cocked his head.

"Do I owe you anything for the canoe?"

The attendant raised his chin. "No, you paid already."

Jeremy spun on his heels and marched off in the direction of the Charles Town west gate.

Mason carried the still heavy rucksack in one hand as he caught up to Jeremy.

"Where to?" Jeremy asked, as he marched forward without looking back.

"Let's see if we can find Captain Darby," Mason said. "We'll ask around at the pubs."

"We should pick up a couple of flintlocks, powder, and shot while we're here. Maybe we should split up."

"Excellent idea," Mason said, as he shifted the rucksack to the other hand. "I was thinking the same thing."

Jeremy kept walking.

"Hold up," Mason said, as he dug into his ruck.

Jeremy stopped, turned, and walked the few steps back to Mason.

Mason handed him a handful of the silver ingots. "Each one is an ounce, which equates to one Spanish dollar. Don't let them cheat you on the rifles."

Jeremy opened the cloth satchel slung over one shoulder, deposited the ingots, and continued his march. "Where we got the supplies last time; the stuff you gave to Mato."

Mason picked up the ruck and continued walking. "When you're done, or if you run into a problem, I'll meet you near the night watch building."

"Will do," Jeremy said, as he quickened his stride with the west gate in view.

◆◆◆

Mason stepped into his fourth pub of the day and waited for his eyes to adjust to the relative darkness. Three men sat at a table, drinking from mugs. The other tables were empty. A single barkeep, an overweight man with greasy hair, was wiping down the heavily stained bar. Mason repeated the same question he had asked in the three previous pubs. This barkeep at least knew who Captain Darby was, but had not seen him in a week.

Mason scanned the mostly empty room, not sure where to go next.

"Maybe I can help," the barkeep said, as he continued to wipe down the bar with a dirty rag.

Mason turned back to the man. "I'm in the market for a boat. Do you happen to know of anyone who could point me in the right direction? A broker maybe?"

The barkeep thought for a moment as he paused his wiping. "Pretty much every day you'll find buyers and sellers up and down the wharf. I'd ask them. They load and off load goods continuously, they might know of a boat for sale."

"Good idea," Mason said. He gave a slight nod, exited the establishment, and began walking toward the waterfront.

Mason gazed at the wharf and the piers jutting out into the Cooper River. He focused on the redbrick building, the headquarters for the town watch. He thought of the morning he'd stood before the provost marshal, being grilled about the dead body found near the pier leading out to his former sloop. He watched as men loaded or unloaded the various merchant ships. His eyes finally rested on a man perched on a three-legged stool. His elbows rested on a small, wooden table as he scrutinized the top paper on a rather thick stack. His right thumb and index finger toyed absently with a feather quill.

Mason approached and came to a stop just to the man's right. When the man didn't look up immediately, Mason cleared his throat.

The man glanced up but immediately resumed his study of the paper. "Yes?"

"My name is Stephen Mason. I'm relatively new to this fine town and was hoping to procure a boat. I thought you might have an idea of what is available."

The man was older, late fifties, maybe early sixties. His long white hair was pulled back into a pony tail that reached nearly to the middle of his back. He was dressed in the proverbial coat, breeches, stockings, and a three-pointed hat.

"A boat, you say. What kind of boat?" He placed the quill on top of the papers and looked up at Mason. He immediately placed a hand over his brow to block the sun from his eyes. "Good God, man, step out of the sun." He motioned to his left.

Mason stepped to the front of the table and extended his hand. "Stephen Mason."

"William Tyler," the man said, as he shook Mason's hand. "Harbor master."

"You're tracking imports and exports," Mason said, as he gestured toward the stack of papers.

Tyler gave a slight nod. "The Crown is entitled to its taxes and port fees."

Mason smiled. "The boat. Forty feet or so, single mast, maneuverable. Shallow draft, for the river."

"A sloop," Tyler said. "Maybe a masted longboat."

"A little larger than a longboat," Mason said. "I may need to run up and down the coast."

Tyler raised his chin and rubbed it with one hand as he gazed out at the harbor. He turned his head to Mason. "I know of the perfect boat."

Mason dipped his head and smiled.

"But it's not for sale."

"I'd be willing to pay a premium for such a boat," Mason said.

"You have cash?"

"I have silver ingots, one ounce each."

"Coins?"

"No, just ingots," Mason said. "Pure silver."

"Meet me back here in an hour," Tyler said. "I should be finished by then."

"See you in an hour, then." Mason dipped his chin and headed off.

He found Jeremy twenty minutes later, coming out of the largest trading post in town, at the north end of Bay Street. "Any luck?"

"They have the flintlocks here. And there's a lumber mill farther up the Cooper, about two miles the man said. There's a road along the river. What about a boat?"

"Maybe," Mason said. "I'm supposed to meet the Harbor Master in an hour."

"This lumber won't fit on a sloop," Jeremy said.

"I know. We'll need to hire a river barge."

"A flat boat," Jeremy said. "The man inside said the owner of the lumber mill also runs a flat boat."

"Convenient," Mason said.

An hour later Mason and Jeremy returned to the spot where Mason had left the Harbor Master. The man was just wrapping up his paper work. Mason introduced Jeremy.

Tyler placed the loose papers into a leather satchel, moved the table and stool next to the redbrick wall running the length of the wharf, and motioned for Mason and Jeremy to follow.

Tyler stopped at the last pier at the south end of the wharf. He motioned with his chin toward a single-masted boat tied up at the pier. The boat rolled softly in rhythm with the water. "Sloop, forty-two feet, tiller, and a small cabin below, in the bow. I use the cabin for storage. Single mast, open deck. Other than the cabin, there's no storage below the deck. There's two anchors, bow and stern."

Mason stepped closer to the boat. "This is your boat?"

"It is," Tyler said. "She was recently careened. The sails are two years old. She's in good condition."

"I thought it wasn't for sale," Mason said, as he continued to peruse the deck.

"Everything is for sale, at a premium," Tyler said.

"May we go aboard?"

"Sure. Take your time and look around. You won't find anything better that meets your requirements."

Mason and Jeremy stepped over the gunwale. Jeremy followed as Mason fingered the sail bundled tightly on top of the boom. They followed the boom to the mast. Mason ran his eyes and hands over the surface of the thick wood, looking for any sign of cracking. Finding none, he gazed up at the rigging, including the two rat lines running from the top of the mast down to each side of the boat. They continued to the forward hatch, just aft of where the bowsprit met the deck. They stepped down the ladder into the cramped space.

"Basically, a V-berth," Jeremy said.

Mason surveyed the darkened space. He saw several coils of line, a rolled-up section of sail cloth, and several planks of wood. "This boat would be perfect,"

Mason whispered. "I wonder how Mister Tyler defines premium."

Jeremy raised an eyebrow.

The two of them returned to the open deck. Mason glanced at the four oars lashed to the hull, two on each side, and the tiller. He made his way to the stern, checked the seams around the transom, and fondled the tiller.

"Like I said," Tyler said, "she's in fine shape."

Mason glanced at Jeremy and saw the subtle tightening of his lips, apparently agreeing with Tyler's assessment. Mason climbed back onto the pier and faced Tyler. "How much?"

Tyler ran his eyes up and down the boat. "She's really a fine boat. I hate to sell her."

"Uh-huh," Mason said. "How much?"

Tyler stared off at the horizon for several moments and turned to Mason. "Seven hundred dollars. Or seven hundred of your pieces of silver."

Mason dropped his chin and massaged his forehead. That was almost double the amount they paid for the prior sloop, and it was larger, with two decks and a full aft cabin. He took in a breath and exhaled as he raised his chin. "Five-fifty."

Tyler shook his head. "Seven hundred."

Mason knew that Tyler knew he had a sucker, or more accurately, a desperate man. Mason glanced at the boat, at Jeremy, and looked back at Tyler. "Deal."

A wide smile appeared on Tyler's face. He stuck out his hand.

Mason shook the man's hand. "How soon can we have her?"

"I can be ready in the morning with a bill of sale. Say, nine o'clock, at the Provost's office. Do you know where that is?"

"I do," Mason said. "In the morning then."

Tyler spun on his heels and stepped off.

"Happy man," Jeremy said.

"Yeah, he is," Mason agreed. He looked back at the boat. "We didn't really have a choice. And it is perfect for our needs."

"It is," Jeremy said. He looked up at the sun. "We have plenty of time. We should check out the lumber mill."

"Agreed," Mason said. "Lead the way."

"Should we stay the night in town, or head back to the plantation?" Jeremy asked as they walked.

"I told them we might have to stay the night," Mason said. "I think that's what we should do. Arrange for the lumber, its delivery, pick up the flintlocks and any tools we might need—we should be able to sail up to the house by early afternoon tomorrow. All in all, this has been a very productive trip."

CHAPTER 6

Nathan, wearing his recovered coat, and Mister Spriggs sat quietly together in the rear of the jolly boat as the three crew members pulled at the oars. They had only the stars and a sliver of moon to light the way as they rowed up the Ashley River.

"You sure you can recognize the house from the water?" Spriggs whispered.

Nathan scanned the western bank. Trees in the distance were perceptible only by their contrast against the night sky. No other details were visible. He rubbed his chin in the darkness as he thought of the possible consequences if he could not find the plantation house. Captain Low had apparently grown used to having Nathan around, hence his continued existence, but that could change on a whim, especially when Spriggs learned there was no additional silver to be had. But the silver's absence wasn't Nathan's fault. Surely, Spriggs and Low would understand. "No problem," he whispered with all the confidence he could muster.

The plantation house stood dark and quiet. The upper half of the top floor was the most visible. It contrasted against the night sky. Nathan was fairly sure this was the house. They had been rowing long enough to get the seven miles up the Ashley River. The house was two stories, and it appeared to be positioned on the land in the right spot. "That's it," Nathan whispered, as he raised his hand and pointed.

Spriggs turned to Nathan. "You're sure?"

"I'm sure," Nathan said.

"And it's just the slaves, two women, and one man, no firearms?"

"That's right," Nathan said.

Spriggs tapped the closest crewman on the shoulder. "Quiet as you approach. Don't be banging the oars around."

"There's a dock," Nathan said.

"Find the dock and tie up," Spriggs said to the crewman.

Ten minutes later the five men stood on the dock facing the still dark hulk of the house. Spriggs held a torch in one hand and a flintlock pistol in the other. He leaned closer to Nathan. "Where would they keep the silver?"

"I don't know," Nathan said.

Spriggs jabbed Nathan hard in the shoulder with the barrel of the pistol. "The silver is here, right?"

"As far as I know," Nathan said. "I helped carry the chest to the house; where it went from there, I don't know."

"Are we going or not?" one of the crewmen asked.

Spriggs poked Nathan in the shoulder again with the barrel. "If this is a waste of my time—"

"I only know where I saw it last," Nathan said. "And I saw it on the porch of that house."

In the dull light of the stars and moon, Nathan saw Spriggs bring the pistol up next to the end of the torch and heard the flint strike the frizzen. With the pistol absent powder, the flint and steel sent a cascade of sparks. Some landed on the torch, which immediately began burning.

Spriggs used his torch to light two others, each held by a crewman. He shoved his pistol into his waistband, drew his cutlass from its scabbard, and took off in a trot toward the house. The others, including Nathan, fell in behind.

◆◆◆

Sylvester stared up at the night sky as he relieved himself against a pine tree. Such was his routine in the middle of each night. He couldn't remember when he'd stopped sleeping through 'til morning—ten, maybe fifteen years. For at least that long he was up at about the same time every night. He was just finishing up when a flash of light in the distance, down by the river, caught his attention. A torch, with its flickering flame, revealed five men. Sylvester couldn't see a lot of detail, but he knew that five men with a torch at this time of night couldn't be good.

He saw two other torches come to life. The combined light identified the interlopers as white men. One of them looked familiar, somehow. Suddenly, all five men set off at a quick pace toward the main house.

Sylvester hadn't known Miss Lisa and Miss Karen that long, but it had been long enough to tell they were good people. They meant well in this less than perfect world. With Mister Jeremy and Mister Mason both gone, the women would be alone.

While still cinching his breeches, Sylvester took off in a gallop toward the house. He knew he could get to the front door before the five men made it to the back. They were moving slower, and they had farther to go. He bounded up the steps, all three in one leap, and slung the door open without bothering with his customary knock. Without slowing, he was up the stairs to the second floor in a flash. He slid to a stop in front of Miss Lisa's room. Again, without knocking, he twisted the doorknob and stuck just his head inside the room. With the bit of light through the single window, he saw Lisa rise up in bed.

"What is it?"

"Sorry, Miss Lisa," Sylvester whispered. "There are five men approaching the house. They are probably at the back door right now."

"It's just Jeremy and Mason," she said. "They must have brought someone back with them."

"It's not Jeremy or Mason," Sylvester said. "They have torches. I could see their faces. They're up to no good."

Lisa tossed the covers, leapt from the bed, and landed in front of the only window in the room. She wore only a short chemise of thin cotton that barely covered her thighs, leaving her long legs exposed.

Sylvester averted his gaze but glanced back with fluttering eyes.

"I don't see any—," Lisa started to say. She turned to a chair and started grabbing at items of clothing. "Wake Karen."

Sylvester closed the door and had taken two steps toward Karen's room when her door opened. She stepped into the hall.

"What is going on?"

"Five men, up to no good, came up to the house with torches," he said.

At that moment, they both froze at the sound of the back door opening. A soft glow emanated up the stairs.

Without another word, she hurried back into her room.

Sylvester heard the swish of cloth behind him. He turned and saw Lisa coming through her door wearing a long petticoat and a waist-length gown. It was the minimum necessary for modesty, obviously thrown on quickly. He turned to the sound of footfalls on the stairs and the increasing light from the three flaming torches. All Sylvester could do was stand there.

◆◆◆

Karen, dressed in a quickly assembled petticoat and short gown, emerged from her room just as the first of the five men stepped onto the second-floor landing. A torch in his hand lit his face and attire. He wore a long sleeved, loose fitting pull-over shirt, long pants, and high black boots. A sword occupied his right hand. The smell of strong body odor immediately filled the hallway as four other men filled the space behind the first. The flames from the three torches flickered about, throwing shadows against the walls. As the last of the five men stepped to the landing, Karen's gaze did a double take. What she was seeing wasn't possible.

"Nathan?" Lisa gasped.

Nathan stepped up next to the man in front. "This is Mister Spriggs," he said, without acknowledging the disbelief on Lisa and Karen's faces.

Karen finally tore her gaze from Nathan and shifted it to the man next to him. She studied the man's face for several moments. There was only one explanation that made any sense. Not everyone on the sloop died. And this Mister Spriggs must be from the pirate ship that Mason talked about. Karen also realized there was no way Nathan knew that Mason had been transported to the future, back again, and was still alive. She thought it better to keep it that way.

She stepped closer to Lisa and grasped her forearm with a firm grip. She hoped Lisa would understand that Karen needed to take the lead. She glanced back to Nathan. "Where are the others?" Out of the corner of her eye she saw Lisa's head spin around to Karen. Karen continued. "On the sloop, where are the others?"

Nathan dropped his chin for a moment. He raised his eyes back to Karen. "Dead. They're all dead, including Mason." He dropped his chin again. "Sorry."

Lisa looked back at Nathan and opened her mouth to speak.

Karen cut her off by tightening her grip on Lisa's arm as she continued to stare at Nathan. She tried to feign surprise, hoping the expression on her face was enough in the dull light. "What do you mean? What happened?"

"They met up with us," Spriggs said. "They elected to fight. Chances are, they would still be alive if they had just given up the silver."

The silver, Karen thought. That's why they're here. Nathan told them the silver was here, probably to save his own life. "Dorothy? Manny? What happened to Mason?"

"All dead," Nathan said. "Mason was apparently blown into the water. His body was never found."

"Of course, we didn't look that hard," Spriggs said with a smirk.

The three crewmen laughed.

Karen let her chin sink to her chest. For several moments she appeared to grieve. She finally looked back up at Nathan. "And you're the only one who survived?"

Nathan nodded. His gaze fixated on Lisa. "Where's Jeremy?"

The two women remained quiet.

"Enough talking," Spriggs said. "He's not on the plantation. If he was, he'd be standing here." He turned his attention to Karen. "Where's the silver?"

Karen looked at Lisa, back to Sylvester, and finally at Spriggs. Nathan was smart enough to know that Karen couldn't tell the truth about the silver—the bulk of it went with Misses Stewart, the previous owner, and the balance had been on the sloop. Telling the truth would probably get them all killed, including Nathan. The only thing she could think to do was stall. "Hidden. You'll never find it without my help." She glanced at Lisa and Sylvester. "I'm the only one who knows where it is."

Spriggs slowly slid the cutlass back into its sheath, handed his torch to Nathan, and took three steps forward. He grabbed Lisa around the neck with one hand, pulled her in until her back was against his chest, and cupped her breast with his free hand. He massaged roughly. "So, we don't need this one then?"

Lisa grasped the hand around her throat with both hands and tried to wiggle free. The man's arm did not relent and appeared ready to lift Lisa off her feet.

Nathan took a step forward with a sudden look of concern.

"If you kill her, you might as well kill me, too," Karen said. "I will not help you, no matter what."

Spriggs pulled Lisa closer to his body. "Who said anything about killing her?" He smiled.

His men jeered and cajoled, encouraging Spriggs to take the women with them.

Spriggs suddenly released Lisa and stepped back as he studied Karen's face. He glanced at Nathan. "I believe her," he said calmly. "But we're not leaving here without the silver." His focus suddenly shifted to Sylvester. "You probably could do without a few slaves. Fewer mouths to feed." He put his hand on the hilt of the sheathed sword and took a step toward Sylvester.

Karen stepped in front of him and raised her hand. "Okay. I'll show you. But it will have to wait until morning."

"Why morning?"

"It's buried," Karen said. "The spot is covered with leaves. I'd never be able to find it, even with the torches."

When it became apparent that Spriggs was considering the proposition, one of the crewmen leaned forward. "What about Ned?"

"He'll wait," Spriggs said, as he kept his attention on Karen. "At first light we get the silver. We'll be back to the ship before breakfast." He glanced at Nathan. "In the meantime—" His hand shot out, grabbed Lisa by her arm, and he began dragging her toward the stairs.

Lisa shrieked and tried to pull away.

"If you harm her, you won't get the silver," Karen said in a raised voice. "I can promise you that."

"It might be worth it," one of the crewmen said, as he eyed Karen.

Spriggs thought for a moment before finally releasing Lisa's arm. "I'm a patient man. This can all wait until morning. But there had better be silver," he said in a low, gruff voice.

Karen breathed a subtle sigh of relief. It was a reprieve, short lived as it might be. Karen had no doubt she and Lisa would end up raped, and probably murdered, whether they found any silver or not, which obviously they would not. She thought of Mason. He would be back the next day, but it would likely be well into morning, maybe the afternoon. She needed to think of something.

"Take your men downstairs," Karen said, as she looked at Spriggs. She turned her eyes to Nathan. "All of your men." When Spriggs finally acknowledged her with a slight nod, she turned to Sylvester. "Go back to the cottages; we'll be alright until morning."

Sylvester looked from Karen to Spriggs and gently made his way past the men and down the stairs.

Spriggs jabbed his thumb in the direction of the stairs and turned to follow his men as they reluctantly began moving. He paused and looked back at Karen. "I'm a light sleeper."

"Just keep your men away from us," Karen said.

He turned and continued down the stairs.

Karen pulled Lisa by the arm into Karen's bedroom. She closed the door and pulled her to the bed. They sat on the edge. "Not a word about Mason or that we already know about the sloop and the others," Karen whispered.

"Mason and Jeremy won't be here by daybreak," Lisa whispered back, "what are we going to do?"

"I don't know," Karen said, "but we have a little time to think about it."

CHAPTER 7

Karen suddenly realized she could see the ceiling, which meant the room was getting lighter. She turned her head toward the window and saw vestiges of color in the early morning sky. Lisa, curled up next to her, purred softly. That girl could sleep through a tornado.

Karen had spent the entire night thinking as she listened to the house's nighttime creaks and cracks. As she saw it, she had two options: fight, or run and hide. Given that all the men, except Nathan, carried flintlock pistols and swords, fighting didn't seem like much of an option. Running and hiding appeared to be the safer idea. The reason she had not already tried to slip out was mainly because that's probably exactly what Mister Spriggs expected. He likely didn't sleep any either. Also, even if she and Lisa were successful with their escape, Spriggs would take it out on Sylvester and the others. She and Lisa's escape would have to play out before Spriggs' eyes so he would know Sylvester had nothing to do with it.

A *thump* from the first floor meant the men were beginning to stir.

Karen prodded Lisa on the shoulder. "Better to deal with this downstairs," Karen whispered, "rather than have them come back up here." She motioned for Lisa to follow. "We'll make a run for it, if possible. Follow my lead."

Already fully dressed, including shoes, they both rose from the bed and shuffled to the door. They stepped quietly along the hall and down the stairs. Just as Karen put a foot on the last step, she startled at the sound of a man's voice.

"Good morning," Spriggs said, standing in the middle of the house's main room.

The others, scattered about the room in various states of repose, began to rise.

Karen glanced at the front door, only a few feet away, before turning her attention to Spriggs. She and Lisa might never have a better time to make a run for it. She tried to judge whether they could make it to the door, open it, and bolt before Spriggs could react. Doubtful. He seemed fairly spry.

"The sooner you show us the silver, the sooner we'll be on our way," Spriggs said.

Karen took the final step to the floor. "And I have your word on that?"

"Of course," Spriggs said.

Wide grins spread across the faces of the three crewmen, now on their feet.

Nathan just stood there, looking stupid. He finally dropped his chin to his chest.

Spriggs motioned with his hand toward the door. "After you."

Karen led Lisa through the doorway, with the five men bunched up behind. Karen immediately saw all the workers, including Sylvester, standing quietly together a few yards from the steps. When Spriggs appeared in the doorway behind Lisa, the workers shuffled their feet and shifted the various tools in their hands, everything from sticks to axes. They began to mumble.

In unison, Spriggs and the three crewmen pulled their flintlock pistols from their waistbands, continued down the steps, and stood shoulder to shoulder.

Nathan, unarmed, moved closer to Karen and Lisa.

"Go back to your work," Spriggs said. "We're here to retrieve what's ours."

The workers remained where they were, obviously unmoved by his words.

Spriggs turned to Karen. "Do you want to see them killed?"

"You can't kill us all," Sylvester said, as he took a step forward.

Spriggs pointed his pistol at Sylvester's chest. "I can kill you."

Suddenly Karen darted forward and stood in front of Sylvester, facing Spriggs. "There is no silver," Karen said. She looked at Nathan. "And he knew there was no silver. Most of what we found went toward this plantation. The prior owner left with the silver days ago. The balance was on the sloop. There is no silver."

Spriggs pondered her words for several moments and slowly turned his head to Nathan.

"Is she telling the truth?"

"The plantation is worth much more than you lost," Nathan said.

Spriggs clenched his jaws. "What are we supposed to do with a plantation?" he spouted.

"Maybe they could borrow against it," Nathan said.

Spriggs pondered that a few moments and looked back at Nathan. "You mentioned a Jeremy."

"That's right," Nathan said, now with more exuberance. "Jeremy could borrow what you're owed and bring us the money." He pointed his chin at Lisa. "He'll do anything to protect these two."

"Us?" Spriggs asked.

Nathan pointed at Karen. "She'll cut my throat while I sleep. I can't stay here."

"He's right about that," Karen said.

Spriggs scanned the workers and glanced back at his men. He stroked his beard as he stared at the ground. Suddenly he lurched, wrapped his free arm around Lisa's waist, and constricted his hold. The muscles in his chest flexed. He raised his pistol and pointed it at Lisa's head.

Lisa screamed and initially tried to wiggle away but finally gave up against the vise-like embrace.

"You tell Jeremy he can have this one back when he brings me the silver."

The workers began to mumble as they inched forward.

Karen held up a hand to calm them. She had no doubt the workers could prevail over Spriggs and his men. But at what cost? Four would die instantly from the pistols. Then they'd start hacking with their swords. Lisa would be the first. "Where?"

A look of panic spread over Lisa's face.

Karen got her attention with her eyes. "Remember what I told you."

Lisa noticeably relaxed but still wore a worried expression.

Karen looked at Spriggs. "Where?"

"There's an inlet thirty miles south, the Edisto. You can't miss it. We'll wait there for three days. Any sign of anyone except a small boat with the silver and she dies." He motioned for his men to follow and began dragging Lisa toward the river. He suddenly stopped and looked back at Karen. "We'll be gone at the end of the three days." He leaned his face closer to Lisa's hair and smelled. "And she'll be gone, too." He continued toward the river, followed by his three crewmen.

Nathan remained behind, staring at Karen.

"If you let anything happen to her, and I mean anything, I'll hunt you down myself," Karen said.

Nathan flexed his jaw as he peered at Karen. He exhaled, turned, and stepped off.

◆◆◆

Mason glanced up at the late afternoon sky and back to the water ahead. He gave a slight push on the tiller to keep the sloop in the center of the river. The jib, filled with a slight breeze, gave the boat enough speed to make maneuvering possible. But just the same, he had Jeremy stationed amidships, port side, with a long pole ready to assist should the boat approach shallow water. So far, the boat had performed beautifully. The copper clad hull did wonders at reducing the amount of growth on the bottom. Reduced growth meant reduced drag through the water. Mason estimated they were doing two knots, with barely enough wind to fill the jib.

"Dock's just ahead," Jeremy yelled.

"Drop the jib," Mason said. "We can coast from here."

Jeremy dashed forward and released the sheet connecting the tack to the bowsprit. He immediately began pulling at the sail cloth until the entire jib was bunched on the deck at his feet.

With Mason working the tiller, and Jeremy a long pole, they were able to ease the boat up to the end of the dock.

"I figure we have about five inches to spare on the draft," Mason said.

"Probably less," Jeremy said. "We could use a tender."

Mason sighted Karen and Sylvester hurrying toward the dock.

Mason helped Jeremy secure the boat to the dock and stepped onto the wood planks just as Karen and Sylvester arrived.

"We have trouble," Karen said.

"Where's Lisa?" Jeremy asked, as he stepped to the dock and looked around.

"They took her."

"Who took her?" Mason asked. "When?"

"Early this morning," Karen said. "The ones who attacked you and the others on the sloop."

"Looking for their silver," Mason said. He thought for a moment and looked at Karen. "How did they know about the plantation?"

"Nathan."

Mason cocked his head. "Nathan? He survived?"

"He was here, in the flesh, with four others. The one in charge was named Spriggs."

"That son of a bitch," Jeremy erupted. "When I get my hands on him—"

"The first thing we need to do is find them," Mason said. He looked at Karen.

"Spriggs said to bring the silver to an inlet about thirty miles south. He also said he'd wait three days, after that he and Lisa would be gone."

"We need to go now," Jeremy said, as he took a step toward the new sloop.

"Go where?" Mason asked, as he halted Jeremy with the back of his hand.

"To Myrtle Beach, to get those four thousand silver ingots you mentioned."

Mason shook his head. "First of all, I only have three thousand buried there. We spent nearly a thousand on the boat, lumber, and guns. I believe Low's chest contained four thousand seven hundred. We don't have enough. And second, even if we could replace all that was in the chest, Low would just take the money, kill us, and keep Lisa. We can't trust a pirate and we can trust Nathan even less."

Jeremy, with lines of worry etched across his forehead, locked eyes on Mason. "We have to do something. Can you imagine what they must be doing to her right now?"

"Their first priority is the silver. We have three days. We can't go off half-cocked. We need a plan."

"And you need more people," Karen said.

Mason lifted his chin. "Yeah."

Jeremy clenched his jaw as he stared at the ground.

"Getting ourselves killed won't help Lisa," Mason said. He turned to Sylvester. "There'll be a barge loaded with lumber coming from town in two or three days. Can you make sure it's off loaded and stacked near the kitchen?"

"Yes, sir, Mister Mason, but you'll need some people to help with getting Miss Lisa."

"I have someone in mind, but thank you," Mason said. He clapped Sylvester on the shoulder.

"He tried to stop them," Karen said. "But there was nothing any of us could do that wouldn't have gotten Lisa killed."

"I know," Mason said.

"Who did you have in mind?" Jeremy asked.

"Colonel Rhett or Captain Darby, maybe both."

"Then we should head back to town right now," Jeremy said, as he started again toward the sloop.

"I'm coming," Karen said. "I can at least help with the boat."

Before Mason could object, Karen fell in behind Jeremy.

Mason turned to Sylvester. "Can you handle things here while we're gone?"

"Don't you worry about a thing," Sylvester said. "I'll take care of the lumber and I'll make sure the place is run just like you were here."

"Hold on," Mason said, as he marched the few feet to the sloop and jumped aboard. He disappeared into the forward berth and returned a minute later. He approached Sylvester with his hand outstretched.

"The barge crew will be expecting twenty of these," Mason said, as he dropped the silver ingots into Sylvester's hand. "If there's a problem, don't get into any kind of argument. Just tell them I'll handle it when I return."

"I'll make sure it's done just as you say."

"If all goes well, we'll be back within that three days," Mason said. As he jumped back aboard the sloop, a thought popped into his mind. *It was conceivable that none of them would be returning.*

◆◆◆

Lisa's anxiety was outweighed only by the stench aboard Edward Low's schooner. She could not believe that men could smell so bad. It was as though none of them had ever taken a bath in their lives. Each was caked in grime, and wore tattered clothes that had never seen a wash pail. The only exceptions were Low, Mister Spriggs and, to a lesser degree, Nathan.

While trying to get her quivering lower lip under control, she scanned the cabin. Practically every inch of the wood planked deck, bulkheads, and overhead were marred and stained. A large brown patch occupied a section of the deck next to where she sat. She was sure it was dried blood. She tried to scrunch away from the stain, but managed only a few inches as she pressed tighter into her corner of the room. She gazed at her bound hands and feet. A precaution, the pirate Low had said as he and Spriggs left the cabin. She had not seen a soul since, and that had been hours earlier. What worried her the most was the growing urge to pee. Even a ship this large probably didn't have a head. Everything went over the side. Doing so was no problem for the men, but for her it would be precarious and embarrassing. Mortifying, really, as she thought about the stares she got as she was escorted across the deck on her way to what was apparently the captain's cabin. She thought about what Spriggs had said back at the plantation. Three days. A person can survive without water for no more than three days. She would have to drink and she would have to pee. She had two choices: endure the leering men above, or use the opposite corner of the cabin. She opted for the latter.

She bent forward until her fingers reached the rope wrapped around her stocking-clad ankles. With just her fingertips she fumbled with the knot until finally it began to loosen. A few minutes of pushing and pulling at the stiff rope finally freed her legs. She got to her feet and, with her hands still tied, made her way along the transom and the starboard hull. At the opposite corner, she lifted her petticoats as best she could, squatted, and relieved herself. She watched as the yellow streams of urine ebbed across the deck in concert with the ever-changing angles of the deck. Just as she finished, the cabin door burst open. She looked up at Spriggs staring down at her.

"There's a place on the main deck for that," he said with a scowl.

"In front of all your men," she countered.

Spriggs stared at her for several moments but finally dipped his chin ever so slightly. "I'll get you a bucket," he said, as he stepped forward, holding a mug in his outstretched hand.

Lisa took the mug, peered into the opening, and smelled the contents.

"It's watered-down rum. I'll be back with that bucket and something to eat." He turned to leave but stopped and looked back at Lisa's unbound feet. He turned and closed the door behind him.

CHAPTER 8

"Good morning, sir," Mason said to the only person manning the landing on the Ashley River. He was an older gentleman with a long flowing beard.

"Mornin'."

Mason motioned to the sloop secured to the dock. "Would it be alright to leave her there for a while?"

"For a shilling it would."

Mason slipped out of his rucksack straps, reached inside, and came out with a single silver ingot. "Would a dollar's worth of silver cover it, we may be a little longer than a while?"

"Four times the rate, sure," the man said. "I'll keep an eye on her for ya."

Mason, with Jeremy and Karen in tow, stepped off toward Charles Town. He stopped and looked back at the man. "Happen to know where I can find Colonel Rhett's house?"

"North on the trail," the man said, "can't miss the gate to Rhettsbury."

Mason dipped his chin and the three of them resumed their march.

Jeremy hurried into the lead, holding a flintlock rifle in one hand.

As they walked, Mason thought of the William Rhett house he had previously walked past at 54 Hasell Street, in modern day Charleston. Mason was as amazed then as he was now that the house was still standing, one of the few buildings to survive. In present day 1720, it would have only been recently built. He was sure the house and land looked nothing like it would three hundred years in the future. And having been built outside the city walls, it would take some scouting to find it.

"What was with the smirk on the man's face?" Karen asked.

"From what little I know," Mason said as they walked, "this is a pivotal time in South Carolina's history. The colony is transitioning from being owned and operated by a group of proprietors, to being governed by King George."

"Why would anyone want that?"

"The people thought the colony was being mismanaged, and vulnerable to attack from the Spanish. They wanted protection from the Crown."

"The man smirked at the mention of Colonel Rhett's name," Karen said.

"Colonel Rhett supported the proprietors, while most of the people wanted protection from the Brits."

"Sounds like you did some reading while you were in the future."

"Had little else to do at night," Mason said, "just read and planned."

"I still can hardly believe you made it back. The odds must be astronomical."

"I couldn't explain it the first time, the second time, and certainly not the third."

Karen smiled. "You're back, that's all that matters."

"I couldn't agree more."

Jeremy, twenty yards ahead, turned left onto the wide trail that would one day become King Street. He looked back just as Mason and Karen stepped onto the trail. "Three days, people. We only have three days, and as of right now, we don't even have a plan."

Mason and Karen quickened their pace and caught up to Jeremy.

"How much are you going to tell Colonel Rhett?" Karen asked.

Mason stared at her for several moments before responding. "We were attacked by the pirate Edward Low on the high seas, he killed nearly everyone in the group, and he has Lisa."

"What about the silver?" Jeremy asked from a few yards farther ahead.

"Yeah, that could be a problem," Mason said. "The silver certainly didn't belong to Low, but it didn't belong to us either."

"Rhett's probably already wondered where we got the money to buy the original sloop, a plantation, and now another sloop," Karen said.

"Let's not get bogged down in the details," Mason said. "Keep it simple. He attacked our boat, he accepted one of our group into his crew, that person has always had a desire for Lisa, they killed the others, and I was presumed dead. Nathan talked Low into kidnapping her for ransom."

"Sounds weak, but mostly true," Karen said.

"Let's keep the focus on Lisa, the kidnapping, and ransom," Mason said. "We'll judge his response to that, and adapt as necessary. I'm hoping Rhett's reputation as a pirate hunter kicks in."

"Sounds good to me," Jeremy said, as he continued his fast pace, without looking at Mason.

"Think that will work?" Karen asked.

"He either helps us, or he doesn't," Mason said. "If it's the latter, we'll try Captain Darby. If he says no, we'll do it ourselves."

"Captain Darby is a merchantman," Karen said.

"Okay, maybe he knows someone," Mason responded. "Let's hope Colonel Rhett has some ideas."

Another mile along the trail they came to a deeply rutted road, cutting off to the right. A small placard on a pole read *Rhettsbury*.

Jeremy glanced at the placard and made the turn, without a reduction in his pace.

Mason and Karen followed.

The road wound through the trees for at least two city blocks before a large house finally came into view.

Jeremy marched up the steps and knocked on the door.

Mason and Karen stepped up behind him and stood on the stoop.

After several long moments, the door swung open revealing an older black woman. Her expression was one of expectation.

"We'd like to see—" Jeremy started before Mason's hand on his shoulder prompted him to stop. He looked around at Mason.

"Is Colonel Rhett available?" Mason asked.

"Who shall I say is calling?" the woman asked.

"Stephen Mason. We met in town."

"Who is it, Martha?" came a voice from inside the house.

An older woman stepped beside Martha in the open doorway. Her style of dress gave her away as someone important.

"Sorry to disturb you, ma'am," Mason said, "we would like to speak to Colonel Rhett, if he is available. It's a matter of some urgency."

"The colonel is not receiving visitors," the woman said, and started to close the door.

"Ma'am, it will only take a few minutes of his time," Mason said. "It's very important that we speak with him."

"Who is it, Sarah?" came a man's voice from deeper inside the house. Mason recognized it as Colonel Rhett's voice despite the hoarseness.

"Two gentlemen and a woman," Sarah replied. "Stephen Mason. Says he met you in town."

Colonel Rhett, wearing a dark blue robe, stepped up behind the two women. "Mister Mason," he said. He coughed. "Please excuse my voice. Been feeling a little under the weather."

"You should be in bed," Sarah said, stepping back from the doorway. "Whatever it is, it can wait until you are feeling better."

"I'm afraid it can't wait," Mason said.

"It's alright, Sarah," Rhett said. "I'm feeling much better today. Do we have some tea we can offer these kind people?"

Sarah turned to Martha. "Please show them into the study and brew a pot of tea."

"Yes, ma'am," Martha said, as she swung the door open wider.

Rhett motioned for the three of them to enter.

Martha led the four of them through the foyer, past a wide set of stairs, and into a wood paneled room. Shelves, with a modest collection of books, occupied one whole corner.

Rhett motioned Mason, Jeremy, and Karen to chairs arranged in a conversation pit at one end of the room. None of the chairs matched, but they all represented fine woodworking, for the period.

"I'll get that tea going," Martha said, as she headed out of the room.

Everyone took a seat, except Rhett. He remained standing. It fit what Mason had read of the man's personality—a bit domineering.

"So, what is this matter of urgency?" Rhett asked, as he scanned the three faces looking up at him.

Mason motioned to Jeremy. "Jeremy's wife has been kidnapped by the pirate Edward Low. It happened early this morning. She was taken from the plantation while Jeremy and I were away on business."

Rhett shook his head. "Why would Ned Low take—"

"Lisa," Jeremy said.

"—Lisa from your plantation?"

"It all started a couple of weeks ago, when Low attacked our sloop, the one we bought through Captain Darby. We were outrunning him until our sail split. He caught up and fired his cannons. I was blown out of the boat and drifted, unconscious. Everyone else was killed except, as it turns out, one person. They showed up yesterday and took Lisa for ransom. They expect us to bring him five thousand dollars' worth of silver in exchange for Lisa's return."

"Where?" Rhett asked, as he paced back and forth.

"Thirty miles south, a small inlet," Karen said.

"I know the inlet quite well," Rhett said. "Mouth of the confluence of several rivers. The South Edisto is the best known."

"What kind of ship? How many guns?"

"Schooner," Mason said. "Ten guns."

"We have been after Mister Low for some time," he said, as he continued to pace. "Unfortunately, I no longer have the political power around here that I once had. Still, I do have associates that feel as strongly about piracy as I do." He stopped pacing and turned to Mason. "When are you supposed to meet?"

"He gave us three days," Mason said.

Martha entered the room carrying a tea service on a serving tray. She set the tray on a small table and poured four cups of the steaming liquid. As Rhett continued to pace back and forth, she handed a cup and saucer to Mason, Karen, and Jeremy. She watched Rhett for several moments, finally shook her head, and exited the room.

Mason took a sip of the tea and sat the cup and saucer on a nearby table.

"I'm worried about what they might be doing to Lisa," Jeremy said, as he stood and placed his cup and saucer on the table.

Rhett stopped pacing, stared at Jeremy for several moments, and turned to Mason. "I'm still not clear on why Ned would follow a stranger to your plantation. He took a serious risk marauding so close to Charles Town."

"That's not clear to me either," Mason said.

"I take it you would like to have Lisa back unharmed?"

"That's our only interest," Mason said, as he glanced at Jeremy.

"Pity," Rhett said, as he stared at the floor. "Without Lisa in the picture, we could block his escape and blast away."

"We need to get Lisa off the ship before the firing starts," Mason said.

Rhett gave a subtle nod, coughed, and pulled his robe tighter at the chest.

At that moment Sarah entered the room. "William, you need to be in bed."

Rhett motioned her away, without looking up.

"I'll be putting *I told you so* on your tombstone," she said, as she turned and exited in a huff.

"She's probably right," Karen said. "You don't look so good."

Rhett motioned at her with his hand as he glanced up. "I'll be fine, young lady. I can't pass up the opportunity to get Ned Low."

"He probably expects us to go straight to you, or someone like you," Jeremy said.

"Ned Low is a cheat, a scoundrel, and a blood-thirsty killer," Rhett said, "but he's also cunning and smart. You are correct, he would expect you to seek help in town."

"Do you have something in mind?" Mason asked.

"The first thing we need to do is round up some firepower of our own. I'll send word into town. In the meantime, we need to figure out a way to get Lisa off that ship." He stared at Jeremy. "You say Lisa is your wife, and they expect you to bring the ransom?"

"That's right," Jeremy said, as he glanced at Mason and Karen.

"Also, they don't know about me," Mason said. "Low and our shipmate think I'm at the bottom of the ocean."

Rhett stared at Mason.

"If these men are cutthroat savages—," Jeremy said, before he choked up.

"That girl is a valuable commodity," Rhett said. "She will be well taken care of until they find out about the silver."

"Where would they be holding her on the ship?" Mason asked.

Rhett thought for a moment before answering. "Nowhere near the crew, probably the captain's cabin."

Rhett yelled for Martha.

Martha immediately appeared in the doorway. "Yes, sir, Mister William."

"Fetch Tom, I have an errand for him."

Martha disappeared.

Rhett walked to a desk at the other end of the room and rummaged for a sheet of paper. He scribbled something on the sheet and was folding it just as a young black man entered the room.

"Yes, sir, Mister William."

"Take this to Mister Charles Sievert," Rhett said, as he stepped to Tom and handed him the folded paper. "You can find him at the town watch. No dawdling, get there and get back."

"Yes, sir," Tom said, as he turned and disappeared.

Rhett walked back to Mason, Karen, and Jeremy, still sitting in the chairs.

Mason placed an empty tea cup back on the table and stood up. "What do we do?"

Rhett eyed Mason for several moments. "Can you swim?"

CHAPTER 9

Tom returned an hour later. Trotting twenty yards behind him was a man, apparently Charles Sievert, trying his best to keep up. Out of breath, the man climbed the steps and stood in front of Rhett.

Mister Sievert was not at all what Mason had expected. This man wore a tattered shirt and breeches, both stained, and a red long coat that had seen better days. A scraggly beard covered his weathered face. The man smelled of body odor and rum as he wobbled, barely able to stand. The only thing decent about the man was the relatively new three-pointed, black hat that sat cocked to one side on his head. Mason had presumed the man worked at the town watch, but apparently he had been incarcerated there.

"Where'd you get the hat, Charlie?" Rhett asked.

"A bit of three-card loo last night at Jacobs Tavern," he said with a slight slur.

"Charlie here was a mate on several of my expeditions. We go way back." He turned his head toward Charlie. "Too much to drink last night?"

"Just a wee bit," Charlie said.

"He weren't able to read the note, Mister William," Tom said. He couldn't focus on the writin'. So, I brung him."

"Good job, Tom," Rhett said. "You can go about your way."

Tom jumped from the porch and ran off toward a field being worked by several black men in the distance.

"We need your help with something," Rhett said to Charlie.

Charlie wobbled. "Anything for you, Colonel."

"Charlie, this is Mason, Jeremy, and Karen."

Charlie's eyes wandered from Mason, to Jeremy, and lingered a little too long on Karen, apparently trying to focus. "Nice to meet you," Charlie said, as he removed his hat. He smiled, with several missing teeth, at Karen.

"These folks have a problem with the notorious Ned Low."

Charlie's expression turned serious as he faced Rhett.

"The conniving pirate kidnapped young Jeremy's wife," Rhett said. "He wants a ransom of five thousand dollars, in silver."

"Paying them won't get your wife back," Charlie said, as he turned his focus to Jeremy. "Give 'em the money and you won't see it, or your wife, again."

"That's what I've been telling them," Rhett said. "But it doesn't matter, since they don't have five thousand in silver."

Charlie looked back to Rhett.

"We have a plan to get the girl back before the shooting starts," Rhett said, "but we need an extra man."

Charlie straightened up but still leaned slightly to one side. "I'm your man, Colonel, you know that."

"I do, Charlie. Let's get some coffee in you and then we'll talk."

◆◆◆

By midafternoon, after a lunch composed of a simple stew and biscuits, Charlie was looking much more alert. Mason was amazed at how much more capable he looked.

"I think I understand my part," Charlie said, as the five of them sat on the porch, "but when do you show up?"

"Sarah won't let me near a ship," Rhett said. He went into a coughing fit, which served to emphasize the point. When he finally stopped coughing, he continued. "But I can arrange to have two sloops of war in position tomorrow night. The governor and I don't see eye-to-eye on much these days, but he'll go along if it means clearing these waters of the likes of Ned Low."

"Tomorrow night," Jeremy said, "that's a long time to leave Lisa on a ship full of cutthroats."

"Can't be helped," Rhett said. "You two can't go in there alone. You'll end up dead. And it will take that long to get the two ships ready to sail."

"I should be the one to go in," Jeremy said.

"I need you to take care of Karen," Mason said. Taking care of Karen was part of it, but also Jeremy's emotional state could turn into a liability. Mason glanced at Jeremy's trembling fingers. He was doing all he could to hold it together. Mason looked at Rhett. "In the meantime?"

"In the meantime, we need information. I think a reconnoiter is called for. We need their exact position and number of ships, at a minimum. He could have friends."

"We can do that," Mason said. "We'll look like a small merchantman. In fact, our boat is a small merchantman."

"Not too close; remain well offshore," Rhett said. "The winds are good. I recommend Jeremy and Karen drop you and Charlie off if Ned Low is where he said he would be. Jeremy can be back in town by late afternoon. If the situation warrants, the two sloops will head out immediately, arriving on station well after dark."

"So, we head out at first light," Mason said, as he got to his feet. "We'll sleep on the sloop at the Ashley

River Landing. If anything changes, that's where we'll be until early morning. Just need to pick up a few things in town." He looked at Charlie. "Do you have what you need?"

Charlie pulled a dagger from a scabbard concealed at the small of his back, under his coat. "This is all I need."

Mason motioned to Jeremy and Karen. "We'll be off then."

◆◆◆

A half hour before sunup, Jeremy pushed off from the dock, while Mason managed the tiller.

The current carried them well into Charles Town harbor where they hoisted the mainsail and jib. The sun was just beginning to peek over the horizon when the wind began moving the boat. They passed Fort Johnston, on the northern beach of Morris Island, and the spit of land that would one day become the home for Fort Sumter. They passed through the river's mouth and finally into the open ocean.

Mason pointed the boat south, veering away from the coast. He wanted to be at least four miles off shore when they passed the inlet. Charlie knew every inch of the coast along the eastern shore, and knew exactly where to look.

The winds were steady at about ten knots, directly from the east, providing a near-perfect broad reach.

Mason didn't know much about apparent wind and wasn't very good at estimating his speed over ground, but they were clicking along at a good pace.

After an hour or so, Jeremy took over the tiller and Mason joined Charlie at the starboard bow.

Charlie glanced up at Mason's approach but quickly turned his attention back to the coast. "Nothing, so far," he said.

"How much farther?" Mason asked.

"Couple hours to the inlet. There won't be anything to see if he has his ship deeper in the mouth of that confluence, but that would be a stupid place to wait. Ned Low is not stupid. He'll have his ship anchored just offshore so he can run for it if he sees anything suspicious."

Mason glanced back at Jeremy, Karen standing next to him, and stepped closer to Charlie. "What are the chances she's still in one piece?"

Charlie took a deep breath, exhaled, and clenched his jaw. He subtly shook his head side-to-side. "Honestly, I don't know. It depends, I guess, on what kind of mood Ned is in and how quickly he gets tired of waiting for something that has a small chance of showing up. He knows that raising five thousand in silver, in three days, is highly improbable."

"But not impossible," Mason said.

"No, not impossible."

"And if we fail?"

"He'll leave with the girl, rape her, let his crew rape her, and feed her to the fish."

"I guess we can't fail," Mason said. "What are his chances of getting past Rhett's two sloops?"

"He'll try to break out with guns blasting," Charlie said. "His schooner is larger, but it also has more sail. He's experienced, and he's escaped before, when his capture appeared to be a foregone conclusion." He glanced at Mason. "His chances are very good."

After another hour, Jeremy joined Mason and Charlie at the bow, while Karen took a turn at the tiller.

The wind held steady, the boat sliced through the water, but still, it looked like they were moving in slow motion against the shore.

The sun was well up when they finally approached the South Edisto inlet, in the distance.

Charlie motioned in that direction. "She's coming up."

All three men squinted as they tried to focus.

Charlie slapped the gunwale. "She's there. Two masts." He cocked his head forward as though the extra couple of inches would improve his vision. "Schooner. Has to be him."

"I see one ship," Mason said.

"There could be another, farther in," Charlie said. "That's something Ned would do. But maybe not, if he doesn't want to share any of the silver with another crew."

"Let's hope," Mason said.

"I've seen enough," Charlie said. "Have Karen veer out to sea, over the horizon, before we turn back."

◆◆◆

Charlie pointed toward the coast. "Head for that break, there."

Mason pushed on the tiller, turning the boat toward the coast. "Are we far enough down?"

"Almost ten miles; this will be fine," Charlie said. "It's the mouth of the North Edisto." He looked up and down the deck of the sloop. "Shallow draft. This will take us right up to the sand."

Mason adjusted the tiller, while Jeremy and Karen trimmed the sails for the downwind.

Forty minutes later, they dropped sails as they passed the sandbar on their way to the southwest shoreline of the river's mouth. The keel slid into the sand a few feet from the beach.

Mason looked at Jeremy. "Rhett should be waiting with the two sloops, at the Cooper River wharfs."

"We know the drill," Jeremy said. "Follow them back at a safe distance and pick you guys up right here. Should be here a few hours after dark."

Mason looked at Karen.

"We'll be fine," Karen said. "Just worry about yourself, and getting Lisa off that ship."

Mason wrapped his arms around Karen's waist and gave her a long, passionate kiss.

"We need to get going," Charlie said.

Mason gave Karen another kiss and stepped back. He leaned closer. "The pistol is in the V-berth, don't be afraid to use it, if needed."

"I know," Karen said.

Mason hefted two gourds filled with water and a buckskin satchel. He put his hand on the butt of the machete sheathed on his left hip, winked at Karen, and joined Charlie. They jumped over the side, into water about three quarters of the way up Mason's black boots. He sloshed the few feet to shore and watched as Jeremy pushed away.

Karen waved and headed back to the tiller.

Mason followed Charlie onshore. He watched Jeremy maneuver the small boat into deeper water, where it caught the outgoing current and was soon being whisked into the open water. With a final wave, Mason turned and followed Charlie into the tree line.

"We have beach all the way to the south inlet," Charlie said. "This is the north inlet, a little less than ten miles. Three hours of walking."

"That will put us there a little before dark," Mason said, as he fell in behind Charlie. In his head, he ran through the plan and how he envisioned the sequence of events would play out.

He saw the whole thing playing out perfectly: with Lisa saved, the pirate vessel sunk, and Ned Low captured or dead. He shook his head. *As usual, there were a million things that could go wrong.*

◆◆◆

Nathan approached the captain's cabin, balancing a bowl of fish stew on top of a mug. "Grab something to eat," Nathan said to the crewman standing guard at the door. "I'll watch her until you return."

The crewman glanced at the closed door, eyed Nathan for several moments, and finally stepped aside. He marched off with a grunt.

Nathan opened the cabin door and took a step inside, still balancing the mug and bowl of stew with one hand. The anticipation of seeing Lisa quickly turned to disappointment as he looked around the empty room. He sat the bowl and mug on the captain's dining table and again inspected every corner of the room. The only thing amiss, other than the room being devoid of Lisa, was one of the three aft windows. The open hatch swung back and forth by its hinges, with the motion of the ship. A single thought occupied Nathan's mind, *They're going to think I set her free.*

Nathan ran to the window and stuck his head through the opening. Schooners generally sit rather low in the water, and this one was no exception. The drop to the ocean's surface was only about fifteen feet.

He scanned the water in all directions. He saw mostly mud flats. The closest real land was the eastern bank of the inlet. Even with the current from the river, the hundred yards were swimmable, especially for an athletic person like Lisa. Nathan had seen her swim farther when they were all marooned on the coast at Myrtle Beach.

He scanned the white-sand beach, but couldn't see much in the dimming light. He turned back to the empty room, eyed the pieces of rope she'd left behind, and stared into oblivion for several moments. He thought of jumping out the same window and swimming for shore. But where would he go? He had burned his bridge to the plantation. He looked toward the open door at the sound of approaching footsteps. "She's gone," he yelled as loud as he could. "The girl's escaped!"

CHAPTER 10

"He must have helped her escape," the crewman said, standing before Ned Low and Mister Spriggs.

"The cabin was empty when I went in," Nathan said. "She was already gone."

"What took you so long to call out?" the crewman asked.

Low turned his attention to Nathan. "That's a good question."

"I, I was in a state of disbelief," Nathan said. "Then I saw the open window. I checked the water and the shore."

"And you saw nothing," Spriggs said.

"That's right, there was nothing to see. She was already long gone." He eyed the crewman standing next to him. "She escaped on his watch."

"So, what I have standing before me is either a total incompetent or a traitor," Low said. He looked at Spriggs. "What do you think?"

"One or the other, for sure."

"She was—" Nathan started, but abruptly stopped when Low raised his hand.

"Get out of my sight, both of you."

Nathan hesitated while the crewman hurried out of the room.

Ned put his hand on the butt of his cutlass and scowled at Nathan.

Nathan scurried through the door.

"Now what?" Spriggs asked. "It'll be pitch black in a few minutes."

"Put some men ashore," Low said. "They can work their way north, while we make sail. We put more men ashore ten miles or so up the coast. They work their way back. We'll find her."

"Tonight?"

"Of course, tonight," Low said with impatience. "Tomorrow is the third day. Besides, I'm tired of waiting."

❖❖❖

"They're getting underway," Charlie said.

Mason jerked his head up from behind the small sand dune and peered through the dimming light. He saw men gathering at the capstan, preparing to lift the anchor, and other men preparing to hoist the sails. "What's going on? Why would they be leaving?"

"I don't know," Charlie said, as he pointed at Low's schooner. "Look, there."

Mason focused where Charlie pointed. He saw three men lowering themselves into the ship's jolly boat, while a fourth waited at the oars.

The oarsman began stroking the water toward the east bank of the inlet, exactly where Mason and Charlie hid behind some brush, near the water's edge.

"We need to move," Charlie whispered.

"So much for our plan," Mason said, as he got to a kneeling position behind the bush. He glanced in all directions and finally pointed toward the deeper swamp to his right. Without a word, he started off in that direction in a low crouch, using the various shrubs and trees for concealment.

Charlie followed.

Ten feet into the swamp's tree line, Mason paused behind a large oak.

Charlie came to a stop next to him. "The only thing that would explain their actions is your girl must have escaped."

"Possibly," Mason said. He thought of Nathan. Would he have finally made a run for it? Mason subtly shook his head back and forth. Not without Lisa. So, either she'd escaped alone, or they'd escaped together. Mason had turned his head toward where they had just come when he heard voices in the distance. He couldn't make out the words, but one of the voices was unmistakable. *Nathan*. That answered one of Mason's questions. He was the third in a three-man hunting party, which meant Lisa had escaped on her own. They must believe she went this way. It made sense. This was the closest land to where the ship was anchored.

"What now?" Charlie asked.

"Lisa must have escaped on her own." Mason pointed in the direction of the voices. "They are after her."

"And setting sail?"

Mason thought for a moment. "Up the coast, put more men ashore, and work back this way."

"If she escaped and headed this way, how did she get past us?"

"Good question," Mason said. "She definitely didn't travel along the shoreline, we would have seen her. She must have gone inland more."

"Or your entire theory is wrong," Charlie commented.

"There is that. But let's presume my theory is correct, that she's traveling through the swamp farther inland."

Charlie shook his head back and forth, barely perceptible in the almost total darkness. "That would be some rough going. Especially in the dark."

"She'll find a place to hole up," Mason said. "That's what—" He cut himself short at the sound of voices getting closer.

Closer to the water, the ocean breeze had kept the mosquitoes at bay. Deeper in the swamp they were alive and swarming. Mason heard their buzzing as they approached his ears for an evening meal. He tried to turn his attention to the sounds of the three men as they walked along the beach. At their closest point, they passed within twenty-five yards of where Mason and Charlie stood.

"We'll let them get well beyond us and then we search for Lisa," Mason whispered.

◆◆◆

"The ship was at the mouth of the inlet," Jeremy said, as he stood on the wharf, facing Colonel Rhett. "Sails were down. Appeared to be anchored."

"Excellent!" Rhett said. "We don't have to wait until morning. We can move on them as soon as we can get there."

"What about Lisa?" Karen asked, standing next to Jeremy.

"Charlie and Mason will make their move as soon as it's dark enough," Rhett said. He waved his arm in a wide arc. "It's already dark enough. They'll have plenty of time to get the job done."

All three turned to the sound of paddles stroking the water. By the light of a torch attached to the city wall a few feet away, they watched as a jolly boat glided to a stop with a *bump* against the wharf.

Two men secured their oars and steadied the boat as two other men got to their feet. They were both well-dressed in the proverbial long coat, breeches, and high boots. They both climbed up on the dock and approached.

"Jeremy and Karen, this is Captain Buckner and Captain Thomas," Rhett said. He shook hands with both men.

Jeremy shook their hands.

Both men bowed slightly and tipped their hats to Karen.

Captain Thomas' gaze lingered on Karen, while Captain Buckner turned to Rhett.

"We're ready to set sail," Buckner said. "We're both well-armed and well-manned."

"Jeremy, here, was just reporting on his reconnoiter," Rhett said. "Low's schooner is anchored just outside the inlet. I suggest you make sail and attack at your earliest convenience."

Captain Thomas faced Jeremy. "Just the one ship, ten guns?"

"We saw only the one ship," Jeremy said. "Anchored at the mouth of the inlet. I suppose it's possible another ship could have been anchored farther in. We were not close enough to see the number of gun ports. But it was a schooner."

Captain Thomas turned to Rhett and raised an eyebrow. "Another ship deeper in would be a Ned Low tactic."

"Without question, but I think not, in this case."

The two captains studied Rhett's face for several moments.

"Right then," Captain Buckner said. "We best be off."

"Jeremy and the young lady, here, will follow with their sloop," Rhett said. "They'll be picking up Charlie, their friend, Mason, and hopefully the young lady."

"If there's nothing else," Captain Buckner said.

The men all shook hands. The two captains tipped their hat at Karen. They returned to the jolly boat, pushed off, and soon disappeared into the darkness.

Rhett placed a hand on Jeremy's shoulder. "I hope you find your wife." He smiled at Karen as she and Jeremy turned toward the sloop tied up farther down the wharf.

Back onboard, they cast off the lines and let the tide wash them into deeper water.

Karen manned the tiller while Jeremy raised the mainsail.

The sail quickly caught the night's breeze and, with Karen's steering, began pulling the small ship toward open water.

Jeremy hoisted the jib and made his way aft until he stood next to Karen. "What do you think?"

"I think nothing ever goes according to plan," Karen said.

◆◆◆

After Nathan and the two crewmen were well past, Mason and Charlie began beating the bushes. About fifty yards of scrub and brush separated the coastline from the line of impenetrable swamp, that no sane person would try to enter in daylight, much less total darkness. The two men concentrated on that fifty-yard strip as they made their way northeast, parallel with the coast. Mason called out Lisa's name in a hushed tone every few yards.

"What happens if the crewmen slow their search, or stop?" Charlie asked. "We'll run right into them. They'll hear us long before we see them."

Mason stopped in his tracks. He had a point. "I think you need to take point."

"Take what?"

"You go on ahead. Don't worry so much about searching. I'll follow at a hundred yards, searching as I go. If the crewmen stop or slow, you hurry back and let me know."

Charlie opened his gourd canteen and took a long swig. He replaced the plug and wiped his mouth with the back of his hand. "Can you find the spot where we were put ashore?"

"Ten miles," Mason said. "I'll find it. Jeremy should be back there in two or three hours. He'll wait."

Charlie slung the canteen strap over his shoulder. "That's where I'll be, unless I run into trouble." He turned and marched off.

When the sound of the bushes rustling against Charlie's clothes subsided, Mason resumed his search.

He called out Lisa's name a little louder as he worked through the brush.

Mason kept at it for well over two hours, to no avail. Lisa was either in hiding farther in the swamp, or she was moving fast and well ahead of Nathan and the crewmen.

At the sound of someone running hard, approaching from the east, Mason stopped. He heard Charlie call out his name in a hushed tone.

Mason responded.

"They have her," Charlie said, as he came to a stop next to Mason.

Mason started walking. "Where, and how many?"

"Half a mile up, on the beach."

"What are they doing right this moment?"

"Waiting. They built a fire. Probably a signal for Low."

"No doubt," Mason said, as he quickened his pace. Making his way in the near pitch dark meant repeatedly running into palmetto bushes, briars, and small trees. It couldn't be helped. Mason just hoped there were no snakes, and that Lisa would be in one piece when he arrived. "What was her condition when you last saw her?"

"Didn't see her," Charlie said, breathing hard. "I heard her scream, and what sounded like her struggling. She went quiet after that. I tried to move in for a closer look, but it was too thick. They would have heard me. I could see the fire, but nothing else."

This is when Mason wished he had brought the Glock. He thought of Charlie's dagger, and the machete bouncing against his thigh as he totted. It wasn't much against probably five or six men.

"We need to slow up," Charlie said.

Mason came to an immediate stop. He cocked his ears, but heard nothing except Charlie's breathing. "How much farther?" he whispered.

"We're close."

Mason began working his way among the trees and brush, toward the coast. It turned out to be closer than he'd thought, only twenty yards. He took a knee behind a bush, right at the tree line. The crash of the ocean waves drowned out most sounds. He could see a small fire, about fifty yards farther down the beach. The flames licked higher as the men added more fuel. They were definitely trying to signal Low's ship.

Charlie wiggled his way up until he was beside Mason. "What do you think?"

"I only see five men," he whispered. "There could be more looking for firewood. One of them is standing close guard over Lisa. She's sitting on the sand, next to the fire."

"She's your girl," Charlie said, "how do you want to do this?"

Mason contemplated the question for a few moments and finally lifted his chin. "The direct approach."

CHAPTER 11

Mason and Charlie worked their way from tree to tree and bush to bush. As they moved, Mason kept his eyes on the group around the campfire. The men, except for Lisa's guard, were still gathering firewood. One or two would disappear into the brush and return with an armload. As far as he could tell, there were a total of only five men, and that included Nathan. Among the four crewmen, there was only one who looked formidable. He would be Mason's first target. None of the men appeared to have a firearm.

Fifty feet from the fire, Mason paused behind a bush.

Charlie did the same next to him.

Mason slipped the pouch and canteen straps over his head and lowered them to the sand. He placed a hand on the hilt of his machete and had withdrawn the blade a couple of inches when he caught sight of target one returning to the Forest for more wood. The others remained around the fire.

Mason let the machete's blade slip back into the scabbard. He leaned his face to within an inch of Charlie's ear. "I'm going for the big one," he whispered.

"Taking him out first will increase our odds." He heard Charlie give a quiet grunt, apparently his way of acknowledging the plan.

Mason stepped off in the direction of where he saw the man enter the Forest. He worked his way slowly from cover to cover. At the sound of the man gathering wood, Mason slowed his approach in the nearly pitch dark. Within a few steps he caught sight of the man's outline, bent over at the waist, apparently feeling for limbs and branches. He appeared to be holding several limbs in the crook of his left elbow.

Mason gauged the distance back to the campfire and how much noise he thought he could get away with. Not much, he estimated. His obvious advantage was the near total darkness. At the sound of someone approaching, the man would assume it was one of his buddies.

Mason raised up to his full height and stepped toward the man. He quickly closed the distance until he stood right next to him, still hunched over at the waist. Mason eyed what appeared to be a large diameter limb, about two feet long, in the man's arm. When the man stood up to acknowledge Mason's presence, Mason removed the limb from the man's stack. "Let me help you with that," Mason said. He swung the limb in a wide arc, catching the man in the side of the head with a loud wallop that had to have been heard by the others around the fire.

The man immediately collapsed, spilling the firewood to the sand.

Mason quickly gathered the limbs in the crook of his own left elbow. He kept the baton-like stick loose in his right hand, raised the wood high to cover his face, and began walking toward the fire.

"What the hell were you doing out there?" one of the crewmen said, as Mason stepped from the tree line.

He walked to where the men were gathered and dropped the pile of wood as he swung his makeshift baton at the man who'd asked the question.

The limb caught the man upside the head at about the same time it registered that something was wrong.

Before the man even reached the ground, Mason was already swinging the baton at the nearest crewman. The man fell to the sand in a heap. Mason turned to the remaining crewman. Lisa was sitting on the sand, next to the fire. Nathan stood next to her.

Everyone stared, wide-eyed in disbelief, especially Nathan.

The remaining crewman broke his trance first. He pulled a dagger from his waistband and began circling toward Mason.

Out of the corner of his eye, he saw Lisa get to her feet and plow a knee into Nathan's groin.

Nathan fell to the ground, curled into the fetal position, moaning in agony.

The crewman, knife hand outstretched, turned toward Lisa. That's when Charlie stepped from the tree line and took a position between the man and Lisa.

Mason flipped the makeshift baton from one end to the other, caught it back in the palm of his right hand, took a step, and slammed it against the man's wrist. At the sound of the loud *crack*, the knife went flying and the man's hand went limp.

The man immediately grabbed his wrist with the other hand, winced in agony, and backed off.

"I thought you would never get here," Lisa said.

"We didn't know you had escaped," Mason said. "By the way, this is Charlie."

Charlie turned to Lisa and gave a slight bow. "Glad to make your acquaintance."

Mason stepped over to the still standing crewman with the broken wrist, placed a hand on his chest, and threw him to ground. "Stay there," he said in an authoritative tone. Mason eyed the man for several moments until he was satisfied the man would follow directions. Mason turned and stood directly over Nathan.

Nathan, still in a fetal position but recovering, stared up with eyes wide with disbelief. "You're supposed to be dead," he groaned. "I saw you blown into the water."

"A temporary state of affairs," Mason said. He turned to Lisa. "Are you alright?" He scanned the four pirates and Nathan. "Any of these dirtbags lay a hand on you?"

"I'm fine. No thanks to this piece of garbage," she said, as she peered down at Nathan.

Charlie stepped over to the one crewman still conscious, the one with the broken wrist. He put a boot on the man's chest as he turned his head toward Mason. "Do I need to remind you that there's a boatload of cutthroats probably moving in on this spot as we speak?"

"Right," Mason said with a nod. "We need to get moving."

Nathan rolled to his haunches with his knees raised in front of him. "What about me?" He glanced at Lisa and back to Mason.

Mason looked at Lisa. "I'll leave it up to you."

Charlie stared at Nathan. "I take it he's one of yours?"

"He was," Mason said. "It's a long story."

"I may regret this, but I say we bring him," Lisa said.

Mason took three long strides over to Nathan, grabbed him with one hand by the back of his coat, and lifted him to his feet. "You heard the lady."

"What about these four?" Charlie asked, as he motioned to the crewmen. Three were still out cold. The other was holding his limp wrist.

Mason wasn't sure what Charlie was asking. Apparently, killing them was an option, in his mind. Leaving them to tell the story of what had happened to Lisa and Nathan might serve to incite Edward Low even more than if he'd found them all dead. Mason had no doubt what Rhett would do, given his general propensity toward pirates. *These are different times*, Mason told himself. Maybe he should start thinking according to the situation, no matter how brutal it seemed. He closed his eyes and rubbed his neck while he contemplated his options. In the end, he couldn't do it.

"Leave 'em," Mason said.

Charlie scratched the back of his head. "That might come back to haunt you."

"I know."

Charlie started kicking sand on the fire.

Mason and Lisa followed suit until the fire was reduced to a few glowing embers and a whiff of smoke. At that point, Charlie stepped off in the lead, to the north, along the coast.

Forty-five minutes later he came to a stop, swiveled his head back and forth in the darkness, and finally turned to the others. "This is it."

Mason couldn't tell much about their location in the dark, but he trusted Charlie to know where they were.

"What's happening?" Lisa asked.

"Jeremy and Karen are supposed to meet us here," Mason said.

"When?"

"Hard to say," Charlie said. "Could be soon, or it could be hours."

"Jeremy's coming?" Nathan asked.

Mason smirked, invisible in the darkness to the others. "And he won't be particularly happy with you."

"Lisa wasn't harmed because of me," Nathan said.

"You had nothing to do with it," Lisa countered. "They left me alone only because I was worth something to Low and Spriggs. You're the reason they showed up at our doorstep to begin with."

"She has a point," Mason said. "Like I said, Jeremy isn't going to be happy with you."

"Then again," Charlie said, "he might be really happy to see him."

Nathan dropped his chin, barely visible in the starlight.

A loud double-tap of *booms* in the distance broke the silence. Mason looked off into the darkness of the ocean just in time to see two rapid flashes, followed by two more *booms*.

"Looks like the sloops found something to shoot at," Mason said.

Charlie stepped closer to the water's edge. "Jeremy shouldn't be far behind."

◆◆◆

The silhouette of the sloop's dark hulk against the slightly lighter sky suddenly appeared. It silently grew larger as it neared the shore.

Mason put his thumb and index finger in the corners of his mouth and blew a loud whistle. Almost immediately he heard a similar whistle from the boat. He turned to Charlie and Lisa, behind a sand dune. "It's them." He turned back to the approaching boat. "That's far enough," he yelled, "we'll wade out to you." Mason and the others stepped into the water.

A few minutes later, the three were aboard the sloop, Lisa was in Jeremy's arms, and Mason and Karen were likewise embraced.

Mason finally broke the bond and stepped back to hold Karen at arm's length. "You don't know how glad I am to see you."

"Oh, I think I do," Karen said.

Charlie, standing nearby, cleared his voice. "What was the shooting about?"

Jeremy released Lisa and turned his head to the dark figure of Nathan, standing alone at the gunwale. "Really, you guys had to bring this piece of shit back with you?"

"It was my decision," Lisa said.

"Uh-huh," Jeremy uttered, as he took the few steps over to Nathan. He stared at his outline a few moments before he suddenly swung a fist, catching Nathan just under his left eye.

Nathan dropped to the deck at Jeremy's feet with a moan. He was down, but not out.

Lisa grabbed Jeremy's cocked arm before he could swing a second time. "That's enough. I'm not defending him, but—"

"But nothing," Jeremy said. "He brought those cutthroats to our house. You and Karen could have been brutalized, raped, or worse."

"But we weren't," Lisa said.

Jeremy finally relaxed his arm and let it slowly drop to his side as Lisa let her grip on his biceps go.

"Let it be," Mason said. "We'll decide what to do with him later."

"They know where we live because of him," Jeremy said.

"It will be awhile before they come knocking," Charlie said, "maybe never. Tell us what happened out on the water."

Jeremy let out a long exhale, took a couple of deep breaths, and turned to Charlie. "The sloops caught sight of the schooner, but it was too far out. It disappeared in the darkness. The last I saw of the sloops, they were giving chase. That's when I turned off and headed here."

"Which direction?" Charlie asked.

"Southwest," Jeremy said. "Away from here, and away from Charles Town."

"That's good," Charlie said. "If the sloops don't have the schooner in sight at first light, they'll return to Charles Town. Whether they find him or not, Edward Low likely won't return to Charles Town for some time."

"We should head out," Mason said, as he turned toward the tiller. He eyed Nathan, still on the deck where he fell, but was now in a sitting position. "Nathan, help with the anchor."

"We should probably wait out the night here," Charlie said. "It's safe enough. The four we left on the beach won't be wandering about at night. And we'll have an outgoing tide in the morning."

Mason considered his own exhaustion as he scanned the other barely visible faces looking back at him. "Sounds good to me."

◆◆◆

Mason woke with a start the next morning, to a rolling deck. The cause was readily apparent—a very stiff onshore wind. He rose from his prone position and poked his head above the gunwale. Gray skies, heavy clouds, and rough water was all he could see to the ocean's horizon. They were obviously in for serious weather. It might even be the beginning of a hurricane, for all he knew. The days of advanced warnings were long to come. Having lived in Florida most of his life, he was well aware of what a hurricane, or even a significant storm, could do. He glanced around the deck at the others starting to rise, including Karen lying beside him. Their little sloop would be hard-pressed to survive serious weather anchored at the mouth of a river open to the ocean. They had to move. Out into the ocean was not an option.

Mason got to his feet, with a hand against the gunwale to steady himself. He surveyed the white sand beach along the west side of the river until his eyes rested on a stand of trees almost at the water's edge. On wobbly legs, he made his way forward to the V-berth hatch. Just as he reached down to open the hatch, Jeremy shuffled to his side.

"We can't sail in this," Jeremy said.

"No, we're here for the duration, but that anchor will never hold." Mason stood up and pointed at the stand of trees. "We need to tie off to those trees."

"Good idea," Charlie said, as he joined them at the hatch. "A small creek on the backside of those trees basically makes this piece of land an island. I'd recommend we hunker down in that creek. It's wide enough."

"Is it deep enough?" Jeremy asked.

"Deep enough for this boat," Charlie said.

Mason pulled the hatch open, stepped down the ladder, and handed up one of the coils of rope to Jeremy. He carried a second coil as he climbed back up the ladder.

"Tie off at the bow," he said to Jeremy. "Wade ashore and pull us down to the creek. Take Nathan with you."

"Is that a good idea?" Karen yelled over the growing wind.

"We tie off the bow to a tree, and anchor the stern out in the creek," Mason said. "It's the best we can do."

"This is looking more like a hurricane," Lisa said, as she joined the group.

"There's nothing about a 1720 hurricane in the history books," Mason said. He winced when he suddenly realized what he had said in Charlie's presence.

Charlie cocked his head. "History books?"

"A figure of speech," Karen said, raising her voice above the wind.

Charlie took the coil of rope from Jeremy. "I'll tie this off and throw it to you on the beach." He looked at Mason. "We need to get this boat moving, or we'll be swamped for sure."

Mason felt the first fat drops of what would soon be a deluge.

CHAPTER 12

"We have two choices," Mason said to Karen and Lisa, standing on the deck beside him. He tested the rope Jeremy had fastened to the trunk of the nearest substantial tree, a tall pine. "Squeeze into the v-berth or ride it out on shore."

"No way I can go down there," Lisa said. She was already looking a little green. "I'll go ashore with Jeremy."

"Sounds fine," Mason said, as he gave a final tug on the secured rope. Against a rolling deck, he made his way aft, with Karen and Lisa following. "That will put you, Jeremy, Nathan, and Charlie on shore. Karen and I will ride it out here, just in case."

"Just in case of what?" Karen asked.

"If the rope were to break loose, we'd lose her if no one was onboard. I'd just feel better staying on board." He bent down to pick up the aft anchor but paused halfway down. He looked back up at Karen. "You okay with staying?"

"I'll be fine; not prone to seasickness as far as I know."

He grabbed the anchor and stood up. "We'll certainly find out." He stared off at the open ocean, just visible around the trees. "This could last for hours. Don't think it's a hurricane, but certainly a tropical storm. We could be looking at sixty mile an hour winds."

"What about those on shore?"

"Sail cloth is all we have to offer," Mason said, as he threw the anchor out as far as he could into the creek. "One of the jibs from below." He secured his end of the anchor rope to the transom, checked the knot, and headed forward.

Mason disappeared into the V-berth and returned with both arms wrapped around the folded extra jib. He rode the rolling deck with his feet wide apart as he shuffled to the gunwale. He handed the sail cloth down to Jeremy and helped Lisa over the side just as the sky opened with raisin-sized pellets that stung when they hit bare skin. A sudden drop in temperature brought goose bumps. He gave a final wave to those on shore and ushered Karen below. He closed the hatch, took a seat next to her, and immediately wrapped an arm around her shoulders. "You warm enough?"

"I will be," she said, as she snuggled closer to Mason's torso.

After a few moments, he shifted his position so he could spread out several layers of sail cloth. He motioned for Karen to join him as he reclined his full length on the makeshift bed.

She joined him, turned to her side, wrapped a leg over his thigh, and an arm around his chest.

Mason turned so they would be face-to-face. "Finally, I have you alone." He brought her face closer with his left hand and kissed her long and hard. After a few moments he felt her fingers manipulating the buttons at his waist and the flap that served as a fly. He lost track of time after that.

Mason woke to the sound of footsteps on the deck above. He quickly tidied himself and roused Karen from a deep slumber. He could still hear rain drops on the deck, but nothing like it had been.

When Karen had reassembled her attire, Mason got to his feet and pushed open the hatch. He saw Charlie at the stern, pulling in the anchor. Mason climbed out and joined him. "Not as bad as we thought."

"No," Charlie said, "heavy rain for about an hour." He turned his head toward the horizon over the ocean. "We should be on our way while there's still an outgoing tide."

Nathan and Jeremy helped Lisa aboard before scrambling over the gunwale.

Jeremy stowed the extra jib in the V-berth. "You guys pole, I'll pull the boat back along the shore," he said, as he went back over the side.

Within twenty minutes, with a moderate wind and lingering drizzle, they were headed for Charles Town, with Mason at the tiller. Nathan stood next to him. "What happened after I was blown into the water?"

Nathan cocked his head.

"When Ned Low attacked us," Mason said. "The original sloop."

Nathan peered at his hands wrapped over the gunwale. "Their canons killed most of them. There were only five of us alive when they came aboard." He closed his eyes for a moment before he continued. "Low's men, but especially Low himself, were ruthless. They checked each person and, without a thought, they hacked any still breathing. I was the last one."

"Why you?"

"I don't know. It just worked out that way. I was on the deck with all of his men gathered around. Low had his sword inches from my throat, ready to plunge. I could see it in his eyes. They were dark and empty."

"What made him hesitate?"

"The silver. I offered to take them to the silver." He turned his eyes to Mason. "You would have done the same thing. Any of us would."

Mason thought about that as he stared into the distance. "For the silver, sure. But with Karen and Lisa thrown into the mix—" He didn't bother to finish the sentence. His facial expression communicated his thought, that he would never risk the women.

"They didn't head straight for the plantation. They sailed north and attacked a couple of merchant ships first."

"What did they do with you?"

"Put me to work in the kitchen, mostly."

"Did any of our people suffer?"

He stared at the water for several moments. "Dorothy."

"I saw her down and covered in blood," Mason said.

"She was still alive. Several of Low's men stripped her and—"

"I get the idea," Mason said, cutting him off.

"They killed Mildred's dog in front of her while she was still conscious."

Mason imagined the mayhem for several moments. He turned his head to Nathan. "You're sure they were all dead when you left the sloop?"

Nathan dropped his chin. "They were dead. Low left the sloop to drift."

Without uttering another word, Mason turned and walked away.

❖❖❖

It was nearly noon when the boat glided into Charles Town harbor. Everyone aboard studied both armed sloops anchored fifty yards out from the wharf. There was no sign of Captains Buckner and Thomas on either deck. Mason, standing at the tiller, figured they were ashore, probably reporting to Colonel Rhett.

Charlie and Jeremy began hauling down the main and jib, while Mason maneuvered the boat to within ten yards of the wharf.

Nathan threw a line to a man standing next to the harbor master, waiting at the spot Mason had vacated the previous day.

"Are the sloop captains with Colonel Rhett?" Mason asked, as he stepped onto the wharf's wood planks.

"They are," Tyler replied. "They are in the provost marshal's office." He helped Karen and Lisa disembark and gave a slight nod to Jeremy, Charlie, and Nathan as they clambered over the gunwale.

"Charlie and I will report in," Mason said to Karen. "How about the rest of you get something to eat? You all must be starving." He looked at Charlie. "Any recommendations?"

"Shepherd's Tavern is new. Heard they have better food than most." He turned to Jeremy. "Cooper Street. About a block down."

"I'll meet you there," Mason said, as he motioned for Charlie to follow.

The two of them stepped into the provost marshal's office, to a meeting already underway. Colonel Rhett stood before a group of about ten men.

Captains Buckner and Thomas were at his side. Everyone turned to Mason and Charlie as they entered.

"The girl?" Rhett asked.

"She managed to escape on her own," Mason said.

Charlie snorted. "Low put men ashore south and north of where they figured she went. They caught her." Charlie motioned with his chin toward Mason. "He bested four men with a stick."

"Well done," Rhett said with exuberance. "Captains Buckner and Thomas were just describing what happened." He turned to Buckner. "Please continue."

"Like I said," Buckner said, "we spotted the schooner in the distance, moving fast to the south. We fired a couple of rounds from our chaser but it was mainly for show. The schooner was out of range. We continued our pursuit, but by morning, his sails were nowhere in sight."

Rhett let out a long exhale. "You did your best."

"That ship of his is fast and capable," Thomas said.

"Just the same," Rhett said, "he won't be returning to these parts for a while. And eventually, someone will catch up with him."

The group of men began mumbling amongst themselves while Rhett and the two captains turned to Mason and Charlie.

"We were about to take lunch at Shephard's," Mason said. "We would enjoy your company, if you have the time."

Rhett cocked his head. "Lunch?"

Mason instantly realized he had probably made a mistake by referring to the midday meal as lunch. He had no idea what they called it, or if they even ate a meal at midday. "Sorry, a term I picked up in the far east."

"You do have an odd vocabulary," Rhett said. He glanced at Buckner and Thomas at his side. "Gentlemen?"

"A pint of beer sounds good to me, no matter what you call it," Buckner said.

The five of them entered Shephard's Tavern, with Rhett in the lead. He immediately spotted Karen, Jeremy, Lisa, and Nathan sitting at a large round table. They were all munching on bread and cheese and sipping from mugs.

Jeremy and Nathan got to their feet as Rhett approached.

"Gentlemen," he said, "I understand you were successful at saving your young lady." His eyes rested on Lisa.

"This is Lisa Jackson," Mason said.

"Very happy to make your acquaintance," Rhett said, as he gave a slight bow. "I hope you were not mistreated."

Mason noted her hesitation to respond. She obviously was not sure of what she should say, or how she should say it.

"She's still a little shaken up," Mason said.

"Of course," Rhett said. He looked around the table. "Mind if we join you?"

"Not at all," Jeremy said.

Rhett extended his hand to Nathan. "Haven't had the pleasure."

"Nathan Sims. I was taken prisoner by Mister Low earlier, while at sea."

"As it turned out, he was being held against his will," Mason said. He glanced at Charlie, who was scratching the back of his head. "He was threatened with death."

"And the rest of the people on your boat?"

"Low killed them all," Mason said, "except Karen, Lisa, and Jeremy. They were at the plantation at the time."

Rhett took the chair next to Nathan. "You'll have to tell me all about your time with Edward Low."

Everyone sat down at the table. The barkeep brought more mugs of beer and another platter of bread and cheese.

As Rhett and the two captains peppered Nathan with questions, Mason interjected as needed, to keep Nathan from saying anything stupid. Overall, the session went well. Nathan was able to provide considerable information on the ships Low attacked, his tactics, and his crew. Several of his crew were fiercely loyal, such as Mister Spriggs, but there were some who were uncomfortable with Low's brutality.

"I've very much enjoyed our conversation," Rhett said, "but I should return home. Sarah will be wondering what became of me." He stood.

"You seem to be feeling better," Mason said, as he got to his feet.

"I do," Rhett said. He stared at Mason for several moments and glanced at Jeremy. "Feel free to stop by anytime. As plantation owners, there is much to discuss."

Mason shook his hand. "Thank you. We'll do that," Mason shook hands with Buckner and Thomas as they stood, as did Jeremy. Nathan finally got up and shook hands with those departing.

"I should probably be leaving as well," Charlie said, as he stood.

Mason shook his hand. "Thank you for all your help. If there's ever anything I can do for you."

Charlie smiled. "Glad to do it."

"By the way, where can I find you? I may be in need of a ship's crew. We plan to transport cargo, and I'll need to make a run to New York soon."

"Colonel Rhett or the Provost Marshal should know."

Mason shook his hand again.

After the four men left the tavern, Mason motioned for Jeremy and Nathan to sit back down. He stared at Nathan. "We need to decide what to do with you."

CHAPTER 13

"I have as much right to be here as any of you," Nathan said with indignation.

Mason, Jeremy, Karen, and Lisa stared back without a word.

"I was on that plane, just like you."

"That's true," Mason finally said. "But your cooperation and ability to get along with others has been less than stellar."

"You were going to keep the silver for yourself," Jeremy said. "You tried to assault Lisa at the pond. You led pirates to our home. You've generally acted like an asshole."

"The fact is, I didn't keep the silver and Lisa wasn't assaulted. Yeah, I made a couple of judgment errors," Nathan said, "you're going to deny my rights because of that?"

Mason looked at Karen. "You haven't said anything."

"Nothing to say. He's right. He's a member of the group and has a right to live at the plantation."

Mason raised an eyebrow.

"But if he steps out of line—"

It was clear from her expression that she was serious, and that she would be watching.

"Okay, then," Jeremy said, "what's next?"

"If we leave now," Mason said, "we can be in Myrtle Beach right at dark. There are some items I need to retrieve from there. We spend the night and head back to the plantation at first light."

"What's in Myrtle Beach?" Nathan asked.

Mason contemplated his response. The silver and extra ammo buried there were the product of his passage through time, twice. But there would be no way to keep that a secret from Nathan if he was to be accepted back into the fold. "I'll explain it once we're on the boat and underway."

"There's no reason for all of us to go," Jeremy said.

"No way I'm leaving Karen and Lisa alone at the plantation," Mason said. "We all go."

An hour later, the mouth of the Cooper River was well behind them. Mason stood at the tiller with Jeremy.

"He gives me the creeps," Jeremy whispered.

"I get that," Mason said. "But he's right. He didn't keep the silver, and he didn't assault Lisa. She did much more damage to him than he did to her. Plus, we could use the extra manpower. We need people at the plantation, and we need to be able to run up and down the coast."

Jeremy subtly shook his head. "I guess. What about Charlie?"

"He's a good man. I plan to use him, if he's willing. But there are aspects of our existence he can't know. We'll have to watch our every word around him, and anyone else outside our group."

Jeremy stared at Nathan, standing in the bow alone. "Of all the people on that sloop, he's the one that survives."

"I know," Mason said. "Fate has a way of screwing with us." He motioned toward Nathan. "Ask him to join me."

Jeremy made his way along the rolling deck. He returned a couple of minutes later with Nathan in tow.

"What's up?" Nathan asked.

"I'm going to tell you something that may be a little hard to believe," Mason said, as he handed the tiller off to Jeremy. He guided Nathan amidships, port side, opposite from where Lisa and Karen sat talking. Mason proceeded to explain his passage back through time, to the future, his time there, and his return in the Cessna. He also told him about the silver ingots and the extra ammo buried in Myrtle Beach.

When Mason stopped talking, Nathan stood staring at him in disbelief for several moments. He finally blinked one time, slowly. "You found a way to return to our time, and you chose to come back here?"

"It wasn't by design. I wasn't even conscious for most of it. I just woke up in Jacksonville."

"But your return was by design. It can be done."

"Yeah, maybe. But we're fresh out of Cessnas."

"Your trip into the future wasn't in a Cessna," Nathan said. "That means it is possible."

"It's obviously possible," Mason said. "But I'm not willing to spend the rest of my life floating around the North Atlantic looking for a storm with a blue haze. It may have been a quirk that might never return."

"So, once again, we're stuck here," Nathan said.

"Looks that way."

"But why would you return to this time? You were back there. You could have picked up your life where you left off."

Mason looked at Karen, still talking with Lisa. "I had a strong motive."

"No way I would have returned," Nathan said.

Mason lifted his chin. "Of that, I have no doubt."

Nathan wandered off toward the bow, still shaking his head. Mason returned to the tiller.

"How'd he take it?" Jeremy asked.

"He's in a state of disbelief," Mason said. "He'll get over it and will soon be back to his normal self."

"That's what worries me," Jeremy said.

◆◆◆

Late the next afternoon, Mason spotted the plantation's dock as he steered the sloop up the Ashley River. Fifty yards short of the dock, they dropped the sails and coasted until the boat bumped against the wood planks. While Nathan and Jeremy tied up, Mason scanned the grounds. He saw men working the fields, as usual, and Sylvester starting to walk toward the dock. The only thing out of the ordinary was a large stack of lumber next to the existing kitchen.

Sylvester met them as they stepped onto the dock. He smiled, but didn't say anything.

"Everything alright here?" Mason asked.

"Fine, Mister Mason. Just fine." He pointed to the lumber. "Wasn't sure where you wanted it."

"Perfect, Sylvester," Mason said. "Right where we needed it to be."

Sylvester smiled again. He swept his arm toward the rice field in the distance. "That rice needs to come up. It's time. Past time."

Mason glanced at Jeremy, Karen, Lisa, and Nathan, who were all staring at him. Knowing nothing about the production of rice, he wasn't sure what to say. He eyed the rice field for several moments and finally turned back to Sylvester. "I'm going to rely on you. The five of us don't have a lot of experience with growing rice."

"That's just fine, Mister Mason," Sylvester said. "It's October already, the rice needs to come up."

"Okay," Mason said, "what's the first step?"

"We drains the fields by opening those gates," he said, as he pointed toward the small canals leading from the fields to the river.

"Okay, let's do that," Mason said. He looked to the sky and back to Sylvester. "Tomorrow?"

Sylvester smiled. "Tomorrow is just fine, Mister Mason." He glanced at the others with his perpetual smile, turned, and walked off.

"Anybody know anything about harvesting rice?" Mason asked.

"Can't be that difficult," Nathan said.

"Probably not difficult, but hard labor," Jeremy said.

Mason snorted. "Thanks, that helps a lot."

"Looks like we may be busy for a while," Karen said, as she started toward the house.

Mason, Lisa, and Nathan fell in with her.

Jeremy stayed behind to better secure the boat and clear the deck.

As Karen and Lisa continued into the house, Mason peeled off, guiding Nathan toward the stack of lumber.

"Rumor has it you know something about construction," Mason said, as he stared at the freshly cut, rough-sawn wood.

"What did you have in mind?"

Mason raised his hand in the direction of the exterior kitchen. "I want to expand the kitchen to include an eating area large enough to accommodate sixty people."

Nathan jerked his head toward Mason. "Sixty? You expecting to throw some kind of shindig?"

Mason pointed to the slaves working in the fields. "From now on, they eat what we eat, and we eat it together."

Nathan cocked his head, thought for a few moments, took in a deep breath and exhaled. "Seems to me, that would be as uncomfortable for them as it would be for the people of this era."

"You're right," Mason said, "which is why we're not going to advertise. When anyone from the outside is here, we eat in the house."

"Seems like a lot of trouble, and may even be risky."

"We can't condone slavery," Mason said. "And while we're limited by this time and place with what we can do to eliminate slavery, altogether, we have to do what we can."

"What about them?" Nathan said, pointing at Sylvester talking to two men at the edge of the nearest field.

"We don't say anything to them. We just make these changes, do what we can, and press on." Mason proceeded to walk off the area that would encompass the additional structure. He described solid walls, roof, wood floor, and tables and benches.

"When?" Nathan asked.

"When the harvesting is done," Mason said. "Couple of weeks, maybe. Spend your time coming up with a plan and getting organized, until then. Let me know what else you need."

Nathan's mind was already on the project.

Mason left him staring at the stack of lumber. He joined Lisa and Karen in the main sitting room, straightening up after the pirate sleepover.

"What were you talking to Nathan about?" Karen asked, as she continued to tidy up.

"We're building a dining hall for all of us, including the slaves."

Karen and Lisa both stopped what they were doing and stared at Mason.

"You sure about doing that?" Karen asked.

Mason shrugged his shoulders. "Not really. But we can't—"

"I get it," Karen said, cutting him off. "We do what we can."

"Exactly."

"With all that reading you did back in the future, did you learn anything about selling rice?" Lisa asked.

"Not much. Nothing about the actual harvesting. As for selling, there's bound to be a commodities broker in town. We'll need barrels."

"Sylvester will know how many," Karen said. "You should ask what else he needs."

Mason took in a deep breath and exhaled as he stared out the window. Two things popped into his mind: what Nathan said about it being possible to get back to the future, and the painting on Mister Mason's wall, three hundred years in the future. The painting depicting Lisa, Karen, and a boy of about ten years old. Based on that painting, and the continued ownership of the plantation in the Mason line, they never returned to the future. He rubbed both temples with his fingers. *One day at a time*.

The next morning, everyone in the house, including Nathan, was up just before the sun. While the others were still getting ready for the day, Mason was outside at first light. He found two of the slave women already busy in the kitchen. He hadn't had time, before, to pay the room much attention, so he took a moment to scan the interior. Wood planks covered the floor and walls. Thick wood beams supported the roof. The wall farthest from the main house enclosed a large brick hearth. Various iron utensils hung from a thick oak beam serving as a mantel above the fireplace. A large iron pot hung from a hook over the fire. Two small windows and the door provided daylight and airflow. Despite the windows and the open door, the room was already hot and a little smokey from the fire burning in the hearth. There were two work tables along one adjacent wall, and numerous bracketed shelves affixed to all the walls. A long, rectangular, sturdy oak table occupied a lot of the room's center space. Barrels, containing what Mason guessed were various foodstuffs, covered half of one of the four walls. The kitchen appeared to have been well-used for many years.

"I don't think we've been introduced," he said to the oldest of the two women.

"I'm Marie, Mister Mason," she said. She motioned to the other woman, in her early twenties. Both were dressed in well-worn petticoats, a long-sleeved gown, and a bonnet. They were both barefoot. "This is Sissy. Breakfast will be ready at the regular time."

Mason almost asked what time that would be, but he caught himself. That would have been a stupid question. "Thank you, Marie." He smiled, scanned the kitchen one last time, and exited. He made a mental note to have Nathan talk to Marie, with regard to the design of the extra space he had in mind. He wanted an adjoining structure but, other than that, he intended to leave the design and construction up to Nathan.

Sylvester was waiting for Mason when he stepped from the open doorway. "You wants me to open those gates now, Mister Mason?"

"Sure. How long before we can start harvesting?"

"Three days, if it don't rain."

"And do you have everything you need?"

"Yes, sir, Mister Mason."

"How about barrels?"

Sylvester cocked his head and stared at Mason for several moments. "We don't use barrels. They sends a boat. We sends the rice to market on a boat. In bags."

Mason scratched his beard as he stared at the ground, wondering if he had bit off more than he could chew with trying to run a plantation. He obviously needed some experienced guidance. What he needed was a manager.

"Alright," Mason finally said. "Did Misses Stewart have someone that oversaw the harvesting?"

"That was Mister Carl," Sylvester said, "but he left during the summer." Sylvester lowered his voice. "I think there was a disagreement between the two of them."

"Was he good?"

"Oh, yes, sir, Mister Mason. Mister Carl was real good. We all had certain jobs. We could take off when finished. Sometimes that was late into the night, but sometimes we finished early in the day."

"Any idea why he left?"

"No, sir. He just up and left one day."

"Alright, Sylvester. Open the gates and do what you would normally do."

"Yes, sir, Mister Mason." He hesitated like there was more he wanted to say.

"What is it, Sylvester?"

"Are you going to ask Mister Carl to come back?"

"I'll see what I can do. Happen to know his last name?"

"Grainger. His name was Carl Grainger."

CHAPTER 14

Sitting at the dining table with the others, Mason took a bite of his biscuit and bacon sandwich. He chewed and swallowed. "Apparently, Misses Stewart had a manager who oversaw the harvesting, and probably everything else related to running a plantation. A Mister Grainger."

"Do we need a manager?" Karen asked from across the table.

"In just a few minutes of talking to Sylvester, I realized we definitely need someone who knows what they are doing." He looked at Nathan. "Hurry up and finish eating, we're heading into town."

"Today?" Jeremy asked.

"Right now," Mason replied. "The sooner we get someone who knows what they are doing, the sooner I'll stop sounding like an idiot." He shoved the final piece of biscuit into his mouth, grabbed his canvas rucksack from the floor next to his chair, and stood up. "Bring the rest of it with you," he said, looking at Nathan.

"What about me?" Jeremy asked.

"I'm not leaving the women here alone. You have the two muskets. Like they say in the movies, shoot first and ask questions later." He lifted the rucksack slightly to emphasize its existence. "I'll have the Glock with me."

Jeremy stood up. "I'll help you clear the dock."

Mason gave Karen a hug and a kiss, motioned for Nathan to follow, and led him and Jeremy out the door toward the river.

Within minutes Mason and Nathan were drifting down the river, the plantation already out of sight.

"Any thoughts on the kitchen structure?" Mason asked, as he maneuvered the tiller.

Nathan stared at the water. "Some. I think it needs to be a separate structure, but connected."

"I was thinking the same thing," Mason said.

"Are you really going to feed everyone at the same time, three times a day?"

"As much as possible. How many times, when, and what, I'll leave up to Marie and Karen."

"I think it's a mistake," Nathan said. "It will just cause a lot of unnecessary confusion. Plus, how do you expect to keep the word from getting out, if you have an outside manager on the plantation?"

"There's obviously a lot we need to work out."

"Do the others know your plans?"

"Yes. But like I said, we need to work out the details."

They tied up at the Ashley River landing and took the well-worn path through the town's west gate. Mason carried the rucksack in one hand, at his side. Their first stop was Jacob's Tavern, already open for business. In fact, it probably never closed. Mason scanned the interior for a familiar face, but saw none. He approached the bar, and the barkeep standing behind it. "Looking for a Carl Grainger?"

The barkeep, an older gentleman with a fat gut, pursed his lips and shook his head. He went back to arranging mugs, without saying anything.

"Friendly chap," Nathan said, as they exited the tavern.

Their second stop was a tavern Mason didn't know the name of. It, too, was devoid of anyone Mason knew and, like the first, the barkeep apparently didn't know a Carl Grainger.

The third stop was Shepherd's Tavern; again, no help.

Mason and Nathan walked to the Provost Marshal's office, adjacent to the Cooper River. Mason immediately spotted Charlie, asleep on the days-old hay, in the holding cell. There was one watchman on duty. He was sitting in a chair, leaned back on two legs against the far wall. He, too, appeared to be asleep, with his arms folded over his chest. Mason walked up to the man in the chair and cleared his voice.

The man's eyes popped open, but he otherwise didn't move from his position.

"Wonder if I could speak to Charlie over there," Mason said, as he pointed.

"What's your business?" the watchman asked.

"I want to offer him a job."

The watchman thought for several moments but finally gave a single nod.

Charlie smelled worse than he had the last time Mason saw him—a combination of rum, beer, and body odor. He was passed out flat on the brick and hay floor, snoring softly.

"Doesn't appear he's going to be much good for a while," Nathan said, as the two of them stared down at the man.

"With Charlie, it appears to be a matter of timing," Mason said. "He apparently has good days, and not-so-good days."

"Now what?" Nathan asked.

At that moment Charlie snorted and stirred. He raised the back of his hand and ran it under his nose. His eyes were open, but it appeared he was having trouble focusing.

"Mason?"

"Yeah, Charlie, Mason and Nathan."

Charlie rolled to a sitting position, with his back against the rough-brick wall. "Is it morning already?"

"Well past morning," Mason said. "Looks like you had an interesting night."

"Not really," Charlie mumbled.

Mason looked around the interior of the holding cell, empty of any other people. "Charlie, do you have a home?"

"I do," Charlie said, "it's wherever I lay my head." He snorted again and sat up straighter, suddenly looking more alert. "What can I do you for?"

"I was hoping you could help me find the former manager of the Stewart Plantation, a Carl Grainger."

Charlie took a moment, swallowing hard. He rubbed his nose again. "He came through town several months ago. Said he was heading north."

"Do you know where?"

"Nope."

Mason took a few moments as he scanned the holding cell again, and the interior of the provost marshal's office. From the first time he'd visited the town's night watch, he thought it was odd there was no door to the holding cell, just a wide opening. Apparently, those placed in the cell knew enough not to wander outside the cell. His eyes went back to Charlie. "Seems I'm in need of a manager, someone who knows how to harvest, process, and sell rice and our other crops."

"That would be Carl Grainger," Charlie said.

"You said Mister Grainger was gone," Nathan said.

"He is," Charlie grunted.

Nathan shook his head and turned away.

"Anyone else you know of?"

"I've worked plenty of plantations," Charlie said.

"You know how to manage the crops?"

"I do."

Nathan turned back around, poked Mason on the arm, and threw his hands up, obviously asking what Mason was thinking.

"You need a job?" Mason asked, as he stared down at Charlie.

"I have a job."

"What's that?" Nathan asked.

"I work for the Colonel when he needs me."

"What do you do when you're not working for the Colonel?" Mason asked.

Charlie swiveled his head back and forth at the other two walls of the holding cell. "Nothing, I guess."

"You want a job for when you're not working for the Colonel?"

Charlie put a finger in his ear and twisted. He grunted and looked up at Mason.

"What did you have in mind?"

Mason glanced at Nathan and back to Charlie. "Managing the harvesting, processing, and selling of our rice and crops."

Charlie pursed his lips as he thought about it. "Sure, I can do that," he finally said.

"You can't take him back like that," Nathan said.

"He's right, Charlie. Is there someplace you can clean up?"

He scratched at his beard. "Yep."

Charlie got to his feet and led Mason and Nathan out of the cell and out of the provost marshal's office. Apparently, he was free to come and go as he wanted. He walked straighter than Mason would have expected as they navigated the main road and down an alley to a single-story dwelling. He stepped up on the porch, knocked on the door, and waited.

A minute later the door finally swung open to reveal a middle-aged woman, on the heavy side, dressed in the proverbial petticoats, blouse, and bonnet. "Wondering when I'd see you again," the woman said.

"I'll be about an hour," Charlie said, as he stepped through the open door.

The woman glanced at Mason and Nathan, standing there gaping. "Make that two or three hours," she said, as she closed the door.

"A couple of hours then," Mason said, as he turned around to face the alley.

Mason and Nathan took the opportunity to stock up on much-needed supplies, including bags or kegs of flour, cornmeal, oatmeal, rice, beans, salt pork, salt, sugar, molasses, and even a few kegs of rum and beer. They also picked out several bolts of linen and wool material. Winter was approaching and several of the workers would be needing warmer clothes. Mason arranged to have all the supplies delivered to the sloop. They also popped into Francois' tailor shop and ordered an extra set of clothes for Karen, Lisa, Jeremy, Nathan, and himself. Francois still had all the measurements from the last time they'd ordered clothes. Francois said the garments would be ready in a couple of weeks. Finally, they grabbed a quick lunch, what the locals called nuncheon, at Shepherd's Tavern. Mason was getting accustomed to beer, bread, and cheese around noon. They were back to where they'd dropped Charlie off, with a little time to spare.

The same lady opened the door, revealing a sitting room. "He's done, but his clothes will take a few minutes more. You're welcome to wait in here."

Mason smiled. "Thank you." He stepped inside, followed by Nathan. "Is this generally open to the public?"

"Within reason," the woman said.

"By the way, I'm Mason. This is Nathan."

"Harriet," the woman said simply. She maintained a neutral expression as she motioned to a fabric-covered settee.

Mason scanned the small room furnished by the settee, two wooden chairs, and a small table with an oil lamp. The wood-slated walls were bare of any decorations.

Thirty minutes later, a much-improved Charlie emerged from a narrow hallway. The former odors were nearly eliminated, and most of the stains from his red overcoat were barely visible. He also seemed more alert.

"What is this place?" Nathan asked.

"Harriet is my wife's sister," Charlie said, as he stepped to the door.

"You have a wife?" Nathan asked.

"I did. She died from the swamp fever two summers back." He turned his eyes to Harriet as she entered the room. "Harriet helps out best she can in emergencies."

"One of these days they'll find you dead in an alley," Harriet said.

"Probably," he replied. He lifted one corner of his mouth into a half smile and pulled the door open.

Mason bowed slightly to Harriet as he and Nathan followed Charlie outside.

"Do you live here?" Nathan asked, as they walked.

"In emergencies," Charlie said.

The three of them made their way through town, through the west gate, and back to the sloop.

"So, you know something about rice?" Nathan asked, as they stepped onto the sloop's deck.

"Everyone around here knows something about rice," Charlie said.

"I mean, harvesting and such."

"You pluck it, you beat it into submission, and you carry it to market," Charlie said. "Not that difficult."

"We opened the gates this morning to let the fields drain," Mason said.

"You're already a little behind, but it will be fine," Charlie said.

The three of them chatted as they made their way up the Ashley River, with clear skies and a light wind. Soon, they were docking at the plantation.

Sylvester met them as they started toward the house.

"This is Sylvester," Mason said. "I've come to rely on him a great deal. Sylvester, this is Charlie Sievert. He's going to help with managing the crops."

"That's just fine, Mister Mason," Sylvester said. "Will he be staying in the rice house? That's where Mister Carl stayed."

"Rice house?"

"Sure," Sylvester said, as he pointed toward the farthest field and a large, single-story rough-wood structure.

"The barn. I thought that was for storage."

"It is. We stores the rice there until we loads it on the boat. There's a extra room."

Mason had inspected the barn and work yard when Misses Stewart first showed him the property. He didn't pay that much attention to it at the time. It was a large barn, that's all he remembered. Mason looked at Charlie. "Would you be more comfortable there? You're welcome to stay in the main house."

"Let's take a look at the rice house," Charlie said, as he started walking in that direction.

The barn consisted of a main section, the largest area, and a wing off of each end. The building partially enclosed the large work yard, dotted with various implements for rice processing. Large mortars and pestles had been fashioned by hollowing out the top portion of logs. And there were several large, square, open containers constructed of wood. Mason's knowledge of rice processing in early Colonial America was extremely limited, but what little reading he'd done on the subject allowed an educated guess as to the purpose of the various implements.

The main section of the barn was completely open. A few loose grains of rice and stalks littered the wood-plank floor, indicating it had, indeed, been used for storage and probably drying.

"This is where we dries the rice and later stores the bags," Sylvester said.

Charlie surveyed the room for a few moments and turned to Sylvester.

Sylvester led the three men through a door into the left wing of the structure and through a second door, into a small room. A fireplace, open to the main section of the barn, backed up to the small room. Mason guessed the heated brick on the back side would keep the room toasty warm during the winter. The room was just big enough for the bunk bed, a single wood chair, and a small table.

Charlie walked around the room, peered at the items of furniture, and turned to Mason. "This will do fine."

"You sure?" Mason said. "Like I said, you're welcome in the main house."

"I'd feel better with my own space," he said.

"Alright, then," Mason said. "Let's walk back to the house. I'll explain what all I have in mind for the near future."

CHAPTER 15

Mason observed the rice operation over the following days. Sylvester and the others required practically no supervision from Charlie. They divided themselves into groups assigned to particular tasks. Charlie pretty much stayed out of the way and let it happen. In Mason's mind, that was the sign of a good manager: get involved only when necessary.

Once the fields were dry enough to walk on, nearly all the workers set out to harvest the rice. They used small sickles, what they called rice hooks, to cut the stalks. Each man, woman, and capable child would grab a handful of the stalks, slice them about nine inches from the ground, and lay the cut stalks of rice back on top of the stubble. This served to keep the rice off the ground. The women began gathering the stalks of rice the next day, tied them in bundles the size of their hand with a length of the stalk itself, and arranged them into sheaves, or ricks, for additional drying. It took several days for the rice to dry enough for the next part of the process.

Charlie explained that the workers didn't need to be taught or closely guided. They were well-versed with growing, harvesting, and processing rice. They brought the knowledge with them from West Africa, where rice was a major food source. The various duties were passed down from generation to generation.

After a few days of drying, the ricks were carried to the work yard where mostly the women began the threshing. This involved beating the bundles against the interior of the large, square wooden containers to separate the rice from the stalks.

Depending on the amount of moisture in the air, the separated rice kernels might need additional drying. That could be done by spreading the rice out on the barn floor.

Once dried, the rice was pounded in log mortars to remove the outer hull and inner bran layer, leaving the lighter grain. This was a crucial step, and required a delicate feel for the right amount of pressure. Too little and the grains would remain unpolished; too much and the grains would break. Both situations would reduce the price at market.

Winnowing was the process of separating the grains from the chaff. This, too, was mostly done by the women. They used large, round, slightly concave baskets to scoop up the rice and toss it in the air, where the wind would blow away the lighter chaff. The heavier grains would fall back into the basket. Charlie explained that weaving the baskets, made of the Bulrush marsh grass, was also a craft brought from

West Africa, and handed down to subsequent generations.

Once milled, the rice was bagged and stored.

Because Mason's crop was harvested late in the season, the price would not be ideal. On average, he would be paid about one and a quarter cents per pound, denominated in British pounds.

During those same days and weeks, Mason helped Nathan and Jeremy on the construction of the addition to the kitchen. By the time the first batches of rice were headed to market, they had completed the floor, framing and battens for the roof, and were beginning the walls, which would ultimately be a single layer of boards. It wouldn't hold out the cold that well, but it was better than nothing.

Because winter was rapidly approaching, they began using the additional kitchen space to feed all the workers as soon as the floor was completed and the tables and benches built. This saved time by eliminating the need for the workers to prepare their own food. This also gave them a few minutes of rest after they ate, before they returned to their various tasks. The quality of their meals also improved which, in turn, improved their attitudes. The communal kitchen went a long way toward increasing productivity.

At first, Charlie thought the communal kitchen would be contrary to good order and discipline among the workers. But once he saw the increase in productivity, he had to agree that it was a good idea. But to maintain Charlie's sense of decorum, a separate table was reserved for the whites. Karen, especially, didn't like the separation or its image of superiority. But Mason was able to convince her that the transition would have to go slow, so as not to upset the order of this time and place.

There was one other transition that became evident during this time. Karen began experiencing morning sickness. This was when Mason privately told her about the ten-year-old boy depicted in the painting he saw on the plantation wall while he was in the future. He didn't mention it before, because he wasn't sure what impact his return might have made on time and space. But it appeared that, so far, his return had made no impact. Karen was pregnant. And based on the timing, conception occurred that night in Charlestown harbor, in the dark of night, on the deck of the original sloop.

A lot was happening, but nearly everything seemed to be falling into place. Each night, lying in his bed next to Karen, Mason stared up into the darkness and pondered their new reality. He had specific ideals he wanted to achieve and a vague notion of how. But the devil was in the details. It was the details he thought about each night: grow the rice, harvest the rice, pay the mortgage to Misses Stewart, give the blacks a better life as much as this period in time would allow, and protect his family and friends. He was comforted by the fact that at this time in history, there were no major threats to Charles Town. The Spanish would not be invading, there would be no major Indian uprisings, and there would be no major wars for many years. He knew that would all change in the future, but for the present, all was good. For the most part.

What Mason didn't realize until he sought payment for his first shipment of rice was that Charles Town, in fact, the entirety of the South Carolina Colony, was in an economic upheaval. Mason learned from Charlie and listening to the town's people complain that the Land Bank, established by the House of Commons, had recently issued a new round of fiat paper money. However, since there was so much fiat paper in circulation, the value of the new issue immediately dropped. Colony paper money, although denominated in British pounds, shillings, and pence, had always been valued at less than an actual pound sterling. But with the Colony's latest issue, it took four Colony pounds to equal one British pound. To make matters worse, South Carolina paper money was practically worthless in any other colony, including that of New York. Misses Stewart lived in New York.

In Mason's mind, the solution was obvious. He would need to ship at least half of his rice directly to New York. When he broached this idea with Charlie, he learned of one giant fly in the ointment. It was illegal.

Since 1705, the British Parliament, under the navigation acts, had designated rice as an enumerated product. That meant all rice had to be sold at the market in Charles Town. From there it would be shipped to England first, and designated portions exported back to the continent. It was a convoluted system, meant to ensure England got its payment in taxes.

Shipping directly to New York was, therefore, out of the question. It would only be a matter of time before the illegal sales would be realized and Mason jailed. He couldn't pay Misses Stewart with worthless paper, and he couldn't ship directly to New York. He needed a solution, and he needed it quick.

◆◆◆

"I think it's a crazy idea," Karen said, as she, Jeremy, Lisa, and Nathan stared at Mason across the dining table in the main house. "I can think of a million things that could go wrong."

"I don't see where we have a choice," Mason said. "England and Spain are in a state of relative peace, and from what I've read, that state will continue for at least fifteen years or so. France is now the major rival to the English, in the New World."

"We would be breaking the law," Jeremy said. "We could end up hanged."

Mason pursed his lips as he thought about that. After a few moments he finally spoke. "Like I said, I don't see where we have a choice. The money here is worthless to us, and we can't ship directly to New York or any other colony."

"What you're proposing is even worse than that," Lisa said.

Mason contemplated her words for a few moments and turned to Nathan. "You haven't said anything."

"I think you're right," Nathan said.

Jeremy shook his head. "Since when did we start listening to him? It's one disaster after another with this guy."

Nathan shot Jeremy a dirty look but said nothing.

"How about if we trade the rice for a different commodity, something not on the restricted list?" Lisa said.

"Like what?" Mason asked.

"What about deer skins?" Karen said. "We could trade with Mato."

"It would take Mato months to gather that many pelts," Mason said. "It would just take too long."

"I'm beginning to see the problem," Jeremy said.

"Trust me, I've lain awake at night thinking about this. Other planters in the area don't have this problem. They don't have a mortgage. Their land was granted to them by the former colony proprietors. The other planters are able to spend locally the money they receive from their crops."

Jeremy almost imperceptibly moved his head up and down.

"It's time we start using our knowledge of history," Mason said. "We know that at this time England is stretched thin. Their economy is unstable, they have potential wars in Europe brewing, they're competing with Spain and France for trade."

"The English and Spanish may not be at war, but they are far from friends," Nathan finally said. "Selling to the Spanish in St. Augustine would be about as close as you can get to aiding and abetting the enemy."

"That was my point," Lisa said.

"You're right," Mason said, "which is why we'll need to use a middle man."

"Any thoughts on who that would be?" Jeremy asked.

"I do."

"What I fear most," Karen said, "is that we know just enough history to get ourselves in serious trouble. History books of the future cover a wide spectrum, generally from limited points of view. The minute details were glossed over."

"Good point," Mason said. "And you're right. We'll need to proceed with extreme caution."

"Okay, say we go along with this idea," Jeremy said. "What's our first step?"

"Two-fold. The first load of rice has already gone to Charles Town. The broker will be back for the next load in a few days. We need to start syphoning off bags of rice."

"Hide it, you mean," Lisa said.

"Yep. Our yield this year just got considerably smaller."

"He saw the fields," Karen said. "He knows how much rice to expect."

"He didn't see the north fields, which is almost a third of the crop," Mason countered.

"And the second part?" Jeremy asked.

"We have to establish communication with someone in Spanish Florida."

"Spanish Florida?" Karen exclaimed. "Are you crazy?"

"Hear me out. We contact the Spanish indirectly, through the Indians there. Many of them came from here."

"How do you plan to do that?" Karen asked.

"Road trip. Or, in our case, a sea trip." Mason looked at Jeremy. "You'll have to remain here and see to the place."

"What about Charlie?" Lisa asked.

"Yeah, we need him on board with the plan," Mason said. "This will never work if he's not with us."

"Have you talked to him?" Karen asked.

"Not yet. I wanted to talk to you guys first." Mason pushed back from the table and stood. "Since we seem to be in agreement, there's no time like the present."

"It's pitch dark outside," Karen said. "He's probably asleep. And I'm not sure we're in agreement."

"He's probably on his second keg of beer," Jeremy said. "He's still up. Want me to tag along?"

"This is something I need to do alone," Mason said. "Just him and me."

"Mano a mano," Jeremy said.

"Something like that." He smiled at Karen. "Trust me, this is the only way."

◆◆◆

Mason carried a torch as he made his way along the well-worn path to the barn, nearly a mile from the main house. Snakes were prevalent and despite wearing his high-top, leather boots he didn't want to step on one. The thick leather would probably protect him from the snake's fangs, but he didn't want to test it.

He saw a tiny flicker of light from the single, glass-paned window of Charlie's small room. Glass panes were somewhat rare at this time, especially for a barn, but Mason wanted to ensure Charlie was as comfortable as possible. The glass was diverted from the few extra panes kept as spares for the main house.

Mason extinguished the torch before he entered the barn. He felt his way along the walls in the dark until he came up to Charlie's door. He knocked softly.

"Who is it?" came a deep grumble.

"Mason."

A few seconds later, the door swung open, revealing Charlie with mug in hand, backlit by a single oil lamp. He wasn't totally inebriated, but he was well on his way. He motioned for Mason to enter. "What can I do you for?"

"I wanted to run something past you."

"Couldn't wait for morning?" Charlie asked as he closed the door and motioned Mason to the chair.

Mason took a seat. "It's rather important."

Charlie poured a bit of clear liquid from a keg into a second mug and handed it to Mason before he took a seat on the bunk.

Mason sniffed the aroma of rum and took a sip while Charlie stared at him expectantly.

"First, let me explain how we came to own this place."

Charlie took a gulp from his mug.

"We bought it from the previous owner, a Misses Stewart. We paid some money down and financed the balance."

Charlie cocked his head. "You did what?"

"We gave her some money up front and agreed to make payments to her over time, one payment per year at harvest time, until the total amount is paid."

"You could have applied for a grant at the Land Office," Charlie said.

"The proprietors closed the Land Office permanently because of all the political turmoil last year," Mason said.

Charlie pursed his lips, indicating he knew that but forgot.

"Plus, we didn't want to start from scratch. We wanted a spot already operating."

Charlie's eyes lost focus for a moment but quickly reacquired Mason. "So, you owe some money to this Misses Stewart?"

"Exactly. The problem is, Misses Stewart moved to New York. Carolina paper isn't worth much in New York. And, as you know, we can't ship our rice directly to New York."

"So, you're left with no way to pay Misses Stewart?" Charlie said.

"Precisely."

Charlie took another gulp of the rum, wobbled a bit, and straightened up. "Sounds like a problem."

Mason wasn't sure how much longer Charlie would be cognizant, so he jumped to the point. "I need to sell the rice where I can get paid in silver."

Charlie wobbled again and focused on Mason. "La Florida."

Mason dipped his chin slightly. "We'd have to divert at least half the rice and ship it south. We would need a middle man, but I have someone in mind."

"If you're caught," Charlie said, "you'll be jailed, maybe even sent to London for trial."

"My plan doesn't include getting caught."

"And you want me to go along with it, maybe even help?"

"I can't pay for the plantation without silver, and I can't grow and sell the rice without your help."

Charlie sat his mug on the small table next to his bed. He dropped his face into both hands and rubbed.

"I'll understand if you can't go along," Mason said. "But without your help, I'll have to turn the property back over to Misses Stewart."

Charlie finally looked up at Mason. "This is something I'll have to sleep on," he said, as he stood up.

Mason got to his feet and stepped to the door. "Sorry to spring this on you, but I just don't see any other way."

Charlie stared into Mason's eyes for several moments and opened the door. "I'll see you in the morning."

CHAPTER 16

"I think you're taking a tremendous risk," Charlie said, as he sat with Mason, Jeremy, and Nathan on the back porch, facing the river. The sun had been up for about an hour and all the workers were busy in the fields or the work yard.

"Like I keep saying," Mason said, "I don't see any other way. We need hard currency to pay the previous owner."

"Who's this middle man you mentioned?"

"When we first arrived, we befriended a small group of Catawba—"

"They killed a great many settlers in this area during the war," Charlie said cutting him off.

"Not this group," Mason countered. "They broke off from the main tribe and were never aligned with the Yamasee. They didn't kill anyone."

"After the war, some Yamasee and others resettled in Spanish territory. I hear there's a town of them near St. Augustine." He paused for several moments while he stared at Mason. "You think your friend may have connections with those Indians near the Spanish fort."

"Exactly."

"There's a lot of moving parts to this plan," Jeremy said. "I may be having second thoughts."

Charlie sat back in his chair. "It wouldn't hurt to talk to your friend. He may not even have a connection. If he does, you wouldn't be the first to transport goods into Spanish territory."

"Nathan and I are heading out this morning. Should be back tomorrow afternoon with word, one way or the other."

"In the meantime," Charlie said, "you want us to start holding back part of the crop."

"Yes. We need at least a third. Half would be better."

Charlie inhaled deeply, exhaled, and massaged the back of his neck. "I'll see what I can do."

The four men stood and parted.

Charlie and Jeremy headed off toward the work yard.

Karen emerged from the back door, stood beside Mason, and watched the two men walk away. "Think he'll keep it a secret?"

"There is something in our favor," Mason said.

Karen turned to face him.

"There's no love lost between Colonel Rhett and the British. From what I've gathered, he is not in favor of the Crown regaining control of this colony from the proprietors. At this time in history, he's sided with the proprietors and the former governor. The whole situation is in flux and, according to what I read, won't be totally resolved for years. I figure Charlie feels the same way. Plus, no one likes paying taxes to London."

"That's pretty weak," Karen said. "No matter how he feels about the Crown, he favors them a lot more than the Spanish."

Mason wrapped his arms around Karen. "Let's hope Charlie has grown on us." He gave her a kiss. "We need to head out."

"To see Mato."

"Should be back by tomorrow afternoon." He gave Karen a final kiss and motioned for Nathan to follow as he stepped off the porch.

◆◆◆

Late in the afternoon, Mason steered the sloop toward the small inlet near their original camp, on the shore of what would become Myrtle Beach.

They dropped anchor behind a small spit of sand and trees that partially concealed the sloop's hull and mast.

"You'll need to stay with the boat," Mason said. "There's a musket and shot in the V-berth, if needed. I'll get back here as quickly as possible."

"You don't mind if I start in on that food Karen and Lisa packed?"

"Have at it. Just stay with the boat. Don't leave for any reason."

"Will do, Captain," Nathan said, with a sloppy salute.

"I'm serious, don't leave this boat. Shoot anyone who even looks at it wrong."

"I got it. See you when you get back."

Mason hesitated as he stared into Nathan's eyes, judging his commitment. After a few moments, he turned, climbed down from the deck holding his rucksack in one hand, and waded to shore. He glanced a final time at Nathan and started off down the beach.

Two hours later he stood at the edge of Mato's village. He scanned the faces of the natives going about their usual routine. Several he knew by name. When they started to notice him, he entered the village and walked to the center hut, smiling and nodding as he went. A native at the hut's opening acknowledged Mason's presence and darted inside.

Mato emerged a few seconds later. "My friend," he said, as he came forward and grasped Mason on the shoulder. He looked around the camp. "You come alone?"

"Yes," Mason said. "Can you walk with me while we talk?"

Mato's expression turned more serious as he fell in beside Mason. They walked toward the far edge of the village.

"Sorry, I don't have a lot of time," Mason said, as he looked toward the sun dropping low in the western sky. When Mato didn't say anything, he continued. "I seem to find myself with a problem."

"How I help?" Mato asked.

"I need to sell the rice for silver. Spanish dollars."

Mato shook his head slightly.

"After the war, some of your people moved with the Yamasee to La Florida."

He gave a slight nod.

"I want to sell my rice to the Spanish there, in St. Augustine, and was hoping you knew someone who could help make that happen."

An understanding expression suddenly spread across Mato's face. "They not friends with the English."

"I know," Mason said, "but I'm hoping they are still friends with you." He paused a few moments to gauge Mato's reaction. "Maybe you could help me meet someone there who can help."

Mato stared at Mason without expression.

"I'm hoping the Spanish desire for rice will outweigh their hatred of the English. At least in this one instance." He watched as the wheels turned in Mato's head. "Your people here, and the people in St. Augustine, will have plenty of rice for themselves."

"Chicos," Mato said, without further explanation.

"Who is Chicos?"

"Brother."

"You split with your brother over the Yamasee War with the English."

"My brother now with Spanish."

"How long since you've seen him?"

"Five summers."

"Are you sure he's still there?"

He dipped his chin. "Some my people come back. They tell me." He turned and stared back at his village. His eyes moved with the comings and goings of the people. He finally turned back to Mason. "When?"

"Soon. Hopefully tomorrow morning. I haven't worked out the logistics—the plan. I have a boat waiting at the inlet near our old camp."

"I meet you at boat morning," Mato said. "I bring two my people. You take us to La Florida."

"It may not be quite that easy, but we can work out the details on the boat."

"Sunrise," Mato said.

"We'll need to make a stop at Charles Town tomorrow and head out the next day."

Mato started back into the village with Mason walking beside him. "You stay here tonight."

"Thank you, but I need to get back to the boat," Mason said. "Don't want to leave it too long."

They parted at the main hut and Mason started back toward the boat.

◆◆◆

Early the next morning, Mato showed up with two of his braves. They carried enough food and water for three or four days, and they each held a musket. The five of them set out as soon as everyone was aboard. The steady onshore winds provided for a quick, uneventful trip back to Charles Town. As he had done several times now, he guided the sloop up the Ashley River with the aid of the slight wind against reefed sails. Soon, they were tied up at the plantation dock.

Everyone gathered on the back porch of the main house to consider their next steps.

"If we follow the coastline, it's about two hundred and fifty miles to St. Augustine," Mason said.

"That sounds about right," Charlie said.

"Why not a more direct route?" Jeremy asked.

"We don't have navigation equipment," Nathan said. He turned to Mason. "Unless you—"

"Navigation equipment?" Charlie asked.

"Compass and sextant," Mason said. "Nathan is right, we're not equipped to navigate the open ocean."

Jeremy's face turned sour, and he was about to respond but Mason cut him off.

"We'll be following the coast. It will also keep us out of the main shipping lanes, and hopefully away from pirates and privateers."

"How long?" Karen asked.

"If we can average seven knots, about thirty-six hours," Mason said. "Day and a half, if we sail through the night."

"Can you do that safely?" Jeremy asked.

"If there's a moon," Charlie said. "There should be enough light for the next five or six days, but you can't just sail into that harbor. They're likely to blow you out of the water. It was only a year ago that we attacked St. Augustine with a small force. We mainly engaged the Yamasee living near the fort, but it amounted to an attack on the Spanish, as well."

"What has been the situation since then?" Jeremy asked.

"Mostly quiet, maybe a few skirmishes with the Indians. The Crown has turned its attention more to the French. Spain, for now, isn't considered a main rival. Merchants from Charles Town have even explored the renewal of trade with La Florida—the Spanish and the Indians. You know how merchants are, they're only concerned with profit. Doesn't matter much where the money comes from." Obviously realizing Mason was about to embark on a similar endeavor, a grimace spread across his face. "No offense intended."

"None taken," Mason said. "We'll be laying up short of the town. The question is whether we should approach that final leg at night, or during the day."

Charlie rubbed his beard for several moments. "Day time you can see what you're running into, but they can also see you. I'd recommend approaching at night, probably early morning."

Mason turned to Mato. "Do you know where to find your brother?"

Mato raised his chin. "Yes. Walk in dark. Find him with sun."

"That means we need to leave now," Nathan said, "or at least in the next couple of hours."

Mason looked at Karen and Lisa. "Can you pack us enough food and water for three or four days?"

Karen and Lisa got up, stepped down from the porch, and began walking toward the kitchen.

"Some of those biscuits," Nathan yelled after her.

Karen raised a hand in the air, without looking back.

"Where do we stand on the rice?" Mason asked, looking at Charlie and Jeremy.

"We've started setting bags to the side," Jeremy said. "We're storing them in the barn for now. The wing closest to the river."

"Normally, we'd use that room for more drying space," Charlie said, "but we'll make do for now. If you are not able to arrange a sale, we'll be right back on track."

"Good," Mason said. "Any problem with the crop so far?"

"Nothing we can't handle," Charlie said.

"Maybe we should take some of the rice with us," Nathan said, "let them know we're serious."

Mason raised an eyebrow. "We're sailing into Spanish territory, they'll know we're serious,"

Charlie cleared his throat. "That brings up a problem. If you plan to transport rice on the sloop, it should be in barrels. The moisture from the sea air, not to mention rain, will ruin bags of rice."

"That's something I hadn't thought of," Mason said. "We'll need barrels." He paused for a moment to think. "How many?"

"The barrels normally used for ocean shipment weigh around three hundred pounds when filled. You'd need seven hundred barrels for two hundred thousand pounds."

"We're talking several trips in the sloop," Mason said. He dropped his head and massaged the back of his neck for almost a full minute before resuming eye contact with the others. "I still don't see any other way."

"If the Spanish are in dire need of food," Charlie said, "they might be willing to meet you half way. Some spot along the coast."

Mason got to his feet when he saw Karen and Lisa returning with their arms full of supplies. "Let's get this first part done. Then we'll figure out the rest."

Jeremy took Karen's load from her and he and Lisa continued on toward the boat.

Mason met Karen as she stepped up on the porch. "With any luck we'll be back here in three days." He stared into her eyes for several moments and gave her a quick kiss.

"Be careful," she said. "Run at the first sign of trouble."

"Will do," he said. The corners of his mouth curled into a slight smile. "We'll be fine." He released her and turned to Nathan, Mato, and the two braves, standing in a group at the edge of the porch. As they stepped off the porch and started walking toward the boat, Mason turned back to Karen. "Nothing too strenuous for you."

"I know," she said. "Just worry about yourself."

He gave her a smile and a wink and turned to Charlie. "Thank you for supporting me in this."

Charlie lifted his chin but said nothing.

Mason gave a slight wave with his hand at Karen and began walking toward the boat.

CHAPTER 17

With the light beginning to fade, they made their way down the Ashley River and into the open Atlantic. About two miles out, Mason turned southwest to follow the curvature of the coast. With steady winds, he estimated they were making about eight knots, maybe nine. When the orange glow in the western sky finally began to disappear, the coastline in the distance lost its detail. Mason navigated based on the North Star and the faint line of contrast between the sky and the darker trees along the coast. Occasionally, he saw the faint glow of a campfire on the beach, probably from a native hunting party.

Mason sent Nathan into the V-berth to get a few hours' sleep. He knew he would not be able to maintain the intense concentration needed to keep the boat on course through the entire night.

He had been steering at least two hours after the sun went down, when the moon finally appeared. Just as he had hoped, the extra light made the coastline more visible, but it remained difficult to judge distance. To keep the boat well away from the shore took constant vigilance on his part. The effort was already leading to a headache. He had been at the tiller for what he estimated to be six straight hours. His arm and his head had had enough.

He tied off the tiller, went forward, and opened the hatch to the V-berth. He could hear Nathan snoring over the sound of the water and wind. He stepped down the ladder and shook Nathan by the shoulder.

Nathan groaned and lifted his head as his eyes shot open. "What time is it?"

"Well after midnight," Mason said.

Nathan emerged from the dark hole rubbing his face and eyes.

Mason climbed back to the deck, untied the tiller, and gauged his position relative to the North Star. He motioned to the star. "Keep it over your right shoulder blade. It's tough to determine distance in the dark. But you need to keep the shore in sight." He paused a moment as he stared at Nathan's mostly obscured face. "Don't run her ashore."

"I know how to steer a boat," he said, as he took hold of the tiller.

"If you see anything out of the ordinary, actually, if you see anything, wake me."

"Get some sleep," Nathan said. "I know what I'm doing."

Mason took in a deep breath and exhaled. He took a final look around the deck, at the shore, at the North Star, and padded off toward the V-berth.

◆◆◆

Mason woke to the sound of the hatch opening and sunlight flooding into his makeshift bedroom. He squinted at the bright light through the opening, and Nathan's backlit hulk.

"Rise and shine," Nathan said.

"How long have I been out?" Mason asked, as he rolled to his knees and poked his head through the opening. The sun was at the nine o'clock position over the starboard bow.

"Long enough," Nathan said, as he let go of the hatch cover and let it slam back against the deck.

Mason climbed the ladder and immediately surveyed the deck, and the boat's position relative to the shore. All seemed okay. "No problems during the night?" he asked, as he came up on deck. He saw Mato at the tiller.

"No problems, didn't see a thing, except an occasional shooting star."

The two braves stood at the bow, peering into the distance.

Mason focused in the same direction. He saw a black dot. A large sailing ship on the horizon, over the port bow. He pointed. "What's that?"

"First I've seen it," Nathan said, as he stared.

Mason immediately went back down the ladder, found his ruck sack, extracted his Glock, two extra magazines, and his shoulder holster. He removed his long coat, slipped into the holster, and back into the coat. He seated the pistol and two magazines in their respective slots and returned to the deck. He looked in the direction of the black dot. "Is it headed our way?"

"I think it's a little bigger," Nathan said. "It looks like it."

"Any chance you speak Spanish?" Mason asked Nathan.

"I can order a cerveza, but that's about it."

Having been stationed in Miami for several years with the Air Marshal's Service, he could speak a little more than that, but not much. He motioned to the V-berth. "Better get the musket, shot, and powder, just in case."

"Is that a good idea?"

"Yes, but keep it hidden on deck. Maybe under a piece of sail cloth."

Nathan disappeared below deck and reemerged through the hatch holding the long rifle, its accessories, and the sail cloth.

Mason motioned for Mato to hide their muskets under the cloth, as well.

Mato said a few words to the braves, who immediately placed their muskets on the deck next to Nathan's rifle.

Nathan covered them all with the sail cloth.

Mason kept his attention on the black dot as it continued to grow in size. "There's two of them."

Nathan stared in that direction. "Maybe we should run for it."

"Nowhere to run," Mason said. "They have us against the shore. Besides, we don't have anything anyone would want."

As the two ships came closer, Mason was able to make out more of the details. "Two masts each," he said. "There's a flag." He squinted. "I don't know all the flags of this era, but it is definitely not English."

"That's good," Nathan said.

Mason exhaled, but finally gave a slight nod. He kept the sloop on course, generally southwest, and about two miles off shore. Everyone on board continued to watch as the two ships approached. When they were a few hundred yards away, their open gun ports became obvious.

The prospect of stopping brought back dark memories. That's exactly what he'd done when Edward Low's pirate schooner was closing in on their former sloop. That decision resulted in the death of nearly everyone on board. *That's not going to happen this time*, he told himself as he scanned the two ships. They both flew military flags. That alone probably ruled out pirate ships, although not entirely. Pirates often flew ensigns in order to lull their target into a false sense of security. Still, against two heavily-armed ships of war, there was nothing he could do.

"We're heaving to," Mason said. "Lower the sails."

Nathan hesitated several moments as he stared at Mason.

"Go ahead," Mason said.

With Mato's help, Nathan lowered the mainsail and the two jibs.

As the tiny sloop continued to glide through the water under Mason's control of the tiller, he watched as one of the ships, the smaller one, a cross between a brig and a schooner, began to lower its lateen-rigged mainsails and two square top sails. It came to a complete stop about fifty yards out, with its port broadside, and five open gun ports facing the sloop.

The larger ship, with square sails on both masts, maintained full sail as it turned off and began a wide arc that would take it back out to sea. Mason presumed it would take up a station farther out and wait for the smaller ship to finish its business with the sloop.

On the stationary smaller ship, Mason could see several people standing on the open stern deck, near the wheel. Three of them wore uniforms. One of the men stepped toward the gunwale and cupped both hands around his mouth. The man yelled something. Mason didn't understand, but it sounded like Spanish.

"We're a small merchant ship out of Charles Town," Mason yelled back.

"English?" the man yelled with a thick accent.

"Yes," Mason yelled back.

The man stepped back to the others. After a few moments, one of the other men stepped to the gunwale.

"What is your purpose and destination?" the man yelled. His accent was also thick, but his English was understandable.

"I wish to trade with St. Augustine," Mason yelled back.

"Trade what?" the man yelled.

"Rice. I own a plantation and I wish to sell my rice."

The man turned to the others. They spoke with each other for a full minute before the man turned back to Mason. "Prepare to be boarded."

The third man, in a slightly more flowery uniform, motioned with his hand.

Several of the crew began lowering the ship's tender. With that done, several scrambled over the side, armed with pistols. The English-speaking gentleman boarded last. Two crewmen manned the oars and began pulling toward the sloop.

When it bumped against the hull, two crewmen jumped aboard and immediately tied off the tender to the sloop. Next, the uniformed gentleman climbed aboard and stood directly in front of Mason. He was tall, thin, and he stood rail-straight. He held his chin high with a sense of superiority. His uniform consisted of a short-in-the-front, long-tailed blue coat with gold and red trim and gold epaulets. The pants were a matching blue with a yellow stripe down each leg. A blue and gold two-pointed hat perched atop his head. A sword dangled from his left hip.

"Manuel Diaz," the man said. "His majesty's royal ship Nuestra Señora del Carmen." The man saluted. He spoke rapidly, in a clipped, direct tone.

"Stephen Mason, captain of this boat." He extended his hand.

Diaz took it with a firm grip. He scanned the deck, bow to stern. "I don't see any rice," he said in his heavy accent, as he turned back to Mason.

"I first need to establish a market," Mason said. "And safe passage. Then I'll begin shipping the rice."

Diaz again scanned the deck. He walked forward, opened the V-berth hatch, and peered inside. Apparently satisfied, he let the hatch cover slam back closed. He kicked at the sail cloth on deck, exposing the barrel of one of the rifles.

"Do you have papers proving who you are? Perhaps signed by the governor of Charles Town?"

"I do not," Mason said. "I own a plantation on the Ashley River. I have two hundred thousand pounds of rice I wish to sell in La Florida, in exchange for silver."

Diaz motioned toward Mato and the two braves standing in the bow. "And these natives?"

"They are friends of mine. I thought I might need to communicate with the Indians near St. Augustine."

"La Florida. Not many English merchants in La Florida in these times. We've been at war with your king." He paused a moment. "But not at the moment." He studied Mason's eyes. "What makes you think we need your rice?"

"Everyone has to eat," Mason said. "I prefer your silver to our paper."

Diaz contemplated that for a moment. "We would escort you directly into St. Augustine," Diaz said, "but unfortunately that is not our destination." He motioned for his men to return to the tender. "You will wait here until I report to my captain."

"I'll do that," Mason said.

Diaz turned to leave, but turned back to Mason. "I've never heard an English accent like you have. Where are you from?"

"I lived for many years in the Far East."

Diaz considered Mason's words. He finally turned to his boat, climbed aboard, and ordered his men to return to the ship.

Mason watched as the boat moved away.

Nathan shuffled up beside Mason. "What do you think?"

"They'll let us go," he said, "or they won't."

All five aboard the sloop watched as Diaz climbed back aboard his ship and reported to the man in the flowery uniform, apparently the captain.

The captain stood silent as Diaz talked.

"This is it," Nathan said. "Our life is in that man's hands."

"If we get past this, I think we'll find that to be the case many more times before this is over."

"What?"

"Our lives in some other person's hands. Much more so in this time, than in our own."

The captain turned to Diaz, said something, and motioned for the crew to bring the tender aboard.

Diaz stepped to the gunwale and cupped his hands around his mouth. "You may go."

Mason gave the man a slight wave. "Hoist the sails, if you will," he said to Nathan. "Let's be on our way before they change their minds."

CHAPTER 18

As the sloop continued its journey along the coast, Mason peered at the trees, inlets, and marshes. It was impossible to see what the area would become in three hundred years. Presently, it was just a lot of mosquito-infested desolation, interspersed with pure white beaches. He thought of how much cleaner the water was, compared to the plastic and chemical filled oceans of the future. He thought of whales tangled in nets, and sea turtles struggling with plastic straws. He remembered something his father often repeated during Mason's childhood in Idaho. *This planet would be a great place to live if it wasn't for the people*. As Mason matured, he came to agree. He realized that what he was living now was just that. A planet with fewer people.

Late in the afternoon, with Nathan at the helm, Mason stood at the mast, using it to balance himself against the rolling deck. The wind had picked up, and they were making excellent progress. His eyes caught sight of a particularly large inlet separating two points of white beach. He checked the position of the sun and estimated that the line of beach was almost perfectly north and south. He made his way along the deck to the helm. Nathan's eyelids were heavy, with each closing lasting longer than the last. He was practically asleep on his feet. They popped wide open when Mason spoke.

"That has to be Fernandina Beach," Mason said, as he pointed.

"Never been there," Nathan grumbled.

"That inlet separates Florida and Georgia. At least it will in the future."

"So, we're entering Florida waters," Nathan said.

"We are." Mason took hold of the tiller. "Why don't you get some sleep?"

"I think I'll do that," Nathan said. He waddled off toward the V-berth hatch.

Mason eyed Mato and one of his braves, asleep on the deck. The other brave was bent over the gunwale. He had been seasick for nearly the entire voyage.

Mason contemplated their position off Fernandina Beach, the distance to St. Augustine, and the number of hours it would take to get there, or near there. The sloop had been beating into the wind for a couple of hours and their speed had dropped considerably. Maybe midnight or so, at their present speed.

◆◆◆

Three hours later, Mason woke Nathan.

With Nathan, Mato, and the two braves standing at the helm, Mason stared at the long ribbon of white beach reflected in the distance from the moonlight.

"Did we pass the St. John's?"

"Not too long after Fernandina Beach," Mason said. "From there it has just been a long strip of beach." He pushed on the tiller. "I think it's time to head in."

"Have you seen any boats?" Nathan asked.

"Several, but all were farther out to sea. I doubt any of them saw us against the darkness of the shore."

Mason steered the sloop landward under a reefed mainsail and no jib. Soon, Mason spotted the white caps of the breakers and heard the sound of the waves lashing against the sand. He continued forward until he felt the surf lift the boat and deliver it safely on the other side of the breakers. "Lower the sail," he said to Nathan. He turned the boat until it was running parallel with the shore. "Mato, drop the stern anchor."

Mato started forward.

"This one," Mason said, pointing to the anchor and rope bundled against the transom.

Mato reversed course, lifted the anchor, and tossed it overboard.

With the sail down, the anchor caught and brought the boat to a stop.

"What's the plan?" Nathan asked.

"Mato and I will walk from here."

"You're going in? I thought Mato was going to arrange an introduction."

"Yeah, I've given it a lot of thought. I need to be there. You and the two braves will stay here with the boat."

"I don't like it," Nathan said.

"I know. There is no perfect way to do this. Hopefully, I can make this happen before the day is out."

"How long do I wait?" Nathan asked.

"You wait until I get back," Mason said seriously. "Protect this boat with your life. You may want to take it back out past the breakers and anchor there." Mason looked at the former seasick brave and turned to Mato. "Your two braves may want to wait on shore, but let them know how important it is to protect the boat."

Mato spoke to them in Catawban. He turned back to Mason. "They will make camp on shore. Watch boat."

Mason looked at Nathan. "Any problems or questions?"

"I guess not," Nathan said.

Mato and the braves gathered their belongings.

Mason retrieved his rucksack from the V-berth, climbed over the gunwale, and began wading the few yards to shore.

Mato and the two braves followed.

On shore, Mato handed his flintlock to one of the braves, said a few more words, and he and Mason started walking down the beach.

Mason had been to St. Augustine several times in his life. The last time had been about three years earlier, when he drove up from Miami for a short getaway with a young lady. They'd spent three glorious days in the sun, and made maximum use of the beaches. Constantly in search of the perfect secluded patch of sand, they'd explored every piece of beach in the area, including the one he and Mato now walked. Getting to it then was easy via the Vilano Bridge over the Tolomato River, about a half mile expanse. Now, getting to the Spanish fort and the actual town of St. Augustine would mean crossing the river, several streams, salt marshes, and mud flats. An impossible task in the time they had, especially at night. They would need a boat of some sort.

Mason estimated they had walked about three miles when they came to the edge of a village. From what Mason could see in the dark, based on the numerous canoes pulled well up on shore, it was an Indian fishing village. Mason guessed it covered most of Vilano Point.

He began thinking about the Glock pistol he carried in the shoulder holster under his coat, and the extra magazines in the rucksack on his back. He contemplated the impact of them being found, should he be searched by either the Indians or the Spanish. If the gun were to fall into either of their hands—.

"Hold up," Mason whispered, as he slung the pack from his shoulders and placed it on the sand at his feet.

Mato stopped about ten feet ahead, glanced back, and began scanning the village.

"Give me a minute while I tend to something," Mason said. In the dark, he removed his coat and slipped out of the shoulder holster. He placed it, the pistol, and the two magazines into the rucksack and cinched it tightly closed. He walked the few steps into the tall grass and found a spot on the backside of a small sand dune. He dropped to his knees and began digging in the soft sand until it was deep enough to conceal the ruck. He dropped the ruck into the hole and pushed sand over the top, completely covering the tan canvas. He pulled the small knife from its sheath on his waist and cut several stalks of the grass. He tied the stalks into a loose knot and stuck the stubble of one end into the sand. The resulting circle of grass sticking above the sand would be enough to find the spot later. At least he hoped it would. With the ruck buried and marked, he stood up, slipped back into his coat and joined Mato on the beach.

The fishing village was quiet in the night. There was no movement that Mason could detect.

Mato suddenly stopped. "We should wait for daylight," he whispered. He stepped to the edge of the dunes and plopped down in the sand.

Mason sat down in the sand beside him, checked both directions, and gradually relaxed.

Mason didn't realize he had fallen asleep until he came awake at the sound of footsteps in the sand near him. He immediately raised up to find the sun peaking over the horizon. Down the beach he saw Mato talking to two natives at the water's edge. Several other natives were coming and going along the beach. Several were pushing long dugout canoes into the surf. So far, everything seemed non-hostile, even though Mason was obviously dressed in typical English attire. Mason got to his feet and started walking toward Mato just as he finished his conversation and parted from the two natives.

"What did they say?" Mason asked when he met Mato and they started walking south along the beach.

"This is Timucuan village. My people are with people from many other tribes, other side of river. Big village there."

"Can we borrow a canoe?"

"Yes," Mato said, as he continued to guide Mason toward the point of land sticking into the inlet.

Once they cleared a line of dome-shaped grass huts, Mason saw a vista of low dunes, short bushes, and wispy tall grass. The coquina stone Castillo de San

Marcos was clearly visible about a mile away on the other side of the Matanzas River.

At the southernmost point of land, they both came to a stop and scanned their surroundings.

Mason had stood in this very spot three hundred years in the future. The inlet was a little narrower than it would be, due to shifting sands, but Anastasia Island on the other side of the inlet was easily recognizable. Mason could see a wood watch tower, maybe twenty-five feet tall and a hundred yards inland, standing prominently on the island. A tall lighthouse would stand in its place in a couple of centuries. A row of tents and several grass huts were grouped between the watch tower and the inlet. Mason saw numerous black men, only black men, in and around the camp. Actually, it would be a garrison, since nearly all of them carried muskets. Armed black men seemed odd, even for Spanish Florida. He turned his attention back to the fort. It would not change much over the next three hundred years. Mason could see two bastions, but he knew there were four. The thick coquina walls would never be penetrated by force, in all the coming years, despite numerous attempts. He stood in awe, mesmerized by the history before him in the land he formerly called home.

Mato and Mason continued around the spit of land, toward the river and the back side of the peninsula. The inhabitants all seemed to be up and about, apparently preparing for another day of fishing. Women were working on nets, hanging fish to dry, and other sundry duties. Twenty or so dugout canoes were pulled up on the beach, and others were in various states of construction or repair.

Mato seemed to have his sights on a thin, lanky native with nearly black skin and long, gray hair. Mason presumed this was the man to see about a boat.

Mato, walking ten feet or so ahead of Mason, approached the man.

Mason stopped well short, but kept an eye on the proceedings. Mato apparently knew a few words of the older man's language, but mostly, he used a lot of sign language. The whole time the two men talked, the older man never took his eyes off Mason.

When Mato stopped talking, the man finally turned to Mato and stared at him. After several long moments, the old man turned to a nearby native working on a thick log.

The native had an axe in the air and was about to take a swing when he stopped in mid stroke, lowered the axe to the sand, and hurried over to the old man and Mato. The old man said a few words as he gestured at Mason.

Mato walked back to where Mason stood waiting. He pointed to the fort on the other side of the Matanzas. "Take us in canoe."

"What about your brother?"

"Only take us to fort."

Mason looked at the stone structure reflecting the morning light. An Englishman showing up without an introduction. What could go wrong? But, once again, Mason seemingly had no other option if he wanted to establish a market for his rice. He removed his three-cornered hat and scratched at his head. "Lead the way," he said, as he replaced the hat.

CHAPTER 19

The native directed Mason and Mato to a canoe pulled up at the river's edge. He motioned for them to get in.

Mason and Mato climbed in and took a seat.

The native was joined by another and together they pushed the canoe into the water, leapt to their positions inside, and began paddling. The slack tide allowed the long, hollowed-out canoe to glide through the water. They headed directly for the fort.

As they drew nearer, Mason could see five soldiers begin to gather at the shore, right where the canoe was headed. Each wore a uniform consisting of a long coat open at the front, over a red waistcoat and blue pants. And they each carried a musket tipped with an excessively long bayonet. Mason began to think this wasn't such a good idea. After all, how could he expect the Spanish to just welcome him? A bad idea didn't begin to describe the situation. It was just stupid. Once again, Karen, Lisa, and Jeremy would be left to struggle on their own, while he languished in prison or worse. He closed his eyes and subtly shook his head while he pinched the bridge of his nose. He thought of one of his favorite movie quotes. *Stupid is as stupid does.*

He came alert when the canoe slid on the sand.

The two natives jumped out and approached the soldiers. They spoke in a language Mason didn't understand, while he and Mato remained in the canoe. Spanish or Timucuan, it was all gibberish to him. Even Mato didn't seem to understand what they were saying. Mason presumed they were explaining how an Englishman and a Catawba came to be in their canoe.

When the natives stopped talking, they all turned and stared at Mason and Mato. After a few moments, four of the soldiers marched forward. Two took Mato's arms and two took Mason's. They were both jerked from the canoe and hustled roughly toward the fort. The fifth fell in behind. No one said a word.

Two other soldiers swung the tall, iron gate open as Mason, Mato, and their escorts approached.

The soldiers, now aided by others inside the fort, roughly pushed Mason and Mato across the courtyard and into a wooden cell built against the coquina walls. The iron gate slamming shut behind them identified the structure as a stockade. With a smirk, the soldiers walked away.

Mason surveyed the cell's interior and quickly deduced that escape was not going to be likely. His arrival to the fort stood in stark contrast to the last time he'd visited.

Mato took a seat on the dirt and oyster shell floor, with his back against the fort's coquina wall.

"You're taking this pretty well," Mason said, as he stared down at him.

"We wait," Mato said with a lot less fear or anger than Mason expected.

"Yeah, I get that. How long, is the question."

"We wait," Mato said again.

Mason stepped up to the iron gate, grabbed two of the bars with both hands, and shook. The gate barely moved, mostly because of its immense weight. "I guess we wait," he said, as he took a seat near Mato.

The sun was at about the 10 o'clock position when four soldiers returned and opened the gate. They each took an arm, lifted Mato and Mason to their feet, and ushered them out of the cell.

"Where are we going?" Mason asked.

The only response was a tighter grasp of his arm by the soldier on his right.

The soldiers took them through the open door of a wooden structure built against the fort's east wall. At the end of a short hallway, one of the soldiers knocked on a door. The door swung open from the inside and Mason and Mato were pushed into the room.

Mason surveyed the interior. It was a well-appointed office, furnished with fine, wood chairs, settees, cabinets, and a massive desk. Behind the desk stood a distinguished gentleman, around forty years of age, in a high-collared, tailored uniform. It was blue with red trim, but it also sported fancy gold epaulets and a single row of gold buttons. The pants were white. The uniform was much tighter fitting than others he had seen, probably to highlight the man's slender physique. His hair on the sides was combed back and flattened with grease, but left curly on top. He stood ramrod straight, with his hands clasped behind his back. He said something in Spanish to the four soldiers.

The soldiers stepped back, but did not leave the room.

The man studied Mason and Mato for almost a full minute before speaking. "I am Antonio Benavides Bazán y Molina, general governor of La Florida." His English was nearly perfect, aside from the accent. "Who are you?"

"My name is Stephen Mason. This is my friend Mato."

"And why are you here?"

"We have traveled from my plantation near Charles Town in search of a market for my rice crop."

"You have a market for your rice, in Charles Town."

"I owe a debt in New York. I need silver to pay that debt. Carolina paper won't work."

The general raised his chin with an expression of understanding. "And you travel here under the authority of Governor Moore?"

Mason hesitated. "Not exactly."

At that moment there was a knock on the door.

One of the soldiers looked at the general. When the general raised his chin, the soldier opened the door.

Another soldier, an officer, escorted a native inside. Based on the native's dress, in full buckskins and a boatload of feathers and ornaments, it had to be someone of importance.

Mason noticed Mato's expression change to one of recognition. Had to be his brother.

The general stepped from behind his desk. "This is Chicos, cacique of the Catawba people here in La Florida." He turned to Mato. "I believe you two are acquainted."

Mason realized the old man at the fishing village must have sent word to Chicos. Mato apparently mentioned they were brothers.

"Yes," Mato said, as he turned to Chicos. "Brothers."

The two of them spoke a few words in their language, but there were no expressions of brotherly love. Mason was aware that Mato's departure from his tribe, prior to the Yamasee War, was not on particularly good terms, but he did not know the relationship between the two brothers. Based on their current interaction, it wasn't that good.

The general let the two Indians finish talking before he spoke. "This is your brother?" he asked Chicos.

"Yes," Chicos replied in English.

"Can you vouch for him?"

"Vouch?"

"Can you stand for him?"

"He is my brother," Chicos said. "That is all."

"Can we believe him?"

Chicos hesitated for several moments before answering. "Yes. He will do what he say."

"Thank you," the general said to Chicos. "That will be all."

Chicos turned to leave only when the officer placed a hand on his shoulder. The two of them left the room.

The general turned to Mason. "We have been at war with England."

"You're not at war now," Mason said.

"Not formally," the general said, "but your people from Carolina continue to attack our missions."

"I don't know anything about that," Mason said. "I'm just here to sell my rice."

The general walked behind his desk and took a seat in the finely carved chair. He looked up at Mason. "Tell me about this rice."

The sudden willingness to discount Mason's origin told him two things. The general was having trouble getting supplies, probably from Havana, and he needed food. The other, he was willing to accept that food from wherever he could get it.

Mason relaxed for the first time since setting eyes on the fort. "I have two hundred thousand pounds ready to transport. I just need the barrels."

"And how much do you want for this rice?"

"Four thousand Spanish silver dollars, plus the cost of the barrels."

"That is not possible," the general said calmly. "Perhaps you will offer a better price if we return you to your stockade." He motioned to the soldiers standing at the door.

"Three thousand," Mason said, "plus the barrels. Any less won't solve my problem. The rice is worth it. And I can do the same next year and the year after."

"And how will you transport this rice?"

"I have a boat."

"You mean the little sloop anchored up the coast?"

Mason stretched his neck until he heard the vertebrae crack. "Yes, that boat."

"Your sloop has been brought into the harbor."

"And the—"

"Your man is unharmed." He turned to Mato. "As are your two braves."

"I believe your man's name is Nathan," the general said. "He is being detained outside." He stared at Mason a few moments, stood, and paced behind his desk. He stopped and turned to Mason. "I believe you, Mister Mason. But you can't carry seven hundred barrels on your tiny boat."

"I'll have to make several trips," Mason said.

"And what if you are discovered? The English routinely patrol the coast. They have garrisons and watch towers. You will eventually be discovered."

"It is my understanding that other English merchants are attempting to establish markets here. With the Indians and the Spanish."

The general said nothing. His expression didn't change.

"I have no choice," Mason said. "I'll have to take my chances."

"You would be chancing my money and my rice."

The general was right, eventually he would be discovered. The more trips he made, the greater the chance of being caught. And, if caught, he would certainly be jailed. Even Colonel Rhett, in his currently reduced status, would not be able to help, even if he wanted to.

The general contemplated the situation for nearly a full minute. He finally faced Mason. "What if you formed an agreement with the Guale to buy your rice?" He bent over his desk, opened a drawer, and pulled out a rolled-up map. He flattened the map over the top of his desk and positioned a lamp and a pewter mug to hold down the edges. He jabbed a spot on the map with his finger. "You know the mouth of the San Juan?"

The general's finger rested on the spot where Jacksonville would one day be built. "I do," Mason said.

The general ran his finger north, along the coast, to another inlet.

Mason knew this spot as well. It was the mouth of the St. Mary's river, the border between future Florida and Georgia, about fifteen miles north of the St. Johns. "I know this river."

"There is a Guale settlement there. I will send word to expect your first shipment, in let's say, ten days."

So far, Mato had not said a word. He just looked on as the two men talked.

Mason turned to Mato. "Do you know this area?"

"Yes," Mato said.

"Are you friendly with these natives, the Guale?"

"I not fight with them."

Mason turned back to the general. "What about the barrels?"

"We load your boat with as many empty barrels as it will hold, here, now. You fill them with rice, deliver to the Guale village, and pick up an equal number of empty barrels." He studied the map. "It will cut some time off your trip. A few hours."

"And I won't be sailing so deep into Spanish territory."

"One day it may all be Spanish territory."

Mason knew that day would never come. The Spanish would lose their grip in the colonies and, eventually, even the land west of the Mississippi. "Of course," Mason said.

The two men smiled.

"And payment?"

"You will be paid in silver for each shipment, totaling three thousand dollars for two hundred thousand pounds of rice."

"And the same next year," Mason said.

"Of course," the general said. "When you are ready to ship next year, pay me another visit."

"If I can lay my hands on a larger ship, this year or next, I may increase the size of the shipments."

"That will be fine. We'll have barrels and silver ready for any shipment you deliver. You may want to stop by the Guale village on your way back, to familiarize yourself with the area. I can assign a Timucua brave from here to make the introduction."

"I think that's a good idea," Mason said.

"And the Guale will want some of your rice for their efforts."

"No problem," Mason said.

"Good, then. I will order your boat loaded with the barrels. You will have a few hours to wait, but I must ask that you wait inside the fort."

"And Nathan?"

"He is already inside these walls."

"I think we have an agreement," Mason said, as he extended his hand. "Hopefully, our two countries can remain at peace long enough to get this done."

"That may be asking a lot," the general said, as he shook Mason's hand. The general reached for a crystal decanter containing a dark liquid. Some kind of wine, Mason presumed. He poured two small glasses and handed one to Mason.

"What about my friend here?"

The general poured a third glass and handed it to Mato. The general held his glass in the air. "To rice."

All three emptied their glass.

CHAPTER 20

Nathan, the two braves, and Mato's brother were waiting when Mason and Mato exited the general's office and stepped into the open courtyard.

Mato and Chicos walked off alone, mumbling in their own language.

The two braves walked with them, several paces behind.

Nathan stood with his head dipped and a grim expression. He looked up when Mason approached. "Sorry. They were on us so quickly, a boat from the sea and a squad from the land. There was nothing I could do."

"Don't worry about it," Mason said. "It all worked out. We have an agreement to sell them our rice. We'll be using an Indian settlement up the coast as a go-between."

"So, we can leave?"

"Not yet. They're loading empty barrels on the sloop. Part of the deal."

Mason explained the agreement in detail, including the multiple trips it would take, the exchange of barrels on each trip, and the stop at the St. Mary's River on the way back.

"Sounds like we're in the black market."

Mason cocked his head to one side and nodded in agreement.

"How many barrels can they get on the sloop without overloading us?"

"I don't know. We'll see."

"And each of those barrels could weigh three hundred pounds when loaded."

"I know. We'll have to work out the details."

Mason and Nathan walked as they talked. Mason took the opportunity to examine every square inch of the fort's interior, comparing it to how the fort would look in the future. The interior was constructed mostly of wood, built against the coquina walls. Nearly all of that would be replaced with coquina in the future. And Mason thought the actual walls were a little higher in the future. Beyond that, the fort was exactly the same. Mason watched the soldiers go about their daily duties. There were people performing maintenance on the many cannons positioned on top of the walls. Some worked on the interior structures, and some were engaged in more menial duties, such as preparing food. The mix of people included soldiers, natives, and a few blacks. He had read something about natives and former black slaves from Carolina finding sanctuary in Spanish Florida during this time. Apparently, he was seeing the product of that policy. It was a shame he would not be able to visit the town of St. Augustine. But, from what he had read, the town structures were mostly built of wood and had been, or would be, burned to the ground several times. What existed here and now was probably nothing like it would become.

Several hours had passed when the same officer approached and announced, in somewhat broken English, that the sloop was ready and Mason's group would be escorted to the harbor. With the officer in the lead and two soldiers trailing behind, they guided Mason and his people through the fort's gate, over the bridge spanning the moat, and down to a longboat pulled up on the sand. The sloop sat out in the middle of the harbor, moving gently with the waves. A Timucua brave was already aboard.

"Tide going out," the officer said.

"Why haven't they built a dock?" Nathan asked.

"Too many shifting sandbars, I suspect," Mason said. "Everything must be ferried out."

Four Timucua braves pushed the longboat off the sand and held it in place.

Mato and Chicos said a few words before Mato and his braves climbed into the boat. Their faces remained emotionless.

Mason and Nathan stepped in, along with the officer and two soldiers. The soldiers took two of the rowing positions. Mato's two braves manned the other two rowing spots.

As they neared, Mason examined the sloop and the many barrels lashed to the deck. The barrels were considerably smaller than Mason had expected. When loaded with rice, he estimated each would weigh around one hundred and fifty pounds. Every inch of the sloop's deck was covered, except for the minimum necessary to operate the boat. The trip home would be cramped, but doable. The load appeared to be well-balanced, with the boat sitting only an inch or two lower in the water. Mason started counting the barrels but quickly gave up. There had to be a hundred or more.

"Will she float?" Nathan asked.

"Let's hope we don't run into a storm on the way home," Mason said.

When the longboat bumped against the sloop's hull, the Spanish officer held the two boats together while Mason and his group scrambled aboard.

Nathan immediately went to the V-berth, opened the hatch, and peered inside. "All our gear is here," he announced.

The Spanish officer pushed away and gave a slight wave, without comment.

Nathan pulled on the anchor line until the iron hook clanged to the deck.

Mason hoisted the main sail as the tide immediately began carrying the sloop farther out.

"Take the helm," Mason said to Nathan. "Hug the coast when you exit the mouth. About a mile up or so, I have something I need to retrieve from the beach."

He went to the bow to watch for sandbars, gave a final wave to the soldiers still rowing away, and focused on the water. He thought about the agreement with the general. He had ten days to return home, load the sloop, and make his first trip to the St. Mary's river with as much rice as he could carry. He scanned the barrels behind him. It would take ten or more trips to transport the agreed-upon rice. It appeared he, Nathan, and probably Charlie, would be busy for two or three months.

Once clear of the sandbars at the mouth of the inlet, Nathan steered north.

About a mile up, just past the fishing village and still in view of the fort's watch tower, Mason motioned toward the beach.

Nathan steered accordingly, converging with the white-sand beach, until he was over the light breakers and about twenty-five yards from shore.

Mato let the sails go slack in the breeze, while Nathan tossed the stern anchor overboard.

Mason removed his boots, coat, breeches, and shirt, leaving them in a pile on the deck. Wearing just his white-cotton boxer shorts, Mason hopped overboard and immediately submerged. He returned to the surface and swam until he could touch the bottom. He waded ashore and rummaged the beach while the others watched from the deck in wonderment, not sure what he was doing.

Mason was a hundred yards farther north when he found the sand dune marked with the circle of reeds. He pulled his rucksack from the sand, brushed it off, and trotted back down the beach. He waded back into the surf and dog paddled to the boat, holding the rucksack high over his head with one hand. He threw the ruck over the gunwale and pulled himself on board, with the help of Mato and one of his braves. Shivering, he quickly pulled his clothes back on while Mato pulled up the anchor. Nathan let the outgoing tide carry the boat a little farther out before Mason set the sails.

◆◆◆

The sloop rode low in the water, but maintained its steadiness through the light waves.

Mason kept an eye on gray clouds to the southeast as he stood with Mato in the bow. It appeared their course would take them out of reach of any rough weather. He estimated it was forty-five miles from St. Augustine to the St. Mary's River. If the wind continued, they could be there just before dark. If not, they would have to anchor short of their destination and wait out the night. Navigating the shoreline and sandbars in the dark would be impossible.

"How did you feel about seeing your brother?" Mason asked.

"He chief of Catawba people here."

"Did he ask you to join him?"

Mato was hesitant.

"Do you want to join him?"

"No."

Mato was never one for a lot of words, but he was being especially tight-lipped. Mason figured he was giving it some thought. "Everything is fine now with the Spanish, but that can change, and likely will change," Mason said.

Mato shuffled his feet to maintain his balance. "With the English, too."

"Very true, my friend." *If he only knew.* "This trip didn't go as I had planned, but I could still use your help."

Mato grunted but said nothing.

"Can you speak the Guale language?"

"Some," he said.

Mason glanced at the Timucua brave huddled with Mato's braves. They watched the coast slide by and occasionally exchanged grunts, gestures, and a few words. He turned back to Mato.

"I'll understand if you need to return home."

Mato continued to stare at the coastline.

Mason walked to the helm, where he took over the tiller from Nathan.

"Probably take longer to get home with this load," Nathan said, as he continued to stand at the helm next to Mason.

"I'm just hoping we can make it to the St. Mary's before dark," Mason said, as he glanced at the sun.

Four hours later, with the sun hanging low in the western sky, Mason began to veer toward the shore just north of Fernandina Beach.

Nathan, who had been napping on the deck next to the transom, blinked his eyes open and looked up at Mason. "You see something?"

"The St. Mary's."

Nathan got to his feet and peered in the distance.

The braves and Mato began to stir at the prospect of heading in. Everyone got to their feet.

They approached the mouth of the river on the downwind, under full sail.

Mason could see a group of what turned out to be native children on the south point of land. With Nathan keeping watch from the bow, he steered the sloop straight into the mouth and along the white sand beach.

The natives stopped what they had been doing and stared at the sloop as it passed within yards of the shore. Several took off running into the trees, presumably to give warning to the village.

Mason followed the beach around until he entered a tributary along the backside of the coastline, basically forming a peninsula. He spotted the village about half a mile down.

Already, people were beginning to mass at the landing.

Nathan lowered the mainsail and the jib.

Mason tossed the stern anchor overboard and did the same with the bow anchor. The two anchors kept the boat stationary in the tributary's current.

The Timucua brave, standing at the port side, spoke to those gathered at the shore, perhaps forty people. They parted to make room as an older native approached and began talking to the Timucua brave.

Mason moved closer to Mato. "Do you understand any of this?"

"Some," Mato said. "He tell chief you will bring rice for them."

A wide smile spread across the chief's face. He waved for everyone to come ashore.

Mason glanced at the sun, just beginning to set over the trees. "Can we stay here tonight?" he asked Mato.

"Yes," Mato said. "You will sit with chief."

Everyone disembarked and waded ashore.

As soon as Mason touched dry ground, the mass of people circled around him while the chief approached.

The old man guided Mason, with the others following, to a large hut in the middle of a clearing.

Mason scanned the village as he walked. The native garb varied, from scant loincloths to buckskin cloaks, to full buckskins. Some wore garments made of cloth. Nearly everyone, except the children, sported feathers, ornaments, shells, and paint. Everyone seemed healthy and well fed, probably from a diet of fish, based on the drying racks built over small, smokey fires. The huts varied, as well. The large hut at the center of the village was basically an A-frame, open at the bottom, with a thatched roof of palmetto. There was one other A-frame hut, a little smaller, next to it, also open at the bottom. The other huts were much smaller—round, about ten feet in diameter—with enough space to house a small family. Some were all thatched with palmetto walls and roofs, others had tree bark walls, and a few even had wattle and daub walls. It was a mishmash of designs, perhaps indicating the tribe itself was a combination of ethnicities.

The old man guided Mason to the larger A-frame and motioned for him to take a seat on the woven, palmetto mat next to a small fire.

Nathan, Mato, and his braves took a seat near Mason, while the old chief sat across from them.

Several young braves sat on the mat behind the chief.

The Timucua brave that had accompanied Mason on the sloop started talking, while the chief and the others listened.

The chief would interject a word or two here and there and listen as the brave continued.

When the brave stopped talking, everyone, including Nathan and Mato, faced Mason. Apparently, he was expected to say something.

"I come in peace," was his first thought.

The Timucua brave looked at Mato.

Mato said a few words and gestured with his hands. He turned to Mason to continue.

"I come back in ten days with rice for your people, and for the Spanish." Mason held up both hands with all ten fingers spread apart. "Spanish meet me here with large ship."

Mato translated as best he could.

The old man listened.

The Timucua brave looked at Mason. "Stay here night," he said in very broken English.

Apparently, the Timucua brave had already explained that the barrels lashed to the sloop were empty and that Mason would return with them full.

"Thank you," Mason said.

With that, the old man gestured and grunted to several of the women standing at the edge of the hut.

The women began scurrying about. Soon, one of them placed a dried fish on a palmetto leaf on the mat in front of Mason. Another sat a wooden mug on the mat, next to the fish.

The old man motioned with his fingers toward his mouth, the universal sign to eat.

Mason hesitated until he saw that fish was being served to the others in his party and began to eat. The fish tasted extremely bland, but nonetheless, Mason smiled and lifted his chin in approval. He only pretended to sip from the wooden mug. Based on the smell, it was likely a harrowing concoction of rum and the juice from local berries, a testament of their interaction with the Spanish, English, French, or all three.

The party continued well into the night, with Mason and Nathan trying their best to understand all the gibberish. They smiled a lot. Nathan even sipped from his mug. As the night wore on, with Nathan suffering no apparent ill effects except for inebriation, Mason finally took a sip, followed by another.

CHAPTER 21

Mason woke in the dim light of early morning. He opened his eyes and immediately felt a stabbing pain in his head. *Never again,* he said to himself, as he rubbed his temples. He scanned the inside of a thatched hut he only vaguely remembered entering. The sound of light snoring got his attention. He turned his head toward Nathan, still asleep on a mat at the other side of the hut. It was just the two of them, leaving Mason to wonder about Mato. He sat up, remained in a sitting position until the dizziness stopped, and got to his feet. With the toe of his right boot, he nudged Nathan in the arm. "Up."

Nathan turned on his side. "Leave me alone," he mumbled, still mostly asleep.

Mason nudged him again, but a little harder. "Up, or I'll leave you here."

Nathan grunted and rubbed the side of his face with one hand but kept his eyes closed. "Ten minutes," he grumbled.

"Ten seconds," Mason said with more authority.

Nathan took in a deep breath and let it out slowly as he rolled to his back. His eyes blinked open. "Ten lousy minutes won't make that much difference."

"I want to be out of here, like, now," Mason said. "Get up."

Nathan lifted his torso to a sitting position, rolled to his knees, his feet, and immediately grabbed hold of Mason for support. "What was that we drank last night?"

"Rum, mostly."

"Must have been extra strong rum," Nathan said. "It hit me like a freight train."

"Hasn't been invented yet," Mason said. He took hold of Nathan's arm and guided him out through the hut's single small opening.

They emerged into a still quiet camp. A fire smoldered in front of the A-frame hut where three women moved around inside. No one else was in sight.

Mason jerked his head toward the water and was reassured to see the sloop still anchored where they had left it the day before. "Let's find Mato," he said, as he started walking.

They went from hut to hut but saw only sleeping natives. No Mato.

"Let's check the boat," Nathan said.

At the water's edge, Mason saw Mato's head pop up from behind the barrels.

Mato got to his feet and motioned for Mason and Nathan to get aboard. "We leave now."

Mason started wading, with Nathan behind him. "Shouldn't we tell someone we're leaving?"

"You say last night," Mato said, "we leave early."

Mason and Nathan climbed aboard, with Mato's help.

Mato's braves were just getting to their feet, mumbling to each other.

Mason rubbed his temples and stepped off toward the helm.

Once in open water, they set the sails and were off, with the sun glaring at them from just above the horizon.

"What happened to the wind?" Nathan asked as he joined Mason at the helm.

"Less than yesterday but at least we're moving." He handed the tiller to Nathan. "Keep us in sight of the coast."

"I know," Nathan said. "You don't have to tell me every little thing."

Mason stared at him a moment before turning away. He joined Mato at the bow. "You didn't drink any of the rum last night."

"No," Mato said.

Mason glanced back at the barrels still lashed in place. "I'll need to take these barrels to the plantation.

Do you mind tagging along? Like I said, I could use your help with the first couple of trips."

"I go with you. You take rice to my people."

"Of course. I'll make sure your people have plenty of rice."

Mato turned to face the coast, as though something was bothering him. His brother, Mason presumed.

Mason decided not to press it, turned, and walked away, leaving him to his thoughts. Mason returned to the helm.

"How long to get back?" Nathan asked.

"With this wind, maybe late afternoon."

"We arrive during daylight," Nathan said. "That's good."

"Yep, that's good."

❖❖❖

Karen and Lisa sat alone in the under-construction kitchen addition. They were finishing a breakfast of oatmeal porridge with molasses. The crowd favorite was actually cornmeal mush, but that took much longer to prepare, so it was served less often, usually on Sundays. The workers, including Charlie and Jeremy, had already eaten and were off tending to the day's jobs. Like everyone else, Karen and Lisa ate from wood trenchers with wood spoons.

Marie and three other women scurried about the kitchen preparing for the next meal. They had adjusted well to cooking for fifty people at a time, and took the daily tasks in stride. Initially, Karen tried to help, but it quickly became clear she was more of a hindrance. So, Marie was in total charge of the kitchen.

Karen and Lisa watched Jeremy and Charlie through a section of unfinished wall, as they worked. Charlie had turned out to be a jack-of-all-trades and had made himself indispensable. He was showing Jeremy how to cleave out shingles, what Charlie called shakes, from a section of sawn log about eighteen inches long. The shakes would ultimately form the top layer of the roof.

Karen sat mesmerized as she watched Charlie use an axe and wood wedges to split the pine logs vertically. Each section of log produced about thirty shakes. Initially, each was in the shape of a thin triangle, from the bark to the log's center. Apparently, the bark would be removed and the shingle further shaped, later in the process. It would take a massive number of shakes to cover the roof, but they had been at it for two days and had already accumulated a lot, all organized in neat little stacks. Apparently, getting the roof done was more important than finishing the walls. Hence, the large section of unfinished wall.

Karen found everything about this era fascinating. She marveled at how people were able to carve a living from the wilderness. And not just survive, but thrive, as they pushed through hardship after hardship. Did she wish she were back in her own time, still working as a flight attendant? Of course. But that was not possible. The five of them, unintended time travelers, were stuck in the past, and she would have to make the most of it. Having Mason made it much easier. She rubbed her belly with the palm of her hand and thought about the life growing inside. According to Mason, based on the painting he had seen, it was a boy. Boy or girl, it didn't matter to her.

She glanced to her left and caught sight of a young black boy peeping at her from around the doorway into the main kitchen. He was around ten years of age and very slender. His eyes were wide with curiosity at the white people who didn't act like your regular slave owners. Karen wondered if he truly understood his situation.

At that moment, Marie took hold of the boy's arm and pulled him away from the opening. "Beggin' your pardon, ma'am. He's being a nuisance."

"No, it's alright," Karen said. "What's his name?"

Lisa looked at the boy and smiled.

He peered from behind Marie's petticoat, probably wondering if he was in trouble.

"Jimmy, ma'am. He won't be no bother. I can send him back out to the field."

Karen shook her head. "How old is he?"

"He's ten, Miss Karen. Been feeling poorly. Thought I'd keep him in for the day."

"That's quite alright, Marie. Please let him stay."

"Thank you, ma'am. He won't be no bother."

Karen smiled at the boy and turned to Lisa. "I wish we could do more."

Lisa picked up a piece of paper from the table and studied the writing on it for several moments. "What's this?"

Karen took the sheet. It was much thicker and rougher than modern paper. "Charlie and Jeremy have been keeping track of the rice." She pointed to the writing. "He's got the number of bags and approximate weight since they started harvesting."

Karen glanced and saw the boy, Jimmy, peering at her again from the open doorway. She motioned for Jimmy to come over, but he didn't budge. She motioned again. "It's alright."

Jimmy took a cautious step.

"You stop being a bother, now," Marie said from deeper in the kitchen.

"It's alright, Marie."

She appeared at the doorway next to Jimmy. She looked at Karen and then down at the boy. "Do what you're told, now, but don't you be a bother to the misses."

Jimmy took another step.

Karen smiled.

Lisa smiled at him, as well.

After several hesitant steps, Jimmy finally made his way over and stood at the end of the table.

Karen held up the piece of paper. "Have you ever seen paper before?"

Jimmy shook his head but said nothing.

"Well," Karen said, "this is paper. People write things on it so they can remember." She held the paper closer. "See the black marks, those are numbers and letters. The letters form words, just like the words I'm saying now." She stared at Jimmy, not sure if he understood.

"We should try and teach him how to read," Lisa said.

Karen cocked her head and turned to Lisa. "I think that's an excellent idea." She thought for a moment. "Marie?"

Marie appeared in the opening. "Yes, ma'am."

"Do any of the workers know how to read and write?"

"Oh, no, ma'am."

"Would any of them like to learn?"

Marie stared at Karen for several long moments, like she was an alien from Mars.

"Read and write," Karen said. She looked down at Jimmy. "We could do it here."

"There's much too much work to be done, ma'am," Marie said. "Jimmy should be helpin' in the fields. I just kept him here today cause he was feelin' poorly."

"No, it's alright, Marie. If Jimmy would like to learn, Lisa and I would like to teach him."

Marie thought a few seconds. "Well, if'n you don't mind, when he's not workin, that would be fine."

"We can start right now," Karen said. She turned to Lisa. "There's a slate tablet in my bedroom. I think Misses Stewart used it for keeping track of things. Can you get it for me? There's a slate pencil with it. In the top dresser drawer."

Lisa got up and left.

Karen turned back to Jimmy.

"Would you like to learn how to read and write?"

Jimmy stared at her.

"We can start by writing your name." She motioned for Jimmy to take a seat on the bench next to her. She looked up at Marie, still standing in the doorway. "It's alright, Marie. We'll be right here."

"If you say so, ma'am," Marie said. She hesitated a few moments before returning to the kitchen.

Lisa plopped on the bench with the slate and pencil in her hand.

Karen took the items and laid the tablet on the table between her and the boy. She used the pencil to scratch Jimmy's name. "This is your name. Jimmy."

◆◆◆

The next afternoon, under cloudy skies, Mason spotted the plantation house as the sloop rounded the final bend in the Ashley River. The thump against the dock was considerably harder than Mason would have liked, but they were home.

While Mato and the braves jumped to the dock and began tying off the sloop, Mason popped into the V-berth and retrieved his rucksack. He followed Nathan onto the dock.

Charlie, walking from a nearby field, was the first to greet them. "Empty barrels?"

"Yep," Mason said. "We have eight days to get them filled and delivered, a full one-day trip. That's seven days to get them filled and loaded."

"It'll be tight," Charlie said.

"What will be tight?" Karen asked as she walked up. She went to give Mason a hug but stepped back. She wrinkled her nose. "You need a bath." She looked at Nathan. "You both do. You smell like rum."

"You missed the party," Mason said.

She cocked her head.

"I'll tell you all about it later." Mason turned to Charlie. "Can you see to these?"

"I'll take care of it," Charlie said.

Mason motioned to Mato and his braves. "They'll be staying with us for a while."

Karen smiled. "They can stay in the house."

Mato scanned the area. "We stay outside."

"Nothing of the sort," Karen said. "It's cold at night."

"They can stay in the barn," Charlie said. "They'll be fine. I keep it toasty warm."

"I'm too tired to argue about it," Mason said, as he started walking toward the house.

Karen fell in next to him.

"Everything okay around here?" Mason asked.

"We've been fine. Sylvester has the rice crop under control; Charlie and Jeremy have been working on the kitchen. And Lisa and I have been busy with school."

"School?"

"The addition is a dining area while we're eating; it's a school the rest of the time. Lisa and I will teach all those who want to learn."

"I read they were educating the blacks in the north during this time, but not down here."

"The Jackson plantation will be an exception."

Mason raised an eyebrow.

"We'll take it slow, only when they are not working. We have to do what we can, plus it will give me something to do." She rubbed her belly. "We already have a student. Marie's son, Jimmy. He tends to get his Es and Is mixed up. He keeps spelling his name with an E."

"Let me know if you need anything."

"I could use more slates."

Mason stopped walking and turned to Karen. "Next time I'm in town, I'll see what they have." He started walking. "Right now, I need a bath."

"Oh, one other thing," Karen said. "Lisa and I have talked about it. We don't want any child younger than thirteen working in the fields."

Mason stopped and stared at her for several seconds. "I'll see what I can do," he said, as he turned and continued walking.

CHAPTER 22

During the next three days, everyone pitched in to fill the barrels with rice. On the morning of the fourth day, Arthur Sullivan, the broker from Charles Town, showed up on a barge with four men, ready for the next load. He was a portly, middle-aged man, well-dressed in a long blue overcoat.

Mason, Charlie, and Nathan met him at the dock.

"This is one of the owners, Mr. Mason," Charlie said. "And this is Nathan."

The three men shook hands.

Nathan nodded to the four men standing on the barge.

"What do we owe the pleasure?" Charlie asked. "Your assistant was more than capable on the last load."

"I wanted to take a look, myself," Sullivan said, as he surveyed the fields. "Looks like a nice operation."

"Unfortunately," Mason said, "our yield is considerably less this year because of the drought."

"Of course," Sullivan said, as he clasped his hands behind his back and began walking toward the nearest field.

Mason and Charlie walked with him.

"I was hoping you could show me around. I need an idea of how much to expect." He glanced at Mason. "I have several buyers ready to take all you have." He stopped at the edge of the nearest field. He bent down and fingered the stubble of a harvested patch. "Seems rather hardy." He looked up at Mason.

"This was our wettest field."

"I see," Sullivan said, as he stood up and stepped farther along the edge of the field.

Mason leaned in to Charlie. "Go tell Jeremy to move those filled barrels into the side room and get the bags ready to load," he whispered. "Make sure there are no barrels outside, empty or otherwise." He looked at Nathan. "Go with him," he whispered.

"Mr. Sullivan," Charlie said, "you'll have to excuse us. Nathan and I have work to tend to."

Sullivan stared at him a few seconds before turning to Mason. "I'm sure Mr. Mason can show me around."

"Glad to," Mason said.

Charlie and Nathan left the two men.

"How many pounds do you estimate?" Sullivan asked, as he scanned the fields.

"Unfortunately, probably just two, maybe three hundred thousand."

Sullivan turned and pondered Mason's face. "You have a very odd accent." He paused a moment before continuing. "I understand you purchased this property from the elder Misses Stewart."

"That's right. I'm sure part of the low yield is due to our lack of experience."

Sullivan cocked his head slightly. "No doubt. But Charlie's a good man. If anyone can coax rice out of this ground, he can."

"We're glad he agreed to join us," Mason said.

"Mind if I take a look at the work yard?"

"Not at all. But I wonder if you and your men would like something to drink up at the house first?"

Sullivan looked back at the barge with the four men standing on the broad deck. He looked back at Mason. "Sure, Mr. Mason. That would be nice."

"It's just Mason. That's what most people call me."

"Alright, Mason." He motioned for the four men to follow. The six of them walked toward the house.

❖❖❖

At the barn, Charlie, Nathan, and Jeremy had every available able-bodied man working hard to move the filled and remaining empty barrels into the side room and the filled bags closer to the front entrance.

Charlie looked in the distance at Mason leading Sullivan and his men to the house. He turned back to Jeremy. "He's giving us some more time." He hurried to the barrels lined up against the back wall, turned one on its side, and began rolling it toward the side room.

Sylvester stopped what he was doing and looked on. "Mister Charlie, we'll take care of that."

"Appreciate that, Sylvester," Charlie said, "but right now, we need every hand moving these barrels." He looked up at Jeremy, standing by the front entrance.

Jeremy hurried to the back wall, turned a barrel over, and began rolling.

◆◆◆

The six men sat on the back porch, facing the river, while Marie served food and drink. The food consisted of a thick, sweet custard poured over a large spoonful of rice, a favorite dessert of the lowlands. They washed it down with beer.

While they ate, Mason tried his best to steer the conversation away from rice. He was mostly successful. As it turned out, Sullivan loved talking about himself. He went into minute detail about his home, his wife, and his six children.

The four men with him remained quiet, preferring to concentrate on their beer, several mugs each.

Nearly an hour had passed when Sullivan finally put his hand over the top of his mug as Marie was about to pour him another.

"We should see to the business at hand," he said, as he stood.

The four men downed their mugs and stood with him.

Mason was amazed that none of the men wobbled from the vast quantities of beer they had consumed.

Sullivan stepped from the porch, with Mason at his side, and began walking toward the barn and work yard.

As they approached, Mason saw a line of workers carrying bags of rice toward the dock.

Charlie and Jeremy stood in the barn's wide opening, behind a wood podium that could be moved into position when needed. As Mason got closer, he could see Jeremy making marks on Charlie's ledger with a quill. Seeing Jeremy use the eighteenth-century writing instrument like he had been born to it just seemed odd.

"They will stack them at the dock until you're ready to load," Charlie said. "Nathan's already down there."

Sullivan turned to his four men and raised his chin.

The four men started off toward the dock.

"We'll compare our counts when all is loaded," Sullivan said, as he peeked inside the barn. His eyes darted from side to side. "You're still harvesting?"

"Got off to a late start," Mason said.

"Misses Stewart usually held the north field 'til last."

"The north field?" Mason asked.

"I brokered for the Stewarts for several years, from when they first started."

"Well, like I said, the yield has been less than we'd hoped," Mason said.

Mason, Charlie, and Sullivan stood chatting while the workers carried bags of rice from the barn. Jeremy kept track with tick marks on the ledger.

Two hours later, the operation moved down to the dock, where the workers loaded the barge and Sullivan's men tracked the number of bags.

One of Sullivan's men supervised the loading.

Nathan remained at the man's side during the process.

At the end, the count was off by only one bag, which was deemed within the acceptable allowance. Sullivan boarded the barge, Nathan disembarked, and Sullivan's men pushed off. The current carried the boat downriver. The four men were armed with long poles to keep the boat in deeper water. They would raise the sail when they neared the open harbor of Charles Town.

"What do you think?" Jeremy asked when the barge was out of hearing range.

"When we're ready to head out in a few days," Mason said, "we'll leave when it's dark." Mason turned and began walking toward the barn. "Any idea of the weight of a full barrel?"

Nathan and Jeremy hurried to keep up.

"Right at one hundred and sixty-two pounds of rice in each barrel," Jeremy said. "Charlie thinks the sloop will accommodate a hundred barrels, maybe a few more."

"So, we're looking at twelve trips?"

"Twelve should do it."

◆◆◆

With twenty-four hours to go before the eighth day, Mason, Nathan, and Mato boarded the fully-loaded sloop in the early morning hours, well before the sun rose. Mato's two braves, not keen on another ocean voyage, would wait at the plantation.

They cast off the lines and used the long poles to keep the sloop away from the shallows as the current carried them toward the Charles Town harbor, and the open ocean. Based on the current winds, one day and night of sailing should put them at the St. Mary's a little after sunup the next day. That was a day earlier than scheduled, but he'd rather be early than late.

Mason pulled his three-cornered hat down lower on his head and fastened the top button of his overcoat against the cool breeze. He wished he had included some padding in the coat when he'd ordered it back in the future. But that would have left Nathan and Jeremy, not to mention Karen and Lisa, lacking. People of this era were hardy and able to weather the elements. He eyed Mato, in his relatively thin buckskins. Mason might as well get used to it. But, just the same, he turned up the collar on his coat.

He thought of Sullivan and the expression on his face at the extremely low rice yield. Black marketing was a common practice at this time in history. Mason wasn't the only planter transporting goods to Florida. Sullivan likely suspected as much. But would he report it to the governor? Or worse, would he be waiting at some point along the route to hijack the load? That was a common practice, as well. Or, perhaps he would require some kind of payoff, maybe with a better margin on the rice being sent to Charles Town.

Mason felt the Glock's slight bulge under his coat. Having the pistol caused as much worry as it did comfort. He eyed Mato again. Could he be made to understand, if Mason were forced to use the pistol in his presence? Probably not. Natives were superstitious. The Glock's firepower would be seen as some kind of witchcraft, even by a close friend. Still, if it meant protecting himself or one of the others, Mason wouldn't hesitate, no matter who was around.

Nearly two-and-a-half hours later, the sloop finally emerged into the open water of the Ashley's mouth, on the west side of Charles Town. The sky was a shade lighter on the eastern horizon, indicating the sun would be peeking over the top soon. Charles Town was still dark, except for an occasional campfire outside the western embankment that served as part of the town's fortification. Mason knew from history that the entire wall would soon be coming down to make room for expansion. They had already started in spots. Trade was booming, and they needed more room for the growing population.

In the subdued light, he scanned the open water in front of him for any movement. There were several anchored ships and boats, but none with hoisted sails. All was quiet.

Mason took the tiller as Nathan and Mato raised the mainsail and both jibs. Within seconds, the sloop was under power from the onshore breezes and Mason steered into the channel well clear of any sandbars. He had made the trip through the harbor enough times to know where they were. Soon, they were in the open ocean. He steered straight out, east-south-east, until he reached the two-mile point. He pointed the bow south-west, against broad-reach winds. Nathan trimmed the sails and Mason settled in for the first watch. He and Nathan planned to switch every four hours. The first three hours on the Ashley and through the harbor didn't count.

He looked to the south-east, at the sun rising from beyond the horizon. He hoped the clear skies would hold; he had no idea how the boat would handle in heavy seas. But over the course of twelve trips, he was likely to find out. That was another advantage of staying within two miles of the coast. He could easily swim that far.

Mason was three hours into his first watch when he caught sight of Nathan staring intently from the port bow. Mason followed his gaze until his eyes locked on a dot on the horizon. Sails. Sails on the horizon was nothing new, there were plenty of merchant and war ships out and about. Mason continued to watch.

"You see that?" Nathan said, as he approached Mason at the tiller. "It's been in that exact position for at least the last hour, maybe longer. Could have been there since we left Charles Town."

Mason adjusted his grip on the tiller. "You think it set sail after we passed through? It would have to be a fast ship."

"I don't know."

"It's probably just a merchant ship."

Nathan stared at the spot for a few seconds. "It's getting bigger."

Mason looked in the distance. He was right, the ship was getting bigger, meaning it was headed at least in the general direction of the sloop. Still, there was nothing particularly odd about that. "Relax, Nathan. I'm sure it's nothing." He thought about the situation a few seconds. "Just the same, go below and check the muskets. Take Mato with you."

Nathan spun around and headed for the V-berth hatch.

He emerged a couple of minutes later and gave a thumbs up.

Mato followed him out and immediately began peering at the dot on the horizon, now recognizable as a single-masted sloop, outfitted with a gaff-rigged mainsail, square topsail, and three jibs. He turned to Mason. "Ship come this way."

"I know," Mason said. "It's on an intercept course."

Nathan, who had been staring at the oncoming boat, turned to Mason. "I believe she has guns."

CHAPTER 23

Mason jerked his head in the direction of the ship. It was hard to tell, but it appeared Nathan might be right. "Can you see how many?"

Nathan, now in the bow, squinted. "Don't see any ports, but there's definitely a chaser."

Mato went to the V-berth, disappeared below deck, and emerged holding his and Nathan's muskets, shot, and powder. He walked to the helm and handed Nathan the musket.

Nathan looked at the gun like he had never seen it before.

Mason continued to gaze at the oncoming ship. "Seems like déjà vu, doesn't it?"

"That's exactly what I was thinking," Nathan said.

"Let's make sure we have a different outcome this time."

"Cannons against pee-shooters," Nathan said, "seems the same to me."

Mason squinted. "How many people?"

Nathan shook his head as he squinted. "I count eight, maybe ten."

"Let's spread out along the deck," Mason said. "No one shoot until I give the word. We still don't know who they are, or what they want."

Mato took up a position amidships; Nathan took cover behind the gunwale in the bow.

Mason turned the boat toward the oncoming ship.

"What are you doing?" Nathan yelled from the bow.

"I'm taking a different tack," Mason yelled back.

When the two ships were a hundred yards apart, Mason ran to the mast and began lowering the mainsail. "Take down the jib," he yelled to Nathan.

Nathan, hesitant to leave his cover, finally did as told.

The crew of the other sloop, ten men that Mason could see, began lowering sails.

When they were fifty yards apart, Mason turned the sloop and ducked below the gunwale.

The other sloop did the same until both ships sat stationary, broadside to broadside.

Mason popped his head up. "What do you want?" he yelled.

All ten men on the other sloop remained standing. They all faced Mason's sloop. One of the men standing at the helm took a couple of steps closer to his gunwale. "We just want your cargo," the man yelled. "Then you can be on your way."

Mason watched as the other nine men suddenly raised a weapon, either a rifle or a pistol. Mason didn't know the range of either one, but was fairly sure it was at least the fifty yards between the two boats.

"We just want the rice," the man yelled again.

Mason thought for a moment as he dropped down behind the hull. "How do you know it's rice?"

The other man went quiet for several seconds. "Just give us the cargo," he finally yelled.

Mato was set to raise his musket and start firing. Nathan, on the other hand, was curled up on the deck. His arms and legs were wrapped around the musket. Mason wasn't sure the man would even fire a shot, if it came to that.

Mason poked up again. "Who sent you to take our cargo?" he yelled.

The man on the other sloop answered with a barrage of musket fire. At least seven of his men had fired.

Mason heard two musket balls whiz over his head. He saw splinters fly from the mast from the impact of another. And he was sure a couple had slammed into the barrels.

Mato suddenly rose up, took aim, and fired.

Mason peered over the railing and saw one of the men on the other boat drop. He heard two more shots. Out of the corner of his eye, he saw Mato drop. He saw blood, but wasn't sure how badly he had been hit. He did know that Mato wasn't moving.

Mason jerked his gaze toward Nathan. "Shoot, you son-of-a-bitch," he yelled.

As Nathan started to stir, Mason looked back at the other boat.

Seven of the men were almost reloaded; two were just starting. The man at the helm, apparently the captain, watched. There was no indication he intended to use his cannons, the bow chaser or a similar weapon in the stern. He was obviously confident his men would prevail with their muskets, and hand-to-hand if necessary.

By this time, the onshore wind had pushed the other sloop to within forty yards.

Mason pulled the Glock from his shoulder holster. He pivoted to a kneeling position as he assumed the standard two-handed grip, lifted the pistol over the top of the gunwale, and took aim. His actions were automatic, smooth, efficient, and without hesitation. His first target was the man standing at the helm. Mason squeezed the trigger until the gun jerked with an explosive recoil. The target fell to the deck, out of sight. Mason shifted the sights to the next man. He was in the process of raising his musket. Mason squeezed. The man dropped. Mason proceeded to acquire targets down the line and squeezed the trigger in rapid succession.

Four men had dropped before the others realized what was happening. The others were mesmerized by the successive muzzle blasts from the tiny gun, but finally took cover behind the gunwale.

Mason took aim at the spots in the hull behind which he estimated a man was hiding. He emptied the magazine, ejected, and slammed in a second. He continued firing. He saw the wood splinter as the rounds peppered their way along the hull. The wood was no match for the 9mm rounds. The projectiles of brass and lead punched straight through. Those that weren't stopped by flesh or some solid object, carried on and splintered other parts of the boat. When the second magazine was empty, he ejected, reloaded, and released the slide onto another full mag.

He slowly rose as he scanned the other boat for movement. Seeing none, he glanced at Nathan, just starting to rise. "Check on Mato," he said, as he stood at the ready position facing the other sloop.

Nathan crawled along the deck to where Mato lay.

Mason glanced as Nathan checked for wounds.

"Looks like he was hit in the head, but it was a glancing blow. His skin at the forehead is separated down to the bone, about an inch long. I think he's just knocked out."

"There's a med kit in my ruck in the V-berth, part of what I brought back with me. Grab it." Still seeing no movement on the other sloop, Mason holstered his pistol as he stepped the few paces to Mato's unconscious body lying sprawled on the deck. He checked for breathing and a pulse. Both were adequate.

The two sloops had continued to close until they were now thirty yards apart. If he did nothing, the two boats would be side-by-side in a few minutes.

Nathan returned from the V-berth with the med kit. He put the black, zippered nylon pouch on the deck beside Mato. "Is he okay?"

"I think so," Mason said. "Keep an eye on that boat. Let me know if you see any movement."

Nathan put both hands on the gunwale and leaned out as he kept both eyes on the boat.

"You may want your rifle."

Nathan retrieved the gun from the bow and resumed his position next to where Mason worked.

Mason pulled a small bottle of antiseptic and a cotton swab from the pouch. He wet the swab and dabbed at the wound. The bleeding was minimal, but the skin was gaped open at the upper right quadrant of his forehead. Another inch to the left and Mato would not have survived. Mason extracted a small suture kit from a pack of twenty-five. It was one of the practice kits available on Amazon. He had only practiced suturing a couple of times, but however it turned out, it would be better than not closing the wound.

He poured antiseptic on his fingers and tore open the paper packet containing the thread and needle. He threaded the small, curved needle, and, with a glance at Nathan, proceeded. He closed the wound with six stitches. It wasn't pretty, but it would work. He dabbed the closed wound with more antiseptic, blotted it dry with cotton, and applied a copious amount of Neosporin from a tube. He wrapped Mato's head with gauze and tied it off.

Just when Mason was beginning to worry about Mato's continued unconsciousness, he groaned. With his eyes still closed, he licked his lips.

"That was a close one, my friend," Mason said.

Mato opened his eyes and spent several seconds trying to focus by continually blinking. He finally focused on Mason's face, hovering above him. He reached up and felt the gauze wrapped around his head.

"You'll be alright. The ball just grazed your head. You've been out for about twenty minutes."

Mato began to sit up. He winced as he raised his head.

"You'll have a headache for awhile."

Mato continued to a sitting position, fingered the gauze at the site of the wound, and turned his face to Mason. He grunted, which for Mato meant thank you.

"Don't mention it," Mason said. He handed Mato a gourd of water, boiled and strained by Karen and Lisa to kill any bacteria.

Mato turned the gourd up to his mouth and took a long gulp. He wiped his mouth with his sleeve and handed the gourd back. He grabbed the gunwale to pull himself up.

Mason helped.

Mato wobbled a bit, but got his balance. He looked at the other sloop, now only a few feet away. The deck was littered with bodies. Two of the men moaned, the captain at the helm, and one other man near the stern. Mato looked at Mason. "You do this?" He examined the full length of the other sloop. "Just like at your camp when you kill the Lenni-Lenape."

Mason nodded. He looked at Nathan. "There's a rope and grappling hook in the V-berth. Let's latch on to that boat."

Nathan went to the berth and returned with the hook and rope. He tossed the hook the few feet to the other boat and began pulling on the rope. When the two boats were side-by-side, Nathan lashed them together at the bow and stern.

The three of them stepped across.

Mason scanned the dead and dying men as he made his way to the captain.

The man, still alive, peered up at Mason with a look of disbelief. He licked his lips.

Mason turned to Nathan. "Grab that water."

Nathan jumped back to the sloop, retrieved the water, and returned. He handed the gourd to Mason.

Mason knelt down, lifted the man's head slightly, and let him take a few sips. "Who sent you for our cargo?"

The man looked into Mason's eyes for several moments. His eyes shifted to Nathan, lingered, and back to Mason. "What makes you think anyone sent me?"

"How else would you know about the rice?"

"Rice is the main cargo out of Charles Town," the man mumbled. His eyes turned to the gourd in Mason's hand.

Mason lifted the man's head and let him take another couple of sips. He lowered his head to the deck and searched for the wound. He found a clean shot to the man's upper chest, just below his right shoulder. Mason stood. He looked at Nathan. "Grab that med kit."

He turned to leave but stopped in his tracks, staring aft.

Mason realized Mato was no longer at his side. He saw him walking back from the direction of the stern. He held his knife. Mason focused on the blood dripping from the blade and then looked past Mato toward the stern. The man who had been wounded but still alive was no longer moaning. All the rest lay motionless, as well.

Mato continued forward until he stood by Mason. "He talk?"

"No," Mason said.

Without hesitation, Mato bent over and plunged his knife into the man's chest. Before Mason could react, Mato repeated the stroke twice more and stood up. "They all dead now."

Nathan staggered back.

Mason stared at Mato. "We don't even know who they were, or who sent them. That man could have told us," he exclaimed.

Mato bent over and wiped the blade on the man's coat. "Better not let them live to try again." He looked around the boat. "You need bigger boat. You have two boat now."

Mason stared at Mato for an eternity but finally tore his gaze away to scan the sloop from their new perspective. The sloop was bigger, longer by about ten feet. She was older and in worse shape, but it floated and was obviously fast. Like Mason's sloop, there was only the single deck. Rather than a V-berth in the bow, this one had a small sterncastle. It was only four feet above the main deck, too small to be a cabin. Mason figured it was mainly for storage, like the V-berth. His gaze landed on an item usually not found on such a small vessel—a binnacle. Basically, it was a wood pillar, square, about waist high, mounted on the deck in front of the tiller. Mason stepped closer and examined the brass and glass enclosed, gimbal-mounted compass. The brass was dark and pitted, but the compass needle pointed to the north, and the gimbal swung freely. The binnacle was obviously not original to the sloop; it had been obtained and mounted, after the fact. Mason turned his gaze to the ten dead men sprawled about. Mason wasn't sure why he was incensed at Mato's actions. After all, Mason was responsible for most of their deaths.

Nathan scrambled back to the smaller sloop, hurried to the far gunwale, and vomited.

Mato grabbed the captain by the armpits, lifted, and dragged him to the side.

When the man's lifeless hand flopped to the deck, something white became visible.

"Hold up," Mason said.

Mato stopped pulling.

Mason bent down and uncurled the man's fingers, revealing a crumpled piece of paper. Mason flattened the paper, a corner of a larger sheet. There was a bit of writing in black ink. Mason stood as he read the scribbles—*27th or 28th – probably morning*. He looked at the man's face again before motioning for Mato to continue.

Mato manhandled the body over the gunwale and into the water.

Mason walked the deck and examined the faces of the other dead men. He recognized one of them. He was one of the four men that had accompanied Sullivan to the plantation. Mason peered at the paper again and back to the man's face. He folded the paper, put it in his coat pocket, and scanned the shore in the distance, still about two miles away. Without a spy glass, no one on shore would be able to recognize Mason or either of the sloops.

Mato was dragging a second body when Mason decided he was right. They now had possession of two boats. Mason gathered all the weapons and stored them in the sterncastle. He then helped Mato with the bodies.

CHAPTER 24

While Mato finished offloading the bodies, Mason jumped back to the smaller sloop and walked directly to Nathan. Mason grabbed him by the bicep and spun him around. "You need to understand where you are. This time and place. They would have killed us for the cargo. They nearly did."

Nathan looked away.

"Sometimes it's kill, or be killed," Mason said. "This is one of those times."

"Fine," Nathan finally screamed. "I get it."

"Do you? You certainly don't act like it. You didn't fire your rifle one time."

Nathan rolled his eyes.

"We took you in after what you did. We expect you to be a part of this team. That means doing what's necessary. You either shape up, or you'll find yourself on the road."

Nathan lifted his chin.

Mason let go of his arm. "I get it, Nathan. Some of this is hard to take. We just have to do what's necessary to survive."

Nathan gave a subtle nod as he stared at the water.

"Can you sail this boat alone?"

Nathan spun around to Mason. "You're going to take their boat."

"I am. They tried to take the cargo, and would have killed us, but they lost. They forfeited their lives and their boat."

"How are you going to explain the boat back in Charles Town?"

"I'm not."

"What about whoever sent those guys?"

"Probably Sullivan," Mason said. "But it doesn't matter who sent them. We're pressing on with getting our rice to market." He motioned to the larger sloop. "The extra boat will help with that endeavor. Can you sail this boat alone?"

"As long as we don't run into a storm, I can handle her."

"You and Mato will continue on to the St. Mary's. I'll follow in the other boat."

"Can you handle that boat alone?" Nathan asked. "It's larger, with more sails."

"I'll just raise the main and one jib. We'll figure the rest out later. I'll be fine, if, like you say, we don't run into a storm."

"We'll both be up for twenty-four hours," Nathan said.

"I've done it before. You have, too. We'll sleep when we get there."

"Fine, the sooner we get out of here the better," Nathan said.

Mason jumped back to the larger sloop. With the bodies gone, Mason found a bucket in the sterncastle. He filled it several times with sea water and sloshed the blood from the deck. "You go with Nathan on our boat," he said to Mato. "Make sure he doesn't fall asleep."

"What you do?" Mato asked.

"I'll be behind you. Keep an eye out. If I fall too far back, there's a problem. You may need to circle around." He began untying the lashes holding the two boats together.

Mato jumped to the other boat and helped Mason push the two boats apart.

"Take it easy with that head," Mason said. "It might be worse than we think. And don't mess with the bandage."

Midmorning the next day, as they approached the St. Mary's inlet, a large ship anchored off shore became visible. With two or three decks, the ship carried two main masts of square sails with a small lateen sail atop the high-backed sterncastle. Seven gun ports were visible along the hull. Mason had never seen such a ship. Apparently, it was too large to navigate the river.

With ropes securing the tiller in place, Mason went forward and lowered the jib. He stepped back to the mast and used it to keep his balance while the boat continued to its destination. He watched Nathan and Mato lower their sails. When Mason figured he was within coasting distance, he did the same with the main sail, then took control of the tiller. Fifty yards short of the ship, with the sloop barely moving, he tossed the stern anchor overboard. It dragged a bit and caught.

Mason watched as a longboat was launched with five men aboard, four at the oars and one man in front. Mason recognized him as the officer from the fort, the one who'd escorted him out of the fort.

The longboat went to Nathan's sloop first. It lingered a bit before the officer pushed away. The oarsmen began rowing toward Mason's sloop.

"Señor Mason," the officer called out.

"I never got your name before," Mason said, as the longboat bumped against the sloop's hull.

"Teniente Diego Alvarez de Ribera."

"Mind if I just call you Lieutenant Ribera?"

Ribera cocked his head in agreement.

"What's the plan?" Mason asked.

"We ferry your cargo to the Nuestra Señora del Carmen," he said, as he scanned the deck of the sloop. "Although, you don't appear to have any cargo aboard."

"Just the other sloop. We acquired this boat on our way here."

"I see," Ribera said. "We can load both with barrels, if you want."

"I do want," Mason said. "I could also use a crew for both."

"That would be up to the capitán."

"Of course," Mason said. "May I come aboard?"

Ribera stepped back to give Mason room to climb down. He motioned for the oarsmen to head back and for Mason to take a seat in the bow. "I presume you will want to monitor the transfer of goods?"

Mason rubbed his eyes and blinked several times. What he wanted was sleep. But that would have to wait. "Certainly."

At the smaller sloop, Mason climbed aboard. Ribera said a few words to the oarsmen, and they immediately headed off toward the Spanish ship. "We will begin offloading shortly," Ribera said as the longboat moved away.

Nathan and Mato walked up. "Don't know about you, but I can't hold my eyes open," Nathan said.

Mato appeared just as tired.

"Catch a few winks in the V-berth," Mason said, "if you can with all the noise we're about to have. I'll monitor the offloading. We'll be loading both sloops with barrels for the return trip."

"Right," Nathan said, as he massaged the back of his neck. He turned and waddled off.

"What about you?" Mason asked, looking at Mato.

"I sleep too."

"How's your head?"

"Head hurt."

"It will for a few days." He looked into Mato's eyes, to compare their pupil size. "I think you'll be fine."

Mato fingered the wound through the bandages. "What you do?"

Mason made a sewing gesture. "Sewed you back together. We'll change the bandage later."

Mato turned and headed off toward the V-berth.

Mason watched as two longboats headed toward the sloop, each powered by only two oarsmen. Ribera and five other men were in the leading boat. Four of them were black men.

With the longboat secured to the side of the sloop, all the men climbed aboard, except the two oarsmen.

"This is John," Ribera said, as he motioned to one of the black men. He and the others will offload your cargo, and the four of them will crew your boats for the remaining trips. They speak English and will fit in better than my men."

Mason stuck out his hand.

John hesitated, but finally took Mason's hand. "Real fast, mistah, we'll get the work done real fast," he said in respectable English.

"Liberated from Carolina," Ribera said. "The four of them. They've found new work as seamen."

Mason looked at each of the four men. They weren't dressed as former slaves. They wore a coat, shirt, pants, and shoes, just like the Spanish seamen. "You alright with returning? We'll be passing by Charles Town."

"The captain said we would stay with you," John said.

"That's right," Mason said. "I'll make sure no harm comes to you."

"Then we do the work," John said. He motioned for the other three blacks and the Spanish seaman to follow. They immediately began removing the barrel lashings.

"I'd like to hold back five barrels for the Guale," Mason said.

Ribera smiled. "Of course, Señor Mason. We will take care of that."

"Five barrels."

"Yes, of course. We want to be the ones to give the rice to the Guale. They are our allies."

"I understand," Mason said.

"El Capitan would like to meet you."

"Aboard your ship?"

"Si, señor Mason. We will leave room in the lancha on the first load."

Mason massaged his left temple. "Be happy to." He excused himself to let Ribera supervise the unloading and went down into the V-berth.

Mato opened his eyes briefly and rolled over on his makeshift bunk.

Nathan snored softly, obviously able to sleep with the pounding and scraping up on deck.

Mason deliberated taking his Glock, still snug in its shoulder holster under his coat. He considered carrying it in the rucksack, instead. In the end, he decided to leave it and the rucksack behind. He removed his coat, the holster and gun, and placed them in the rucksack. He pushed the ruck as far up into the darkness of the bow as it would go. It wasn't exactly hidden, but it was better than leaving it out in the open. He slipped back into his coat and exited the berth.

He and Ribera chatted idly while the men transferred barrels to the longboat. Three one-hundred-pound barrels, like those commonly used in Charles Town, would have taken some kind of block and tackle. But the smaller barrels could be handled by two men.

With the boat finally loaded, Ribera and Mason joined the two oarsmen and began the trip to the Spanish ship. As soon as they vacated their spot against the sloop's hull, the second longboat moved into position.

At the Spanish ship, Ribera ascended the ship's ladder first. Mason climbed up. When he stepped onto the deck, he was met by an older gentleman wearing an impeccable uniform. Mason admired the deep blue long coat, with red trim and gold buttons. The buttons and trim ran the full length of both sides of the front, highlighting the pure white waistcoat and wide black belt. Matching white pants were tucked into high black boots.

"Capitán Miguel Medina," the man said, as he extended his hand.

"Stephen Mason," he said, as he shook the man's hand. Mason quickly scanned the deck. The captain did have a block and tackle, with a net, ready to lower over the side. Several seamen stood ready, including several black men.

"Señor Mason, would you like to join me for a glass of sherry while my men transfer your cargo?"

The captain's English surprised him. It was flawless. Alcohol was the last thing he wanted, but declining would be an insult. "Thank you, Captain."

"My quarters, then," Medina said, as he motioned for Mason to walk with him.

As they walked, Mason noted the seven cannons on each side of the main deck, the general orderliness, and the discipline of the men. "You command a fine galleon."

Medina smiled. "Patache, Señor Mason. The Nuestra Señora del Carmen is a patache, much smaller than a galleon."

"Sorry," Mason said. "I'm not familiar with Spanish ships."

"Of course, Señor Mason. The English think all our ships are galleons."

At the sterncastle, the captain opened the door and ushered Mason into what would be the captain's quarters. He went directly to what Mason would consider an antique cabinet, opened the double doors, and withdrew a bottle of dark liquid and two glasses. He motioned Mason to a wood-framed chair in front of a small desk. The desk was covered with charts and papers.

Mason stood next to the chair and waited for the captain.

Medina poured both glasses, handed one to Mason, and raised his own in a salute.

Mason raised his glass and took a sip.

Medina walked around the desk and took a seat. He motioned for Mason to sit. "Tell me about your plantation, and Charles Town."

Mason hid a yawn behind his hand. "Purchased from the previous owner who now lives in New York. I'll be making payments for a while."

"I see. And this is why you need our silver?"

"Yes. We both benefit."

"Si, Señor Mason. We both benefit." He stared at Mason for a few moments. "Tell me about your Governor James Moore."

"Never met the man," Mason said.

"The citizens no longer want proprietary rule and wish for the king to intervene."

"You're better informed than I am. You must understand, Captain, I'm relatively new to the area. I've been far away in the east for several years. And since arriving, I've been busy with the plantation. There's been no time to delve into politics."

"But you have spent time in Charles Town, correct?"

"Some."

"What is the state of the fortifications there?"

Mason massaged the back of his neck. "I understand you're a military man and that your country has been at odds with the English. But I really can't help you. My only interest is getting my crops to a market that pays in silver."

Medina studied Mason from head to toe. "You refer to the English as though you are not one of them."

Mason took a moment to think, to clear his groggy head. "Like I said, I'm new to the area."

"I see. You seem tired, Señor Mason."

"I could use some sleep."

Medina stood. "I will have someone return you to your vessel."

Mason stood.

"I have enjoyed our chat. Perhaps we can continue when you are rested. Or maybe the next trip."

"That would be fine," Mason said.

"It will take most of the afternoon to unload your cargo and reload both vessels with barrels," Medina said. "I presume you will depart tomorrow morning."

"Very early, if not tonight," Mason said. "I plan to return in five or six days with both boats loaded."

"We should have a count soon on the barrels offloaded. I believe the agreed upon price was two Spanish dollars per barrel."

"Two point forty-three per barrel," Mason said. "One hundred barrels would be two hundred and forty-three Spanish dollars."

"Of course, Señor Mason." Medina extended his hand. "I will ensure you are paid."

"And the Guale get their five barrels."

"Yes, of course, señor."

The two men parted and Mason was rowed back to the larger sloop. He wanted to get some sleep before they started loading it with barrels.

CHAPTER 25

Mason was curled up asleep in the tiny storage locker when a loud *thump* on the hull brought him fully awake. The thump was followed by voices and foot falls on the deck.

Mason had no idea how long he had been out, but there was still plenty of light streaming through the cracks between the hatch and the jam. He rousted himself and emerged from the locker to find several men on board, carrying barrels in the late afternoon.

A second longboat came alongside with more barrels and a passenger.

Lieutenant Ribera climbed aboard. He held a small pouch in his hand, which he raised to Mason. "One hundred barrels; two hundred and forty-three Spanish dollars."

Mason took the pouch.

"You may count if you wish," Ribera said.

"Not necessary. Are we agreed to meet back here in six days, seven at the most?"

"We are agreed, Señor Mason." He glanced at the men loading the barrels and turned back to Mason.

"You will be loaded before dark. John and his men will be aboard, and you will be ready to leave."

"Thank you," Mason said. "And please thank Captain Medina.

Ribera smiled.

"I wonder if you would mind ferrying me to my other sloop?"

"Of course, señor. Step aboard."

Ribera left Mason on the smaller sloop and set off for another load of barrels.

Mato leaned against the mast and watched the operation.

"Where's Nathan?"

"Sleep," Mato said.

Mason looked up at the sun hanging low in the sky and judged he had been asleep for about three hours. "How is your head?"

"Head still hurt," he said. A spot of blood was visible through the bandage.

"A few days, my friend, you'll be good as new."

Mato's expression didn't reveal much, and it didn't change.

"I'm sorry I won't have time to run you back to your village, but you can sit out the next trip if you want."

"I go with you," Mato said.

Mason put a hand on Mato's shoulder for a moment. He turned and surveyed the barrels lashed to the deck. He checked several of the ropes, tested their tautness, and determined the load was well balanced. He estimated there were about as many barrels as there were before. The larger sloop would be able to handle more. At the current rate, he figured a couple more hours to finish loading. At that point he intended to depart.

Mason leaned against the gunwale and watched the longboat deliver empty barrels to the other boat. Several men onboard, including John and his three compatriots, shuffled the barrels around the deck and lashed them securely. He pondered the attack by the ten men, and the piece of paper. The one man he recognized worked for Sullivan. That was prima facie evidence that Sullivan was behind the attempted hijacking. He thought of the paper. The previous day had been the 28th of October. Lucky guess, Mason supposed. Still operating with not enough sleep, Mason let it go. He would figure it out later. He heard footsteps behind him and turned to see Nathan approaching. "Get some sleep?"

Nathan looked toward the sun. "A few hours, I guess."

"They'll be finished loading in awhile. I plan to head out then."

Nathan looked stunned. "I thought we'd leave in the morning."

Mason motioned toward the Spanish ship. "The captain loaned us a couple of seamen for each sloop. Former slaves from Carolina."

"Seamen?"

"They've apparently served on Spanish ships and know the ropes. He assured me they would be fine."

"And they're okay with returning to Charles Town?"

"Won't be there long, and they'll be staying with us. You and Mato take this boat. Don't be hard on them. Like I said, they know what they are doing. You and Mato can take turns standing watch."

"Fine," Nathan said.

With the final load of barrels aboard the larger sloop and lashed down, the Spanish crew members left two of the black seamen aboard and then rowed toward Mason, Nathan, and Mato, standing on the deck of the smaller sloop.

John and the fourth black seaman boarded. John introduced the fourth man as Skinny.

Mason asked the oarsmen to wait a moment while he introduced everyone and made sure Nathan had no questions or problems. He went to the V-berth, rearmed himself with the Glock, grabbed the rucksack, and returned to the deck. He said a few final words to Nathan and Mato and climbed down to the longboat.

The Spanish oarsmen ferried him to the larger sloop and departed with a final wave.

Mason introduced himself and learned the two men were named Sebastian and Slim. "Is Skinny your brother?"

"No, sir, Mista Mason. He's just Skinny."

Mason considered Slim's own thin physique before continuing. He explained they would be hugging the coast back, and helped with hoisting the anchor and the sails.

The sails took the light wind, the boat heeled a few degrees, and Mason steered the tiller.

They were on their way, with Nathan bringing up the rear.

With the boat two miles offshore and on course, he turned the tiller over to Sebastian. He looked at Slim and suggested he might want to get some sleep, since he would be taking over in a few hours.

Slim looked around the deck.

"There's room in the storage locker. Just move the rope and extra sail cloth around to make room."

"Thank you, Mista Mason," Slim said. He ducked inside the locker.

Mason rubbed his eyes and scanned the deck. With everything in order and the sky clear, he turned back to Sebastian. "I'm going to get some sleep right over here," he said, as he pointed to an open spot between the barrels. "Wake me if you see anything weird."

"Weird, Mista Mason?"

"Sorry, anything that doesn't look or feel right. Like vessels headed our way."

"That's fine, Mista Mason."

"Three or four hours, wake me."

"Yes, sir, Mista Mason."

Mason took a seat on the hard deck, leaned against a couple of barrels, and was soon asleep.

◆◆◆

When Mason opened his eyes, his surroundings were much lighter than he expected for the middle of the night. He took a moment to orient himself. He was still on the deck, the boat was still moving, Slim was at the tiller, but it was morning. He jumped to his feet. He eyed the smaller sloop, keeping pace behind them. He relaxed a bit and went to the helm. "I told Sebastian to wake me."

"He say to let you sleep."

Mason rubbed a crick in his neck as he looked toward the shore in the subdued light of very early morning. "Where are we?"

"Sebastian told me to keep two miles off shore."

"That's good," Mason said, as he began to relax more. "Did you eat something?"

"Yes, sir, Mista Mason."

Mason couldn't remember the last time he ate, but he was starved. Karen had packed bread, cheese, and salt pork for the trip, but that was all on the other sloop.

"There's biscuits, Mista Mason." He pointed to the storage locker.

"Thank you, Slim."

Slim spread his lips, showing all his teeth. They were surprisingly white, considering the conditions of this era.

At about that moment, Sebastian emerged from the storage locker. "Everything alright, Mista Mason?"

"Considering I apparently slept through the night, everything is just fine."

"You looked like you needed the rest," Sebastian said.

Mason studied Sebastian for a moment. As a seaman, one would think he would understand an order. But then, Mason rather liked a person who could do what was needed without being told. "Slim said something about some biscuits?"

"Yes, sir, Mista Mason." He ducked back into the locker and returned with a cloth bag. He handed the bag to Mason.

Mason opened the bag and peered inside. *Ship's biscuits.* Nathan had told him about the ship's biscuits when he was aboard the pirate ship. Hard as a rock and inedible, unless soaked in something. Water would do, if there was nothing else around. He extracted a biscuit and studied its contours. He knocked it against a nearby barrel. When the biscuit didn't crumble, he looked at Sebastian.

"Beer," Slim said.

Sebastian ducked back inside the locker and returned with a gourd and a mug. He filled the mug and handed it to Mason.

Mason considered his stomach's empty feeling and its grumbles against the prospect of a ship's biscuit and beer. In the army he had learned to eat everything available, even bugs and grubs on occasion.

"You breaks it up and lets it soak in the beer," Sebastian said.

Mason placed the cloth bag and the mug on top of the barrel. He pulled his knife from its sheath on his hip and used the butt to pound the biscuit against the barrel. He scooped up the pieces in his hands and dumped them in the mug. He waited a full minute and took a gulp. He chewed on the little pieces of now softer biscuit. The conglomeration tasted terrible, but he swallowed it, just the same.

Mason scanned the coastline while he drank from the mug. He peered at the smaller sloop, keeping pace about two hundred yards behind. He ran through his mind the sequence of filling the barrels, loading, and the return trips. Probably six trips. He just wanted to get it done, get Misses Stewart paid, and concentrate on the plantation and the coming year. Life had become very simple. Perilous, maybe treacherous, but simple. He pulled the collar up around his neck. It didn't do much to block the brisk wind. He looked at Sebastian and Slim and thought of John and Skinny on the boat behind them, all examples of what a little freedom could accomplish. He thought of Karen, the baby, Lisa, and Jeremy. He looked back at the trailing sloop and contemplated Nathan's role in their life on the plantation. If nothing else, it would be interesting.

While Sebastian managed the tiller, Slim began making his way among the barrels, checking the lashings as he went.

Mason placed his empty mug on top of one of the barrels and followed along until they were both at the bow. Mason swiveled the small brass cannon, discolored from the ocean spray. "You ever fire one of these?"

"No, sir, Mista Mason," Slim said. "I just carry the powder and shot."

"So, you know how to fire it?"

"Yes, sir, Mista Mason."

"That's good to know, Slim," Mason said. "What's your real name?"

"Slim," he said, "I've just always been called that."

Mason thought of asking how his life was before he escaped to Spanish territory but decided it didn't really matter. "I appreciate the four of you taking this risk."

Slim smiled and returned to checking the lashings.

Mason joined Sebastian at the tiller. "I think it would be better if the four of you slept and took your meals on the boats."

"I was thinkin' the same thing, Mista Mason. That's alright by us."

Mason took in a deep breath and exhaled.

The remainder of the day passed slowly. It was dusk when the two sloops rounded the final bend in the Ashley River. They secured the smaller sloop to the dock and the larger sloop to the smaller. They also tossed out the bow and stern anchors for both boats, as added security against the river's current.

While Nathan and the others were putting the final touches on securing the two boats, Mason met Charlie, Karen, Lisa, and Jeremy at the foot of the dock.

"You leave with one and come back with two, how did you manage that?" Charlie asked.

"Some people tried to hijack us," Mason said.

Lines of concern etched across Karen and Lisa's faces. Karen wrapped her arms around Mason's torso.

"We're alright. Mato was slightly wounded, but he'll survive."

Everyone looked to the sloops and saw Mato beginning to unleash the barrels.

"What happened to the hijackers?" Jeremy asked.

"Let's just say they didn't fair very well."

"But how did you—"

"Right now, we just need to get the barrels filled and the boats reloaded," Mason said, cutting Charlie off.

"Will someone come asking about the other boat?" Lisa asked.

"I don't know," Mason replied. "I'll deal with that if it happens. For now, we have two boats, which means we can get all this done in five or six trips."

Nathan and John joined the group.

"This is John," Mason said. He pointed to the three black men still on the sloops. "The captain of the Spanish ship loaned them to us to help crew the boats."

"They're slaves," Charlie said. "Runaways."

Mason turned to Charlie. "I can't speak for the past, but right now they are citizens of La Florida and temporarily our guests."

"There'll be hell to pay if anyone from Charles Town sees them," Charlie said.

"I know," Mason said. "We need to make sure that doesn't happen."

Charlie pursed his lips, barely visible behind his scraggly beard. "I don't know."

"What don't you know?" Jeremy asked.

Charlie removed his hat and scratched his head. "I mean, they're slaves. Their owners want them back."

John looked at Mason. A hint of fear entered his eyes.

Mason glanced at Karen, Lisa, Jeremy, and Nathan. He motioned for John to stay where he was, put an arm around Charlie's shoulders, and started walking. Charlie had no choice but to walk with him. They walked toward the house, away from the group at the dock.

"Charlie, you've probably seen that we don't operate this plantation the way most people would."

"I have noticed that," Charlie said.

"It may be apparent by now that we think of the workers here as more than slaves."

"I've been meaning to talk to you about that. You know, Karen and Lisa have been educatin' some of them."

"I know." Mason took a moment to consider his words. "We're not from here, Charlie. Where we come from, people don't have slaves."

"Where's that exactly?"

"It's a long way from here. The point is, we're not really used to having slaves, or people even being slaves. We think of people as, well, just people, no matter what their skin color."

Charlie turned his head. Both eyebrows were raised.

"Charlie, we hope to build something here, something different. Trust me when I say, the world won't always be this way. Things will change, and change drastically."

"How do you know that?"

"Let's just say, I'm pretty good at seeing the future."

"The people here will fight you on the issue of slaves."

"We don't want to fight anyone. And trust me, we plan to take things slowly, minor changes here and there."

"Like the combined eatin' area."

"Exactly," Mason said. "Small things that will make a difference for the better, for all of us." He glanced at the fields in the dimming light. "You've probably noticed an increase in productivity."

Charlie gave a slight nod.

"Small changes can make a big difference."

"What about them slaves you brought? Where you planning to put them up?"

"It's just temporary. There's no sense in mixing them in with the rest of the workers. They'll be staying on the boat."

"I guess that will work," Charlie said.

"It's just five or six trips." Mason stopped walking and turned to face Charlie. "You alright with this?"

"I'll let you know when I ain't," Charlie said.

Mason cocked his head. "Fair enough." He looked back at the group still on the dock. "Starting tomorrow morning, early, we have five days to get those barrels filled and the boats reloaded."

"I'll get to it first thing," Charlie said, as he turned to leave.

"And Charlie—"

Charlie stopped and looked back.

"If you have any problems or questions, you come straight to me. If I'm not here, then Jeremy."

"I'll do that," Charlie said. He turned and resumed walking.

Mason returned to the group at the dock. John stood a few feet from the others. "I spoke to Sebastian about the four of you staying on the boats," he said to John.

"That'll be fine, Mista Mason. Just fine." He turned and headed toward the boats.

Mason looked at Karen. "Can we get some food and something to drink brought down for them tonight, and breakfast tomorrow?"

"Of course," Karen said. She looked at Lisa and the two of them started off toward the kitchen.

Nathan walked off toward the house, without a word, leaving Mason and Jeremy on the dock in the nearly pitch dark.

"What's his problem?"

"The attempted hijacking on the way there was pretty brutal."

As they began walking slowly toward the house, Mason described the attack, the firepower of the Glock,

Mato getting wounded, the stitches, the two men he'd stabbed, and dumping the bodies into the sea.

"I recognized one of them."

Jeremy stopped walking.

Mason stopped and faced him. "One of the four men with Sullivan."

Jeremy thought for a moment as he studied Mason's face in the dark. "What does that mean? Sullivan tried to steal the cargo? How did he even know when you were leaving?"

"Lucky guess, I suppose," Mason said.

"So, you think Sullivan figured out we were going to black market part of the crop, and he wanted his share?"

"I don't know. But that's my working theory for now."

They started walking, but Jeremy abruptly stopped again. "Did Mato see you use the Glock?"

"He was out cold at the time," Mason said.

"What if he hadn't been?" Jeremy asked.

Mason tossed his hands in the air. "When our lives are in danger, shoot first and explain later."

"That would take some tall explaining."

"Yeah, I got lucky this time."

The two men resumed walking.

CHAPTER 26

"And you think Sullivan might have been behind it?" Karen asked, lying in bed next to Mason.

Mason pondered the question in the early morning light. "I don't know," Mason finally said. "That's what it looks like."

"What happens when he shows up for the next load of rice? Could be as early as today."

"If he shows up."

"Why wouldn't he? If he was behind it, he'll think you're lost at sea."

"True." He stared at the ceiling. "And if he wasn't, he'll show up like normal. What I don't get is, the load was relatively small compared to the overall crop. Two hundred and forty-three Spanish dollars. That wouldn't mean much to a man like Sullivan."

"You don't know that. Or maybe it's a matter of principle. He may feel entitled to a portion of the profits on everything that goes to market, no matter which market."

"I suppose," Mason mumbled. "What's been happening around here?"

"Lisa and I have two students, now. Jimmy and Monroe, both about ten. Jimmy catches on quickly."

"How are the adults taking it?"

"Marie isn't sure what to think."

"But she's going along with it okay?"

"So far. Sylvester has even shown an interest. He tends to linger after supper, when we break out the slate." Her expression turned more serious. "But I'm worried about these trips you're making."

"With the two boats, we have half as many trips."

"And you can trust this General Molena?"

"I don't think we can trust anybody. But he's getting the rice he needs, and we're getting the silver," Mason said, as he turned on his side, facing Karen. "Can we talk about this later? You and I haven't had a lot of time together lately."

Karen studied his face for a moment before running her hand under the covers to his bare thigh and beyond.

Her touch just added to the already apparent issue.

"Certainly," she said.

◆◆◆

"What have you two been doing?" Lisa asked. "Breakfast is over and the men are at it. They already have those barrels unloaded."

"We were catching up on some us time," Karen said, as she took a seat on the bench.

Mason arrived with two bowls of steaming porridge. He placed one of the bowls in front of Karen as he took a seat across from her. He immediately started eating.

"He must be hungry," Lisa said.

Karen smiled.

Mason had taken two bites when Jeremy stuck his head in the doorway. "Sullivan's barge is coming down the river. I've already told John and his men to stay out of sight until he's gone."

Mason paused his chewing and rapidly shoved three heaping spoonfuls into his mouth. He rose from his seat, still chewing, dipped his chin in Karen and Lisa's direction, and headed for the door.

"This should be interesting," Karen said.

◆◆◆

Mason and Jeremy hurried to the dock. Mason saw Charlie headed the same way, from the work yard where nearly all the workers were stowing the barrels in the barn.

They stood in silence as the barge drew closer and began heading for an open spot against the dock.

"This place is getting crowded," Jeremy said.

"Yeah, let's see what Sullivan has to say about the extra boat we have," Mason said.

"I don't see Sullivan," Charlie said. "That's Mister Harris, his assistant, in the bow."

Mason studied the other men on deck. He spotted three of the four from their last trip. The hijacker had been replaced by a new man.

Jeremy and Charlie walked onto the dock and caught the lines thrown their way. They tied off the barge and stood waiting for Harris.

Mason lingered at the foot of the dock and nudged the butt of his Glock under his coat with his bicep.

Harris stepped from the boat and immediately shook hands with Charlie and Jeremy.

"Where's Mister Sullivan?" Mason asked, as he walked up and extended his hand.

Harris shook it. "In town." He glanced back at the four men still on board. "We do most of this for Mister Sullivan."

"You're missing one," Mason said.

Harris cocked his head. "How's that?"

Mason motioned toward the boat. "Your men, you're missing one."

"Oh, you mean Burton. Don't know where he got off to. Been missing for a couple of days."

Mason said nothing.

"Looks like you got yourself another sloop," Harris said. He studied the boat for a few moments. "That looks like the Adams boat."

Mason looked at him quizzically.

"Tom Adams. He transports for planters up and down the coast."

"We ran into Mister Adams a couple of days ago," Mason said. "I ended up with the boat. He said something about retiring."

Harris raised his chin and pursed his lips in a noncommittal expression. He looked at Charlie. "We'll take what you have ready."

"Mister Sullivan feeling alright?" Mason asked. "Not sick or anything, is he?"

Harris turned back to Mason. "Feeling just fine. Same as always."

Mason put his hand on Charlie's shoulder. "Let's load him up with what we have."

Charlie started walking toward the work yard, with Harris following.

"What do you think?" Jeremy asked when Charlie and Harris were out of earshot.

"I don't think Mister Harris knew anything about it," Mason said. "The jury's still out on Sullivan."

"The sooner we get him loaded and out of here," Jeremy said, "the sooner we can get back to the barrels."

"Where's Nathan?"

"Work yard," Jeremy said as he started walking.

Mason stepped off.

❖❖❖

With the last of the bags headed toward the barge, Mason glanced at Jeremy making a final entry on the paper, now bound with other pages into a ledger. Mason turned to Harris. "Are we agreed on the count?"

"We are," Harris said, as he scanned the yard and barn for any other bags.

"That's the last of it going to market," Mason said. "We'll keep what's left for personal consumption, and maybe trade some with the local natives."

Harris extended his hand. "Your rice will be on the next ship to London."

Jeremy closed the ledger and shook Harris' hand.

Mason shook the man's hand and began walking him toward the dock, with Charlie in tow. "I'll stop by tomorrow for the final total."

"That will be fine, Mister Mason. I'll look forward to seeing you then."

Mason and Charlie let go the docking lines and watched the men on board begin poling the barge into the river's current. Mason gave a wave to Harris, standing in the stern.

Harris waved back and turned to the man at the tiller.

"We lost most of the day," Charlie said. "Getting those barrels filled and loaded in time will be tight."

"Let's get to it while we still have light."

◆◆◆

Early the next morning, Charlie let go the bow line as Mason jumped aboard the smaller sloop with Jeremy already on board.

"Anything you need from town?" Mason asked, as they began moving away from the larger sloop.

"As long as we have plenty of rum, I'm good," Charlie said.

"I'll add it to the list," Mason replied.

Charlie smiled and gave a wave. He turned to leave when the sloop was beyond talking distance and began walking toward the work yard. Approaching, he heard Nathan's voice yelling from inside the barn. Charlie quickened his pace. When he stepped inside, he saw Nathan berating two of the men. A barrel at their feet lay cracked open, with rice spilled out. The numerous other men inside, including Sylvester, kept at their work except they were all moving with considerably less urgency than usual. "What's the problem, Nathan?"

"These bumbling idiots broke open one of the barrels."

The two men stood quietly with their chins pointed to the floor.

"Let me take care of it," Charlie said.

"Fine," Nathan yelled. "But they should be whipped, or at least go a day without food."

"I can deal with it," Charlie said.

"How about if I deal with it?" Nathan said in a low rumble as he turned his head to the two men.

One of the men was nearly twice Nathan's size.

"Mason and Jeremy hired me to oversee the rice and crops, let me do my job."

Nathan stood staring at Charlie for several long moments. "Take care of it, then."

"I'd prefer to deal with it on my terms, alone." He stared at Nathan.

Nathan's jaws flexed, but he finally walked out of the barn.

Charlie turned to the two men. "Just sweep it up and get back to work." He scanned everyone in the barn, all now staring at him. "Everyone back to work. It's a broken barrel, it's not the end of the world."

Everyone started moving.

◆◆◆

At supper that night, everyone listened to Mason describe the trip to Charles Town and the supplies they had acquired, including two slates and pencils.

"Sullivan wasn't there, but Mister Harris paid us for the rice," Mason was saying.

"Paper money," Jeremy said.

"We picked up some more tools. When this kitchen addition is finished, I'd like to start working on the cabins. We can cut most of our own lumber this time."

"The slave quarters," Nathan said.

Mason cocked his head. "Just cabins."

"What did you have in mind?" Charlie asked.

"Replace the ones that need replacing, maybe increase their size and comfort level."

"More comfort means happier workers and more productivity," Charlie said.

"Something like that." He turned to Nathan. "I'd like for you to focus on this building. We need to finish the walls and get the place ready for winter."

Nathan glanced at Charlie and back to Mason. "Will I have help?"

"Jeremy and I can pitch in. Charlie will be busy with the workers and the crops."

"So, you want to keep me away from the slaves?"

"Workers," Mason said. He tossed his hands in the air. "Not particularly. You're the construction guy, we need you to construct."

Nathan glanced at Charlie again.

Charlie stared at his bowl as he chewed.

"Is there something going on that I'm not aware of?" Mason asked. He glanced at Karen and Lisa.

They both shrugged their shoulders.

"I'll get back to the kitchen in the morning," Nathan said.

"Thank you." Mason looked at Charlie, still staring at his bowl. "How are we on the barrels?"

"Coming along just fine," Charlie said. "Should have both boats loaded day after tomorrow."

"Can you make the trip this time?" Mason asked, looking at Charlie.

Charlie glanced at Nathan.

"Nathan will sit this one out." Mason scanned the interior of the dining space and focused on the large section of unfinished wall. "We need this place finished before we all freeze to death."

"Sure," Charlie said. "Sylvester knows what needs to be done."

"Anything else we need to discuss?" Mason asked.

With no further issues to discuss, they resumed eating and chatting.

CHAPTER 27

For the next two days, Mason helped Nathan with the kitchen addition while Jeremy and Charlie concentrated on filling the barrels, getting them loaded, and processing more rice.

As usual, when they weren't needed, Mato and his braves spent their time hunting and fishing. They had already brought in one large buck. They would continue to hunt and fish at the plantation until the transfer of rice was completed. Mason's mind rested a little easier knowing they were there while he was gone.

By the evening of the second day, the boats were loaded, and the walls were finished. Mason considered leaving that night, but decided to get some extra sleep instead.

Early the next morning, before the sun rose, Mason woke to the sound of rain hitting the roof.

The drops were fat and steady, dropping from black skies. Despite the heavy rain, the wind remained moderate. But without the Weather Channel for updates, Mason had no way to know what was coming.

"What do you think?" Jeremy asked, standing next to Mason in the open back door. They both peered into the darkness at the river and the silhouette of boat rigging, barely visible against the slightly lighter background. "Could be a bad storm."

"Short of a hurricane, Captain Medina will have his ship on station as agreed," Mason said. He slowly shook his head. "On the bright side, the crops are happy."

"We need the water, that's for sure," Jeremy said. "But we don't need to lose the rice, not to mention the boats and crew." He looked at Mason.

"Can you wait a day?" Karen asked, stepping up behind them. She pulled her shawl tighter.

Mason turned and put his arm around her shoulders.

"This is a cold front," she said. "There could be freezing temperatures and ice on the back side of this."

"We don't know how long this will last," Mason said. "And it's only the beginning of November."

"This is not Miami," Karen said.

Mason turned his head to the glow becoming visible through the exterior kitchen's single west-side window. "It's just another morning for Marie." He rubbed his face and beard. "We head out as planned."

"It might not be just another day," Karen said.

He turned to her and wrapped both arms around her waist.

She rested her head on Mason's chest.

"If the wind starts to pick up, we'll find a cove," Mason said. He stepped back and placed both hands on her shoulders. "We'll be fine."

"I need to get dressed," she said, as she turned and disappeared.

Mason turned to Jeremy. "You okay being here with Nathan?"

"I have a stout hickory limb picked out if needed."

"Let's hope it doesn't come to that. He'll want to stay inside with this weather. Let him."

"You sure?"

"Karen and Lisa will be in the kitchen most of the day, and you'll be here at night," Mason said. "But just the same, keep the hickory limb handy."

◆◆◆

"Which boat do you want?" Mason asked Charlie. Both men stood on the dock, facing the two sloops still lashed together. Both men wore buckskin shirts, pants, and black leather boots. Mason wore a poncho, basically a buckskin with a hole cut in the middle for his head.

Mason pulled his three-pointed hat tighter with one hand. The other held his canvas ruck containing a gourd of water, a day's worth of food for three men, his Glock, and extra magazines.

Charlie held a satchel containing four days' worth of food, enough for all six men, even though they hoped to be back in two, three at the most. A keg of beer had already been loaded onto both boats, along with a keg of boiled and strained water.

The sun was up, but hidden behind a thick cloud cover, rendering the scene dark, gloomy, wet, and cold.

"Do they know what they're doing?" Charlie asked, as he motioned to John and his men readying the two sloops.

"They do."

"I'll take the big one," he said, "should plow through the waves a little easier."

The two men stepped over the gunwale of the smaller boat. Charlie continued on and joined Sebastian and Slim on the larger one.

Mason immediately stashed his ruck in the V-berth.

Both boats were crammed with barrels of rice, lashed tightly to the deck. As with the previous trips, the cargo left only enough room to maneuver fore and aft, with a small cutout port and starboard.

John and Skinny greeted Mason with smiles. Both were dressed in only their regular coats, shirts, pants, and shoes, all soaked through, but neither man appeared chilled.

Mason looked toward the house and saw Karen, Lisa, and Jeremy standing together on the porch, barely visible in the dull light and drizzle. Mason waved. He saw Karen raise her hand a few seconds later.

A gust of wind rocked both boats and sheets of rain came down in buckets. It lasted only a minute or so before returning to a steady drizzle.

Mason shivered against the cold air finding its way through the openings in his buckskins. This is when he wished he had brought a more substantial, and waterproof, overcoat from the future. He glanced at John and Skinny and saw that they seemed to take the cold and wet in stride. This wasn't even winter to them. Technically, it wasn't winter for Mason either. He shivered again.

Mason helped unlash the larger boat from the smaller, while John and Skinny stood ready at the anchor lines.

When the larger boat began drifting away, Mason signaled John and Skinny to hoist the anchors. With only a few yards of line out, fore and aft, the anchors were aboard within a minute.

Mason released the dock lines and jumped back aboard.

The sloop immediately began drifting with the current.

Mason manned the tiller while the two seamen kept the boat away from the shore. It took both men pushing together on one side to move the boat, due to its increased weight.

Three hours later, both sloops emerged into the Ashley River's mouth. With room to maneuver, the two men raised the main and both jibs.

Mason steered to take advantage of the onshore winds, which he estimated at twelve knots. His steering took the sloop on a zigzag course, almost exactly in the wake of Charlie's boat. Once past James Island and Morris Island, Mason steered due south behind Charlie.

About two miles out, with the coast barely visible, both boats turned to a southwest course with beam reach winds that Mason estimated at fourteen knots churning five-foot seas. The cold water routinely splashed over the bow and was picked up by the wind.

Mason's buckskins hung heavy from his shoulders and waist, drenched and soggy from the rain and ocean spray. It was the most miserable conditions Mason could remember, made even more depressing by the thought that it could, and probably would, get much worse, especially at night. The only redeeming factor was they were clicking along at a pretty good pace.

With John and Skinny standing next to him at the helm, Mason explained that he wanted two men on duty at all times, while the third rested or slept. He was conscious of the fact that the V-berth was the only relatively dry and warm spot on the boat, and that's where he stored the ruck and the Glock. He had removed the food and water from the ruck before he stashed the canvas as far up into the bow as it would go. He'd left the food and water in plain sight, leaving no reason to go searching for anything. He hoped that would be enough.

Two hours after entering the open sea, the wind increased.

Mason ordered one reef in the mainsail and one of the jibs lowered. Instantly, the keeled over boat righted itself a couple of degrees.

The increase in wind brought higher waves and lower troughs. The water now crashed over the bow nearly every time the it dipped. Mason actually considered turning back. But neither John nor Skinny seemed all that worried. And it would be impossible to catch Charlie. Mason put the thought out of his mind and pressed on.

He turned the tiller over to John, which was the plan—switch the helmsman every two hours. Mason used the time to make his way about the deck, sliding and slamming against one stack of barrels and then another, as he checked and rechecked the lashings. Keen on his mind was the prospect of loose barrels and a shifting load. In these seas, such would prove disastrous.

They fell into the routine—two hours on, two hours off, and two hours of rest or sleep.

Actually, sleep was impossible. Just being in the V-berth during heavy seas was dangerous. The constant pounding against the waves, and sudden drops into the troughs, tossed everything inside the tiny space against the hulls, deck, and overhead.

Fortunately, by nightfall the rain had subsided to a light drizzle, and the winds had backed off to about twelve knots. The water's surface calmed. The lingering overcast, however, made it practically impossible to orient the boat against the shore, two miles in the distance. As it got darker, the coastline got less visible. The usual contrast between the tops of the trees and the sky beyond was nonexistent, which presented a serious navigation problem.

Mason walked to the bow and peered at Charlie's boat, nearly half a mile in the distance and fading quickly. With no moon or stars, it would soon become impossible to keep an eye on the leading boat in the pitch dark. As he continued to watch, two things happened. The larger sloop made a course change. It was slight, only a degree or two to the south. Charlie obviously intended to steer more away from the coast, to increase the distance between their course and the potential hazards closer to shore. The other thing Charlie did was to light the boat's stern lantern. The glow wasn't much, but it would be enough as long as they remained within a mile or so of the sloop's stern.

Mason returned to the helm and pointed out the lantern and the course change to John, at the tiller, and Skinny, standing next to him.

John steered accordingly.

"And we'll keep the reef in the sails," Mason said. "Unless we lose the lantern during the night." With their acknowledgements, Mason stared at the last vestiges of the coastline as the evening got darker.

◆◆◆

During the night, Mason might have gotten an hour's sleep. He spent most of the time on deck, shivering, either at the tiller or at the bow, keeping Charlie's lantern in sight. He lost all track of time and began wishing for daybreak hours before it actually came.

The morning brought an end to the rain, fewer clouds, and cooler temperatures. But it also brought open seas in every direction. The coastline was no longer in sight. Charlie's sloop, still visible in the distance, did a lot to comfort his nerves. It was two or three miles ahead, but still very much in sight.

Mason removed the reef in the main and raised the second jib. The sloop gradually closed on the larger boat.

At that point, Charlie changed to a more northerly course that would take them to the coast. As it turned out, they weren't that far off course. Four hours later, both sloops were anchored next to the Spanish ship at the mouth of the Saint Mary's River.

While the Spanish crew began transferring the barrels of rice, and John and his men got some much-needed sleep, Mason introduced Charlie to Lieutenant Ribera and Captain Medina, aboard the Spanish ship. As before, Medina insisted on a glass of sherry in his quarters for the four of them, along with a platter of cheese and bread, freshly baked aboard his ship. And, as before, Captain Medina pressed for information on Governor Moore and Charles Town. Charlie followed Mason's lead and was able to steer clear of providing any tactical information.

With Charlie and Mason barely able to keep their eyes open, especially after a second glass of sherry, the captain finally suggested the two men return to their sloops for some rest. Captain Medina assured Mason he would be awakened when the count was completed and the sloops were reloaded with empty barrels.

They thanked Medina for his hospitality and caught a ride on the next longboat to their respective boats.

With John and Skinny occupying most of the room in the V-berth, Mason curled up in the bow, pulled his buckskin cloak tighter around his shoulders, and tried to rest. He was able to achieve that twilight realm, never a deep sleep, because of the constant voice commands to the Spanish crew, and the bumps and scrapes of barrels being moved about. Around midafternoon he gave up trying and began pacing the deck in his groggy state, trying to stay warm.

At dusk, with both sloops loaded with empty barrels, Lieutenant Ribera came aboard with the final count. The count was off by two barrels, in favor of the Spanish, but Mason was too tired to worry about it. He accepted the silver coins, over twice as many as the first payment, thanked the lieutenant, and arranged to meet again in seven days. He gave a final wave as Ribera's oarsmen pulled away and headed back to the ship.

Fifty yards away, Charlie stood at the stern of his sloop, watching the transaction. "Can we head out?" he yelled, obviously anxious to get back to his warm room and mug of rum.

"We're ready," Mason yelled back, as he motioned with his arm to weigh anchor. He turned to John. "Get us underway, if you will," Mason said. "Remain behind Charlie, as before." He looked to the sky. "We should be able to keep the coastline in sight this time."

Mason lingered a couple of minutes to ensure John and Skinny did what was necessary to get the boat underway. He then retired to the V-berth and passed out.

◆◆◆

The subsequent four trips went off without a hitch. Mason alternated between Charlie and Nathan to command the larger sloop with Sebastian and Slim.

On the last trip, Mason and Charlie lingered with their sloops as the Spanish ship weighed anchor and headed out to sea. Mason took that opportunity to visit the Guale, once more, and present them with two barrels of rice that had been stowed in the V-berth. The Guale chief invited him to stay and appeared disappointed when Mason declined. He promised to see them again after the next harvest.

The final trip back to the plantation was long and tiring, given that John and his men had remained on the Spanish ship, leaving just Mason and Charlie to pilot the two sloops.

By the 5th day of December, 1720, the two hundred thousand pounds of rice had been transferred, Mason possessed three thousand silver Spanish coins, and two boatloads of empty barrels occupied space in the barn.

Mason and Captain Medina, speaking for General Molina, had agreed on the sale and purchase of at least that many pounds the following year, starting with a full load delivered directly to Saint Augustine. Captain Medina gave Mason a letter, signed by Governor General Molina, giving free passage should Mason be stopped by any Spanish vessel.

CHAPTER 28

Mason felt someone poking his arm. He opened his eyes to find Karen staring down at him.

"You've been asleep for at least sixteen hours," Karen said. "The sun's been up for hours."

"How do you know?" Mason asked, without moving a muscle.

"Know what?"

"How many hours. You don't own a watch."

"Trust me, you've slept long enough. Even Nathan is up and about."

Mason took in a deep breath and exhaled while he rubbed his face. He swung his feet off the bed and came to a sitting position. "Damn, woman, it's freezing in here."

"Put some clothes on," Karen said.

"How about if I don't, and you come back to bed?"

"That ship has sailed for the day," Karen said. "I'm sure you have something that needs doing."

"I do, in fact," Mason said. He smiled.

"Besides that."

He frowned. "Well, speaking of sailing ships—"

"What?" Karen said, cutting him off before he could continue.

"Mato and his braves need a ride to Myrtle Beach. And I might as well continue on to New York to get Misses Stewart paid for the year's harvest."

"You're heading out so soon?"

"It's only going to get colder. The harbor in New York might freeze over, for all I know. The sooner, the better. Plus, like I said, Mato is anxious to get back."

"I think New York harbor is noted for not freezing over," Karen said.

"I still want to get this trip over with."

"You'll load Mato up with rice and vegetables?"

"Of course," Mason said, "plenty of rice and some vegetables."

"The least you could do, after him getting shot and all."

"The wound healed. It hardly left a scar. He was impressed with my stitching."

"When are you leaving?"

"Tomorrow. The small schooner; it's easier to sail. I figure five or six hundred miles. Should be able to do two hundred miles a day. Three days up, three days back, and a day or two in the city. I should be back, easily, in ten days."

"Who are you taking?"

"Nathan and Jeremy. Jeremy needs a break from the plantation."

"And Charlie has agreed to stay on?"

"So far," Mason said. "He hasn't said anything about leaving."

"I guess it has to be done," Karen said, as she took a seat on the bed beside Mason.

Mason put one arm around her shoulders, the other hand on her stomach, and snuggled closer. "Everything okay?"

"Yeah, except you're gone a lot."

"One more trip."

Karen smiled and put her hand on top of his.

"Given any thought to the baby, the delivery?"

"I suppose we should explore the midwives in town."

"Probably a good idea," Mason said. "As soon as I'm back." He paused a moment before continuing. "There's something else we haven't talked about."

"What?"

"Well, marriage. We haven't talked about that, at all. We can't let Jeremy and Lisa have all the fun."

Karen stared at a wall for several moments. She finally faced Mason and exhaled. "You know I've been married before. Twice, actually. I was working on a third." She stared into Mason's eyes. "I haven't been all that lucky when it comes to marriage."

"Actually, I didn't know that. You've never mentioned it, and I haven't asked."

"We've both been occupied."

"Children?"

"No. Neither marriage lasted long enough."

"Okay, the mayhem is behind us," Mason said. "And we have a son coming."

Karen said nothing as she turned her head and stared into space.

"Your life before. That was a different time and place."

"But I'm the same."

"So, what are you saying?"

"I guess I'm saying that in this time and place, for now at least, I don't need a piece of paper to feel married. Subconsciously, maybe, I don't want to jinx what we have. I may feel differently later." She rubbed her stomach. "Our son will be named Mason. Let me ease into the rest of it."

"I can do that. But in the meantime—" He raised both eyebrows.

Karen stood. "Like I said, the day's half over."

Mason smiled. "It is," he said, as he took hold of her arm, pulled her to the bed, and slung the quilts over the two of them. "And since we're not getting married today, we might as well find something else to occupy our time."

◆◆◆

Mason spent the rest of the day getting organized for the trip. He ensured Charlie would mind the place while he, Nathan, and Jeremy were gone, and he provisioned the boat with plenty of food, water, and quilts, along with some rum and beer. If it got cold enough, the drinking water might freeze.

He loaded five barrels of rice on board. He also transferred the hijackers' six muskets and most of the powder and shot from the larger sloop for Mato and his tribe. He kept the three pistols and the remaining powder and shot. He also gave Karen and Lisa a quick lesson on how to load and fire the ancient weapons. The three pistols would remain with the women, in the house.

Following a hardy supper, a good night's sleep, and an even hardier breakfast, Mason, his small crew, along with Mato and his braves, were ready to head out by midmorning the next day.

Charlie, Karen, Lisa, and Sylvester waved from the foot of the dock as the sloop caught the current and began drifting downriver.

Mason and Jeremy gave a final wave just before the first bend.

"I guess we're headed for New York City," Mason said, as he turned to Jeremy.

"Probably not much of a city," Jeremy said. "Any idea what we can expect?"

"Didn't do a lot of reading on New York. I know it's small, probably not much bigger than Charles Town. It was a fairly busy port, even at this early time."

"We follow the coast?"

"Yeah, and keep the coast in sight," Mason said. "Two miles seems to work well."

Mason, Jeremy, and Nathan each wore two layers of long pants, two or three shirts, and their heaviest coat and neckerchief. Mason wore the buckskin poncho over his coat. It looked silly, but it added that much more of a barrier against the wind and any ocean spray. Mason made a mental note to have Francois make everyone a heavy wool coat.

They expected the traffic to be much greater north of Charles Town. Merchant ships, small and large, left Charles Town almost every day, most destined for the West Indies and London. But a few headed north to New York, Philadelphia, and Boston. Most of that traffic would be farther out. Captains of larger ships tended to keep their distance from the coast.

Mason had no idea where Misses Stewart's home was located in New York. He had an address on Gold Street, but it would take some footwork to find the right house. Finding the house was the least of his worries. He had three full days of open ocean sailing ahead of him. He just hoped the weather and adequate winds remained favorable. Stay alert and take it one day at a time; that's all he could do.

◆◆◆

The end of the first day, with plenty of sun remaining in the sky, brought them to Myrtle Beach. They made a beeline to the little inlet where Mato and his braves had boarded, weeks earlier.

Mason dropped the sails and tossed out the bow anchor.

Mason and Jeremy helped Mato and his two braves over the side and handed them the mountain of supplies. Each barrel of rice, alone, took two men to handle.

Mato and his braves stacked the barrels at the edge of the pond, and piled the additional bags and weapons on top. Mato directed one of the braves to hoof it to the village and bring back enough natives to carry all the items in one trip.

The brave took off running.

"Thank you, my friend," Mason said, standing on the deck. "Is there anything else your people need? I can stop here on my return trip."

"This plenty," Mato said, as he stood in thigh-deep water. He extended his hand.

Mason took Mato's hand with a firm grip, held it for several moments, and released. Mato was a good friend. Mason likely would not be alive if it were not for Mato's assistance in those first days at the camp. Mason only wished his village was closer. "We have plenty of room at the plantation, if you want to move your village there."

"Too many white man," Mato said. "We stay here."

"I understand completely," Mason said. "I sometimes feel the same way." Mason motioned to Jeremy and Nathan to hoist the anchor. "I'll visit as much as I can," Mason said to Mato. "You know where to find me."

Mato simply turned away. He waded to the shore and watched as the sloop drifted to deeper water.

Mason gave a final wave and moved to the tiller as Jeremy and Nathan kept the boat in the center of the outgoing current. With enough distance between the boat and the shore, they raised the main sail, both jibs, and resumed their northerly course.

◆◆◆

Mason felt like he had just crawled under the quilts when either Nathan or Jeremy was poking him on the arm for his shift. In the early morning hours of the next day, everyone was pretty much a walking zombie. And they all made up for the lack of sleep at night by dozing on deck during the day. That meant there was often only one man awake, for hours at a time.

Beginning the next night, they switched to three-hour shifts. That was a long time to be at the tiller, especially at night, but on an extended haul it was the only solution for a three-man crew. At least everyone got some sleep.

Just after sunup on the third day, Mason recognized the white, sandy beaches of what would become Atlantic City. He envisioned the hotels and casinos that would one day occupy most of the shoreline. He had been there several times and had visited all the major casinos. For some strange reason, he didn't miss the future. He didn't miss any of it—the big cities, lights, noise, people. He especially didn't miss the crowds of people.

Off the coast of Atlantic City meant he was about sixty miles from New York, six or seven more hours if the wind held. It was possible they could roll into town well before dark. He yelled for Jeremy, who was on duty with him at the time, to trim the sails. Mason wanted to get every last knot possible out of the broad reach winds. Everyone would be able to get a good night's sleep that night, in an actual bed.

Late that afternoon, they entered what would become America's largest metropolitan area. At this time in history, he wasn't expecting much, but the reality of seeing it still froze him in awe.

Jeremy and Nathan were likewise glued to the gunwales, peering out, heads swiveling back and forth.

As they made their way through the Lower Bay, along with several other vessels, Mason scanned the shores of New Jersey to the south, and Staten Island and Brooklyn to the north. From a couple of miles out, the entire coastline appeared desolate and empty. He saw an occasional plume of smoke, likely from a campfire, but the scene was otherwise devoid of human content. He saw only tree-lined shores.

The number of encampments increased as they entered the Upper Bay, and as they rounded what would be Brooklyn's west side and continued north, Mason got his first glimpse of New York.

CHAPTER 29

Perched on the tip of Manhattan sat the bastions, ramparts, fortifications, and walls of Fort George. Mason had read about it. Originally built by the Dutch, the fort went by many names, but finally settled on George, under the British. From a mile out, the fort appeared to be a combination of stone, brick, wood, and earth. Cannons protruded through the parapets in all directions, and garrisoned British soldiers in their red uniforms could be seen walking about.

"Where to?" Jeremy asked from the tiller.

As they passed by the future home of the statue of liberty on the left, and Governors Island on the right, Mason pointed to the East River and the wharf along the southeast side of Manhattan. Numerous ships and boats were docked there. Some were very large, with three and even four masts. He spotted a section of smaller, one and two-masted vessels. "Find a spot along there," he said as he pointed. With Jeremy at the tiller and Nathan amidships, port side, Mason walked to the bow for a better view.

Most of the brick and wood buildings and homes, some two and three stories, were concentrated on the very tip of Manhattan, running maybe a half mile across and a mile to the north. The streets, some wide but most narrow, were mostly dirt. He spotted one paved with cobblestones. Every facade appeared dingy, likely from years of caked-on dust and grime.

The wharf was buzzing with activity. Barrels and bags were stacked along the entire length. Men, mostly black men, scurried about, moving more barrels and bags on and off the ships.

Mason glanced at Jeremy and pointed to a relatively inactive section of the wharf, with an empty spot large enough for the sloop. They would be able to tie up directly to the wooden pier.

Jeremy steered accordingly, as Mason and Nathan lowered the sails. The sloop continued forward but was quickly losing steam in the river's current.

A man appeared on the dock and motioned for Mason to throw him a line.

Mason grabbed the coil of rope at his feet and tossed it.

The man caught hold, pulled the sloop up to the pier, and tied off the bow line. He walked back and received Nathan's stern line.

With the sloop secured, Mason climbed up onto the dock. "Thank you," he said to the man.

"Think nothing of it, mate," the man said. His accent was thick, Scottish or Irish, maybe.

"Can you tell me who I see about docking?"

"That would be O'Holleran," the man said, as he pointed. "We call him Pappy."

Mason spotted a tall, slightly overweight gentleman, middle aged, with thick, curly red hair. He wore black long pants and a black, heavy coat.

"Thank you," Mason said to the man. "Will he allow us to leave the boat here for a day or so?"

The man gave a slight snort. He surveyed the sloop's deck. "If you're loadin' something, the harbor master takes a percentage based on weight."

"What if we're not loading?"

The man cocked his head. "Talk to Pappy."

Mason thanked the man again and turned to Jeremy and Nathan, still standing on deck, peering up. "Wait here until I figure out the process." He reached into his coat pocket and fingered the small, buckskin coin pouch containing thirty or so of the silver ingots he carried most of the time. He had a second pouch, with a hundred more, hidden in the sloop's V-berth.

He approached the man standing at a barrel. He was making entries into a leather-bound ledger. The late afternoon sun highlighted his red hair.

"Excuse me," Mason said as he approached. "Are you Pappy?"

"What's your business?" the man asked in a gruff tone, without looking up.

"Well, I have business in town. Day or two." Mason pointed, even though the man had still not looked up. "The sloop over there is mine."

Finally, Pappy stopped writing, looked at Mason, and toward the sloop. "Cargo coming or going?"

"Neither," Mason said. "Just need a place to park her."

"How long?" Pappy asked in an even gruffer tone.

"Day. Two, at the most."

Pappy studied Mason's face, surveyed the sloop again, and raised both eyebrows. "There's no loitering here, cargo on or off, that's it." He resumed making notations in the ledger.

"I can pay for the spot," Mason said.

Pappy paused his notations. He looked up and down the wharf. "How long you say?"

"Day or two."

Pappy pursed his lips as he stared at Mason. "Ten quid," he finally said.

"I have silver. Let's say, ten one-ounce ingots?"

Pappy looked up and down the wharf again and gave a single nod. He stuck out his hand.

Mason produced the ten ingots from his pouch and placed them in the man's hand. "Will I need to leave a man on board?"

"Nobody'll touch your boat, day or night."

"Thank you," Mason said, as he extended his hand.

Pappy shook with a vise-like grip and returned to his ledger.

Mason returned to the sloop and jumped aboard. "We can leave it here."

"I wouldn't leave the silver." Jeremy said.

"No, we take that with us, and anything else of value, including the muskets," Mason said.

"That silver alone is two hundred pounds," Nathan said.

"Roughly one eighty-seven," Mason corrected, "about sixty pounds each."

With no objections, Mason led them to the V-berth and began extracting the sacks of Spanish dollars, each around thirty pounds in weight. Mason put two of the sacks into his rucksack.

"This place really stinks," Nathan said.

Mason paused for a moment. He was right. The place stunk worse than Charles Town. He detected a combination of rotting fish and flesh, hopefully animal flesh, with a few unidentifiable odors mixed in. And the two men Mason spoke with both stunk of severe body odor. "You'll get used to it."

Nathan placed his two bags in a small, buckskin duffle.

Jeremy tied his two bags together with a piece of rope and slung them over his shoulder. He winced at the weight. "As long as we don't have to go far."

The three men hefted their load and climbed out of the sloop. Nathan and Jeremy each carried their muskets, as well. Jeremy additionally carried the small ledger from the plantation, containing the year's accounting for the rice and crops, income, and expenses.

"Where to?" Jeremy asked.

Mason thought for a moment. He looked up at the sinking sun. "Room for the night, or find Misses Stewart's house?"

"All I know is, this stuff is getting heavy," Nathan said.

Mason scanned the buildings along the wharf. He spotted what were obviously shops and warehouses, an exporter or two, several taverns, and even what was apparently a brothel. Several women lingered outside the establishment, soliciting men as they walked by. His eyes finally locked on what appeared to be an inn. It was a wood, three-story structure, with numerous windows. "Let's try that," he said, as he pointed to the building nearly a hundred yards down the wharf.

The three men entered through a windowed door. A small fire in a stone fireplace took the chill out of the room.

Nathan and Jeremy lowered their loads to the floor while Mason, carrying his rucksack in one hand, approached a young woman, maybe thirty, standing behind a short, oak counter. She wore several petticoat layers, a tight top over a generous bosom, and a wool shawl over her shoulders. The woman smiled as Mason approached.

"Would you have a room for the night?" Mason asked. "Three men."

"One will have to sleep on the floor," the woman said.

"That's fine," Mason said, as he looked around at Nathan and Jeremy, still standing just inside the door.

"That will be two dollars for the night," the woman said.

"I have one-ounce silver ingots, each is equal in weight to a Spanish dollar. Will that do?"

"It will," the woman said.

Mason lowered his ruck to the floor and produced his coin pouch. He extracted two of the ingots and placed them in the palm of the woman's hand.

"Up the stairs, second room on the right. You have a view of the water."

"Thank you," Mason said. He smiled at the woman, lifted his ruck, and motioned for Nathan and Jeremy to follow.

The room was more spacious than Mason had expected. The floor was plain wood planks, probably pine. The ceiling was covered with hardwood panels carved with linear designs. But it was low. There were only a few inches above Mason's and Jeremy's heads. The walls were also wood paneled. Furniture consisted of two simple, wood-frame beds, each with a straw mattress and two folded quilts. Against the wall stood a carved wood table with four legs, somewhat like a short sofa table. A mirror hung on the wall behind the table. And there were two wooden, straight-backed chairs against the wall. Two double-hung, six-pane windows provided light and a view of the wharf, although the light was fading fast. The only amenities were a pitcher of water and a bowl on the table, a towel folded to one side, a half-burned candle in a pewter holder to the other, and a copper pot in one corner. The room was not that different from the rooms at the plantation house.

Nathan dropped his duffle on the floor and immediately took a seat on one of the beds. "I have dibs on this one."

"Age before beauty," Jeremy said, as he removed the two bags from his shoulder and lowered them to the floor. He looked at Mason. "You can have the other one. Probably has bedbugs, anyhow, or who knows what."

Nathan looked down at his mattress with a concerned expression, ran his hand over it, but finally relaxed.

"We'll get a couple of extra blankets for you," Mason said. He stepped back to the door and examined the knob. "No lock. We can't leave the silver here, unguarded."

Nathan reclined on the bed. "I'm starved. I think we should eat first."

Mason turned to Jeremy. "Why don't you stay here? Nathan and I will find something and bring it back."

"Maybe there's room service," Nathan said.

Mason and Jeremy looked at each other. "Worth a shot," Jeremy said.

Mason motioned for the two of them to stay put. He returned to the lobby and learned there was, indeed, room service. The woman, named Matilda, employed a young man to fetch food and drink from a nearby tavern. She said the stews were good and this time of year the beer was cold. Mason ordered three servings of whatever was on the menu, paid in advance, and also asked for two extra quilts.

"We have room service," he said as he slung the door open. "Should be here shortly."

Nathan was still lying on the bed.

Jeremy stood at the window, peering out. "We can see the boat from here."

Mason joined him at the window. "Excellent."

Jeremy faced Mason. "So, what's the plan?"

"The town's not that big," Mason said. "Eat, figure out where Misses Stewart lives, and play the rest by ear."

"Sounds good to me," Nathan quipped from the bed.

He turned to Jeremy. "Mind staying with the silver while Nathan and I track down the address? We'll all three deliver the money."

Jeremy gave him a knowing look. "Sounds like a plan."

A few minutes later, dinner arrived. It consisted of a thick beef stew, with potatoes and carrots, in a wood bowl, a pewter spoon, and a pewter mug of beer.

Mason's coin pouch included a few copper pence coins he had picked up along the way. The delivery boy seemed happy with two of them.

Fifteen minutes later, with the sun setting, Mason and Nathan exited the room carrying the empty dishes, which they deposited with Matilda, still at the counter. The two of them stepped out onto the street to a frenzy of activity.

"The proverbial party town," Nathan said, as he scanned up and down the wharf.

Men and women were shuffling by, many of them already totally inebriated. The brothel had the most activity, followed by the two taverns. Men spilled out of all three establishments. A pair of candle lanterns hung at the doorway of the three buildings. Other buildings sported much brighter torches affixed to a pillar or post.

"Any idea where she lives?"

"She told me it was the only brick house on Gold Street, two stories. Said I couldn't miss it. Apparently, her brother-in-law owns one of the grain mills around here." Mason held up a finger, indicating he would be right back. He ducked back inside the inn and approached the counter. "Any idea where I can find Gold Street?"

Matilda gave him directions, and he rejoined Nathan, still standing outside.

"The women are interesting," Nathan said, as his head rotated back and forth.

Mason studied the street a few moments. The only women he saw were clad in dingy, stained clothing. Many of them staggered as much as their male counterparts. And a few smelled worse. Most lacked at least one tooth in the front. "Before you get any ideas, diseases are as rampant in this time as they are in ours. Only difference is, they don't have a cure for any of them."

"You think I don't know that," Nathan said with indignation.

"Not sure what you know," Mason said, as he stepped off. "Gold Street is this way." As it turned out, nearly all the buildings and houses were numbered, and many of the street names were marked, either on the corner of a building or with a sign. He led Nathan up an alley, which ended at Queen Street, about half a block up. Mason crossed the street and continued walking.

The alley turned into the slightly wider King Street. Two blocks up they came to William Street, one of the few paved streets in town, and it also had sidewalks.

They turned right and began dodging the strollers, many of them walking arm-in-arm. Their manner of dress, and their styles, improved considerably once away from the wharf. Men wore more fashionable coats and pants; the women wore colorful petticoats, tops, and shawls.

As Mason and Nathan walked, both men swiveled their heads back and forth, capturing the people and buildings of a very early New York City. Some of those people spoke a highly accented version of English, and many spoke languages Mason didn't recognize.

A block past a meat market, now closed, but identifiable because of the stench, Mason turned onto an unmarked, considerably narrower street. A hundred feet farther, the street made a sharp left.

"This is Gold Street, according to Matilda," Mason said.

"Who?"

"The woman at the inn."

Trees and stately houses lined both sides of the dirt-covered street.

Mason continued on until he came to the first brick home. It was wide, with two stories and plenty of windows. Mason saw the flicker of candles through two of the windows.

"Shall we knock?" Nathan asked, as he started for the front porch.

"Let's just come back in the morning. With the payment. No sense in disturbing them at this late an hour."

Nathan stopped. "Whatever," he said, as he turned to Mason, already walking away.

CHAPTER 30

The next morning, loaded with the silver and their other possessions, the three men exited the inn and began walking the same route as the night before. The streets were much less crowded. Those out and about appeared to be working people—dock workers along the wharf, merchants conducting business, usually on the street, itself, and women out to gather the foodstuffs needed for the day.

The meat market was open for business. In the daylight, the source of the awful stench became evident. Animal and fish remains littered the area around the building. It even spilled into the street.

"I can't even imagine the bacteria and germs residing here," Jeremy said. He swiveled his head up and down the street. "This is worse than Charles Town."

"Their immune systems must be on afterburner," Nathan said.

Mason pressed on without comment, anxious to get Misses Stewart paid. Walking around with three thousand in silver, in such a rowdy town, was probably not the brightest of ideas. The muskets probably helped ensure their safety.

With Gold Street now fully illuminated, Mason could see that the brick house he'd found the previous evening was the only brick house on the street. With Jeremy and Nathan trailing slightly behind, he stepped up to the porch and knocked on the solid oak door.

A few moments later, an older, rather well-dressed, black gentlemen opened the door. "Yes, sir?"

"I'm Stephen Mason, from Charles Town." He motioned to Jeremy and Nathan. "We're here to see Misses Stewart."

"You mean Miss Wilma?"

"Yes. Wilma Stewart."

"Who is it?" came a woman's voice from inside the house.

The man turned. "A Mister Mason from Charles Town. Says he's here to see you."

"Yes, of course, Ernest, let him in."

Ernest took a step back, opening the door wider. He motioned for Mason to enter.

Mason removed his hat and stepped inside. He immediately caught sight of Misses Stewart, standing in the middle of the room. She was dressed in a fine ensemble of petticoats and tops.

"Mister Mason, I wasn't sure when to expect you."

He smiled. "Sorry for that, Misses Stewart. We got off to a late start on the harvest." He slung the ruck from his shoulders and lowered it to the floor. The ruck landed with a very audible *thud*.

"Good heavens, what are you carrying in there?"

"Your payment," he said, as he turned to the side and motioned toward Nathan and Jeremy, both standing with their hat and musket in one hand, and the silver in the other. "You remember Mister Jackson and Mister Sims?"

"Of course," she said, as she stepped forward. "You gentlemen have come a long way. I hope your journey was not too arduous."

"Came by boat," Mason said, "not at all difficult."

Nathan and Jeremy lowered their loads to the floor, but remained where they were standing, just inside the door.

"Please, come on in," Misses Stewart said. She turned to the black man now standing at her side. "Ernest, tea for our guests. In the parlor."

"Yes, ma'am, Miss Wilma." He turned and disappeared deeper into the house.

"Place your muskets in the corner there," Misses Stewart said. When Nathan and Jeremy deposited the weapons, she directed the three men to the room directly off the foyer, to the right.

Mason lifted the ruck and followed Misses Stewart.

Nathan and Jeremy followed with their silver. Jeremy additionally held the ledger.

Mason studied the interior as he walked. Wide stairs led to the second floor. The walls and ceilings were finely carved hardwood panels, cherry maybe. The floors were polished narrow planks, covered with intricately patterned wool rugs. The parlor included a small fireplace with a crackling flame. All the furniture was exquisitely crafted.

Misses Stewart directed the men to three straight-backed chairs arranged in a semi-circle facing an ornate, upholstered settee, mostly white. She reserved the settee for herself, probably to avoid any dirt the three men might be harboring.

The three of them took their seats. Everything was lowered to the floor except the ledger Jeremy held in his hands.

"Your home is beautiful," Jeremy said.

"Thanks to my sister and brother-in-law. They are both out at the moment. My two nephews are with their father, at the mill."

"So, you're happy with the move to New York?" Jeremy said.

"Very much so. That land was too much for me to handle."

"How is living in New York?" Nathan asked.

"Like everywhere, it has its good points and bad. Opportunities for the young are unsurpassed, or so I'm told by Johnathan."

"Your brother-in-law?" Mason asked.

"Yes. Johnathan moved here with Ella, my sister, ten years ago. He said the money was on the processing end of grain."

"Apparently, he was right," Nathan said.

Misses Stewart smiled.

They chatted a few minutes more about living in New York, until Ernest entered the room with a silver tray of porcelain cups, a tea pot, and what Mason presumed was sugar, in a matching server with a pewter spoon. He sat the tray on the salon table separating the three men from Misses Stewart and poured the tea. He left the room, returned a few seconds later, and placed four matching dessert plates and a loaf of cake or bread on a serving dish. The loaf was already sliced, revealing dried fruit and nuts.

"Please, gentlemen, help yourselves," she said.

Nathan was the first to move. He glanced at Mason and Jeremy and leaned forward. He used a pewter server to slide one of the slices onto a dessert plate, placed it on his lap and returned for the cup of tea.

Misses Stewart smiled at him and raised her eyebrows at Mason and Jeremy.

They both followed Nathan's lead.

Mason broke off a small corner of the bread and placed it in his mouth. He was expecting something along the lines of a fruitcake, but Misses Stewart's version turned out to be much lighter and less sweet.

He followed the morsel with a sip of tea. "This is wonderful."

"I'm glad you like it," Misses Stewart said. She turned to Ernest, still standing next to the salon table. "That will be all, Ernest."

Ernest turned and left the room. He slid a pair of pocket doors closed behind him.

"Now tell me about the harvest," Misses Stewart said, looking first at Jeremy, and then Mason.

Mason looked at Jeremy.

Jeremy finished chewing and took a sip of tea. "Well, you know we've had a drought."

"Yes, of course, my dear man. I was there only a few months ago."

Jeremy glanced at Mason before continuing.

"Well, despite the drought, Charlie and Sylvester were still able to harvest more than we expected."

"Who's Charlie?"

"He's the overseer we hired," Mason said.

Jeremy placed his cup and plate on the salon table and picked up the ledger from the floor, next to the two bags of silver. "May I?" he asked as he went to rise.

"Yes, of course," Misses Stewart said. She patted the settee next to her, apparently satisfied he was clean enough.

Jeremy shifted seats and opened the ledger so Misses Stewart could see. "I've recorded every bushel harvested and processed, and tracked the amount shipped to Charles Town, the amount we still have on hand, and what we transported to Saint Augustine."

"St. Augustine?" Misses Stewart asked with a bit of alarm in her voice.

"We made an arrangement with the governor there," Mason said, as he kicked the ruck at his feet, "which is why we can pay you in silver."

"Silver?"

"Yes, ma'am," Jeremy said. "Spanish dollars."

"How many?"

Jeremy directed her back to the ledger and pointed to the bottom of the page. "Three thousand."

Misses Stewart stared at the ledger for several moments. She finally looked up at Jeremy.

"Carolina paper is highly inflated and practically worthless here in New York," Mason said.

"I hadn't really given it that much thought," Misses Stewart said. She looked at the two bags of silver next to Jeremy's chair. "And you brought me three thousand Spanish silver dollars?"

"Yes, ma'am," Jeremy said.

"We plan to do the same next year," Mason said. "Half the crop, as agreed."

Misses Stewart placed her tea cup on the salon table. "Gentlemen, I never expected—" She closed the ledger and placed it on the salon table. "I'm impressed. I never expected you to go to this much trouble."

"That was our agreement," Mason said. He picked up the ledger and thumbed to the last page. He examined the page for a moment, flipped to the previous page, and back to the last. "Roughly, half a million pounds at today's prices in Carolina amounts to six thousand dollars."

"Yes, I saw that," Misses Stewart said. "But, Saint Augustine. How on earth did you manage that?"

Mason returned the ledger to the salon table. "It took some doing." He reached down and opened his ruck. He pulled out the two pouches of silver coins. He placed them on the floor against the salon table leg.

Nathan did the same thing, followed by Jeremy.

Jeremy picked up the ledger, opened to the last page. "Wonder if I could get your signature acknowledging the payment?"

"Of course," she said, as she took the ledger from his hand, walked to a small desk, and signed the page with quill and ink. She returned and handed the ledger to Jeremy.

The four of them continued to chat as they finished their cake and another cup of tea. Finally, Mason placed his empty plate and cup on the serving tray. He glanced at Jeremy and Nathan. Seeing they were also finished, he stood. "It has been very nice seeing you again, Misses Stewart. And I'm glad you remain in good health."

Jeremy and Nathan stood with Misses Stewart.

"You, as well," she said, as she shook each of the men's hands. She took the few steps and opened the pocket doors. "And I'll look forward to seeing you again."

Ernest was waiting at the front door, which he opened when they approached.

"Until next time," Mason said, as he gave a slight bow.

Jeremy and Nathan retrieved their muskets.

Misses Stewart shook the men's hands again as they exited, gave a final wave from the open doorway, and closed the door.

"That's a load off our shoulders, literally," Jeremy said, as he led the others to the street.

"Now what?" Nathan asked.

"I don't know about you gentlemen," Mason said, "but I'd like to see more of New York."

Jeremy and Nathan agreed. The three of them started walking.

They followed Gold Street back the way they had come, crossed over William, and continued west. They passed homes and businesses. Some were modest, but some extremely nice.

"There appears to be money in this town," Nathan said. "The place is buzzing. People from all over."

"From what I read, New York at this time was largely a concentration of grain mills, slaughter houses, and processing plants," Mason said. "There is money to be made."

They walked by numerous public wells, with people extracting water with a hand-cranked bucket. And they examined nearly every shop they passed. They finally made their way out to Broadway, by far the widest street they had seen so far. It was also one of the few paved with cobblestones. They walked the entire length, south to Fort George, and made their way back around to the wharf. The sloop was docked right where they had left it.

"Now what?" Jeremy asked.

"I say we grab something to eat," Nathan said.

They began walking west along a narrow alley which ended in back of another meat market. Like the other one, it stunk of rotting flesh. They kept walking west, past the market, and found themselves on a wider street, running east and west.

"Look at that," Nathan said, pointing to a placard on the corner of a building. *Wall Street*. "Where's the wall?"

"I think that was dismantled years ago," Mason said. "But there was a wall at one time."

At the end of Wall Street, across from what appeared to be some kind of government building, Mason spotted a tavern open for business. He began walking in that direction.

They entered the establishment and stopped just inside the entrance, to let their eyes adjust. There were only three patrons, one standing at the end of a long bar, and two more at a table. The fortyish or so barkeep stood behind the bar, wiping a pewter mug. He wore the standard long pants, linen shirt, and wool coat.

"What can I get for you gents?" the man asked.

His English was the most understandable Mason had heard since being thrown back in time.

"Something to eat and drink," Nathan said. "What do you have?"

"I have the finest ale in town. The only food I can offer is bread and cheese. A hearty beef stew will be ready in a couple of hours."

"Ale, bread, and cheese then," Nathan said. "For three."

"For three, coming up," the man said, as he stepped away and disappeared into a back room.

Nathan and Jeremy leaned their muskets against the bar railing. Jeremy placed the ledger he had been carrying on top of the bar.

Mason glanced around the interior. It was nicer than the other taverns he had seen, and well furnished with solid-looking tables and chairs. Three simple, pewter candle chandeliers hung from the relatively high ceiling, evenly spaced along the length of the tavern. None of the partially burned candles were lit. Mason suspected the tavern catered to a higher clientele, which would make sense, being so close to the government building. He examined the three patrons. All three were better dressed than anyone he had seen on the wharf, or in town, for that matter.

The barkeep returned with a wood platter of bread and cheese. He sat the food on the bar in front of Nathan and began filling three mugs.

Nathan and Jeremy started munching from the platter.

"From where do you gentlemen hail?"

"Charles Town," Jeremy said. "Up here on business."

"What sort of business?" The man pursed his lips and cocked his head. "Excuse my directness. You three are different from most."

"We own a plantation near Charles Town," Mason said. He stuck out his hand. "Mason, Stephen Mason. This is Jeremy Jackson and Nathan Sims."

"Forrest J. Gerber," the barkeep said, as he shook Mason's hand. He proceeded to shake Nathan's and Jeremy's hands. "Plantation, you say? Rice?"

"That's right," Mason said.

"Up here to sell your crop?"

"Not really," Mason said. "Other business."

"We get all types through here."

"You from the area?" Jeremy asked.

"I've lived all over. Arrived here about ten years ago."

"And you own this place?" Nathan asked.

"I do now. Had a partner, but he died a couple of years back. The fever."

"Sorry to hear that," Mason said.

"The two of us had been friends for a very long time," Gerber said. "Bill, was his name."

"This seems to be a very active town, especially at night," Nathan said.

"It is that," Gerber said. "All the crazies come out at night; most are from the building across the way."

Mason glanced out the door. "The government building?"

"City Hall."

They chatted a while longer, until Mason, Jeremy, and Nathan had eaten and drank their fill.

"It's been very nice talking with you Mister Gerber," Mason said.

"Forrest. Just call me Forrest."

"Will do, Forrest." Mason motioned to Jeremy and Nathan. "We should be on our way," he said. He placed two silver ingots on the bar. "Will that cover it?"

Gerber picked up one of the ingots and examined it closely. "Yes, these will do."

"Plantation near Charles Town," Gerber said.

"The Jackson plantation, on the Ashley," Mason said. "Stop by if you're down that way. Anyone in town can give you directions."

"I may do that," Gerber said. "It's been a long time since I was in Charleston."

Mason stared at the man. "You mean Charles Town."

"Yes, of course, Charles Town."

"Where did you say you were from?" Mason asked, as he stepped back to the bar.

The man stared into Mason's eyes for several long moments. "Like I said, here and there," Gerber finally said.

"Well, Forrest, the invitation is open if you find yourself in Charles Town."

"Thank you," he said. He touched the outstretched fingers of his right hand to his forehead, just above the eyebrow, in a sort of salute.

Jeremy and Nathan picked up their possessions and started for the door.

"Military, by chance?" Mason asked.

"I spent some time with the navy."

"Army," Mason said, as he extended his hand again.

Gerber shook Mason's hand. "Nice talking to you Mister Mason."

"Mason. People call me Mason. At the Jackson plantation."

"I'll remember," Gerber said.

Mason turned to follow the others.

CHAPTER 31

"I see no reason why we shouldn't head out now," Mason said, as he caught up to Nathan and Jeremy.

"I'm all for that," Jeremy said. "Like to get back as soon as possible."

"I think we should stay another night," Nathan said. "Get to know the place."

"Why don't you do that," Jeremy said. "We'll pick you up on our next trip."

"We head back," Mason said.

The three men returned to the wharf. Mason checked in with Pappy and joined Nathan and Jeremy at the boat. He let go the stern and bow lines and jumped aboard as the current and tide began moving the boat away from the pier.

Jeremy stowed the muskets, bags, and the ledger in the V-berth, while Mason manned the tiller, and Nathan readied the sails.

The mainsail caught the wind and immediately began pushing the boat while Nathan went forward to hoist the jibs.

Jeremy joined Mason at the helm. "Think this weather will hold?" he asked, as he scanned the sky.

"Hold the tiller while I check my smart phone," Mason said with a smirk. He glanced at the sky. "Yeah, I think the weather will hold."

They dodged other, usually larger, vessels as they navigated their way back through the upper and lower bays and out into the open ocean, where Mason steered to the south.

The three of them stood at the helm and studied the coastline as it slid by in the early afternoon sun. No one said much as they settled in for the three-day trip back.

After two mugs of beer, three in Nathan's case, all three men took turns at the bow and urinated over the side. It was the logical spot, with the wind usually blowing from the stern.

Standing there, with one hand on a rigging line and the other ensuring the flow made it over the gunwale, Mason thought of the large sailing ships with hundreds of seamen taking care of nature's call.

He finished, returned to the helm, and took over the tiller from Jeremy.

"And we do it all again next year," Jeremy said. "Grow the rice, harvest, sell it, and pay Misses Stewart."

"It's a living," Mason said. "It provides us a home. But it is a lot of work. A far cry from the life I had in Miami."

"You miss it?"

"Only once or twice a day," Mason said. "Actually, not really. You?"

Jeremy scratched the back of his neck. "Not really. I would never have met Lisa if that plane had landed as usual. I wasn't sure what I wanted to do in life. Now I am."

Mason glanced at Nathan at the gunwale, staring at the coast. "Funny how things turned out."

They were quiet for a several moments. The wind rushed through their hair and ruffled their coats. Salt from the ocean spray began to accumulate on their skin and hair.

"So, we work on the plantation this winter?" Jeremy asked.

"Yeah. Maybe install a small hearth in the kitchen addition. With fifty mouths to feed, Marie could use the extra capacity. I'd also like to improve the cabins for the workers. And I was thinking about a shower."

"Shower?"

"Yeah, we erect a structure closer to the river and mount a large barrel, maybe two or three, on top. Gravity feed."

"We'd have to fill them with buckets," Jeremy said.

"Yeah, but wouldn't it be nice to take a shower? And maybe we could devise a pump."

"In the summer it would. Not so sure about the winter."

"We devise a way to heat the water. One step at a time, my young friend. We make our lives as comfortable as possible, but without getting too far ahead of history."

"Nothing wrong with that," Jeremy said. "How's Karen and the baby?"

"So far, so good."

Jeremy was quiet for a moment. "Karen told Lisa about the painting you saw in the future, with the one child. Lisa told me."

Mason knew immediately what he was thinking. One child—Karen's child at ten years old. It meant he and Lisa apparently would never have children. Mason never told Karen the worst part about that painting, that Jeremy wasn't in it, just Karen, Lisa, and the child. "History is fluid, it can change."

"You believe that?"

"I do."

Jeremy stared off at the coast. "Was I in that painting?"

Mason hesitated several moments before answering. "No. But neither was I."

"You were in the future at the time," Jeremy said. "It wouldn't have made sense for you to be in the painting."

"None of this makes sense, Jeremy. Me coming back will have an impact."

"How so? Karen's pregnant, just like in the painting."

"Okay, here it is. The man I spoke to in the future, at the plantation, was a Fred Mason. He knew about you. He said you died two years after acquiring the plantation. Rumor passed down was that you caught one of the fevers from working in the fields."

Jeremy ran his hand across this face as he stared at the deck.

"But that was before I came back. You're not working in the fields. And even if you did catch some kind of disease, I brought back antibiotics. I can't change you and Lisa's ability to have a baby, but I can change whether you get sick and die."

"I guess we'll find out," Jeremy said.

Mason placed his hand on Jeremy's shoulder. "Don't worry about it. There are plenty of other things you can die from." A smile spread across his face. "Might get eaten by a bear."

Jeremy cocked his head. "That's refreshing."

Mason tilted his head up to the sky. "Why don't you take the tiller while I get a nap. Didn't sleep much last night with Nathan's snoring. In two or three hours, turn it over to Nathan and wake me."

"Will do."

Mason gave Jeremy a final pat on the shoulder, handed off the tiller, and went to the V-berth. He opened the hatch, stepped down the ladder, and began moving things out of the way to make room to lie down. He shifted the muskets to one side and picked up the ledger. He went to set it aside, but opened it instead. He flipped to the last page, where Misses Stewart had signed for the receipt of the silver. He flipped back to the previous page and studied the entries for several moments. Something looked familiar about the writing on the previous page.

He put the open ledger to one side and fished in his coat pocket. He came out with a wadded piece of paper, wrinkled and balled up from having been wet more than once. He unrolled the ball and flattened the paper against his palm. The paper was weathered, but still very much readable—*27th or 28th – probably morning*. Mason picked up the ledger and compared the writing style on the two documents. He flipped to the last page, and to the page before it. The writing styles on the two pages were different. The style on the prior page appeared to be very similar in style to what was written on the note.

Mason folded the note and put it back in his pocket. With the ledger in hand, he climbed back up the ladder and out of the hatch. He approached Jeremy, standing alone at the tiller. Mason opened to the last page of the ledger. "Who wrote that?"

Jeremy glanced at the page. "I did."

Mason flipped to the prior page. "Who wrote that?"

"Nathan. That's his hen scratching." He looked into Mason's eyes. "Why?"

Mason's faced suddenly turned red and angry. He felt his heart thumping in his chest as his blood pressure went up. Without another word, he closed the ledger, pivoted, and locked his eyes on Nathan, standing at the gunwale. He marched over, grabbed Nathan by the arm, and spun him around. "It was you," he screamed.

Nathan moved away from the gunwale as he stared at Mason. "What?"

Jeremy checked the sails and began tying off the tiller to keep the boat on course.

"The hijackers. Burton. You told Burton. Burton told Adams. You told them when and where."

"What are you talking about?"

"What was your plan?" Mason yelled.

"Have you gone insane? I didn't tell anyone anything."

"You're right," Mason said, as he reached in his pocket. He unrolled the small piece of paper. "You gave Burton this note."

Nathan glanced at the note for a millisecond. "You have completely lost your mind. I didn't write that."

Mason jerked the ledger open, flipped to the next-to-last page, and put the note against the page. "The writing is the same. You wrote this in the ledger, and you wrote this note." Mason glared at him. "You sorry son-of-a-bitch."

Nathan took a step back and pulled the knife from its sheath on his hip. He pointed the knife at Mason.

"You've wanted me out of the picture since day one," Mason said.

"You're right. Day one. That first day, on Myrtle Beach."

Mason thought back. The day the airliner went down. The day the survivors made it to shore. The first day in the camp they built. He drew a blank about Nathan.

"You made a fool of me in front of the others," Nathan said. "The bottle of soda."

"The bottle of soda I told you to put down because we had to conserve what we had? That bottle of soda?"

"Yeah, that bottle of soda. I swore to myself then and there that I would repay you for that."

"So, you were willing to let Adams and Burton kill me and Mato over a bottle of soda?" He stared at Nathan for several moments. "Adams gets the load of rice, and you get what?"

"The boat." He glanced around. "This boat. I was leaving, and I needed a way to travel and make a living."

Mason shook his head with his jaw locked. "Sullivan?"

"Wasn't part of it," Nathan said, as he raised the knife. He looked as though he were about to lunge, but before he made another move, there was a loud *whack*. The knife clanged to the deck and Nathan crumpled at Mason's feet.

Jeremy stood there holding a solid oak belaying pin plucked from the rigging's pinrail. "I always knew he was an asshole and couldn't be trusted."

A small amount of blood began to appear on the deck next to Nathan's head.

Mason knelt and put two fingers on his neck. Feeling a pulse, he looked up at Jeremy. "Find a rag or something. Need to stop the bleeding."

"Throw him over the side," Jeremy said.

"It may come to that, but for now, just find something to stop the bleeding."

Jeremy disappeared into the V-berth and came back with Mason's rucksack. He opened the ruck and pulled out the small first aid kit. He opened the kit and extracted a gauze contained in a paper wrapper. He tore open the wrapper and handed the gauze to Mason.

Mason put the gauze against Nathan's wound. "I think he'll be alright. Hand me some bandage so I can wrap this."

Jeremy handed him a length of bandage. Staring down at Nathan, Jeremy's jaw muscles flexed. "I say we put him over the side. Here and now."

"We can't do that," Mason said, as he finished wrapping Nathan's head. He tore the bandage at the end and used the two pieces to tie a knot, securing the bandage. "Let's move him to the berth."

Jeremy hesitated until Mason looked up at him. He reached down and helped lift Nathan's considerable weight.

They half dragged, half carried Nathan to the berth, and eased him down the ladder.

Mason positioned him in the spot he had cleared. "We'll decide what to do with him when we get back."

The two men returned to the deck. Jeremy resumed his position at the tiller.

They took turns through the night at the helm. Two-hour shifts each. One man at the tiller, the other sleeping, or at least resting, on deck against the transom. Every few hours Mason checked on Nathan.

Through the night, Nathan remained unconscious, taking shallow breaths.

In the very early morning, Mason opened his eyes and rubbed his face. He got to his feet and joined Jeremy at the tiller. "How long was I out?"

"I don't know, two or three hours probably."

"You should have woken me."

"You needed the extra rest."

Mason shook his head and stepped off for the V-berth. "Did you check on him?"

"Nope."

Mason opened the hatch and climbed down.

Nathan was in the exact same position Mason had last seen him.

He put two fingers to Nathan's neck, felt for a moment, felt a different spot, and a third. He placed the palm of his hand on Nathan's chest.

Mason sat back. He peered at Nathan for several moments before getting to his feet and climbing the ladder. He walked back to Jeremy. "He's dead."

"You said he never fired his musket at the hijackers," Jeremy said. "That's why, he was part of it. He was with them. Now can we dump him over the side?"

"Like it or not, he was one of us, one of the survivors. We take him back and bury him."

"An unmarked grave, I hope," Jeremy said, as he stared straight ahead.

◆◆◆

Two days later, back at the plantation, Mason stepped to the dock and helped Jeremy secure the sloop. He glanced at the larger sloop, now secured to the other side of the dock. He stood up and saw Karen and Lisa walking toward them. The sun, low in the west, highlighted their hair.

"How was it?" Karen asked, as she reached Mason and wrapped her arms around his chest.

"Misses Stewart is paid."

The four of them began walking toward the house, with the two couples intertwined.

Karen suddenly stopped and looked back at the boat. "Where's Nathan?"

Mason took in a deep breath and exhaled. "He'll remain on the boat until morning. Then we'll bury him."

###

A REQUEST FROM THE AUTHOR

Thank you for reading *The Planters: A Ripple In Time Book 2*. I hope you enjoyed the story as much as I enjoyed writing it. I do have one request. I ask that you please take a few moments to enter a product review on your Amazon Orders page. Independent authors depend on reviews to get their books noticed. And reviews also help make my future books better. A few moments of your time would be much appreciated. I look forward to reading your thoughts. —**Victor Zugg**

ABOUT THE AUTHOR

Victor Zugg is a former US Air Force officer and OSI special agent who served and lived all over the world. Given his extensive travels and opportunities to settle anywhere, it is ironic that he now resides in Florida, only a few miles from his hometown of Orlando. He credits the warm temperatures for that decision.

Check out the author's other novels—*Solar Plexus (1)*, *Near Total Eclipse (Solar Plexus 2)*, *Surrounded By The Blue*, and *From Near Extinction*.

For information on his latest project, visit his Facebook page—'Victor Zugg Author.'

Printed in Great Britain
by Amazon